SPUR OF THE MOMENT

KARLEY BRENNA

Spur of the Moment

Copyright © 2024 by Karley Brenna

All rights reserved.

No part of this book may be reproduced in any form or by any electronic or mechanical means, including information storage and retrieval systems, without written permission from the author, except for the use of brief quotations in a book review.

This is a work of fiction. Any names, characters, places, brands, media, and incidents are either the products of the author's imagination and used in a fictitious manner. Any resemblance to actual people, places, or events is purely coincidental and fictional.

Do not copy, loan, sell, or redistribute.

Paperback ISBN: 979-8-9888184-1-0

Edited by: Bobbi Maclaren

Cover: Dirty Girl Designs by Ali Clemons

You can have it all – ride the horse and *the cowboy.*

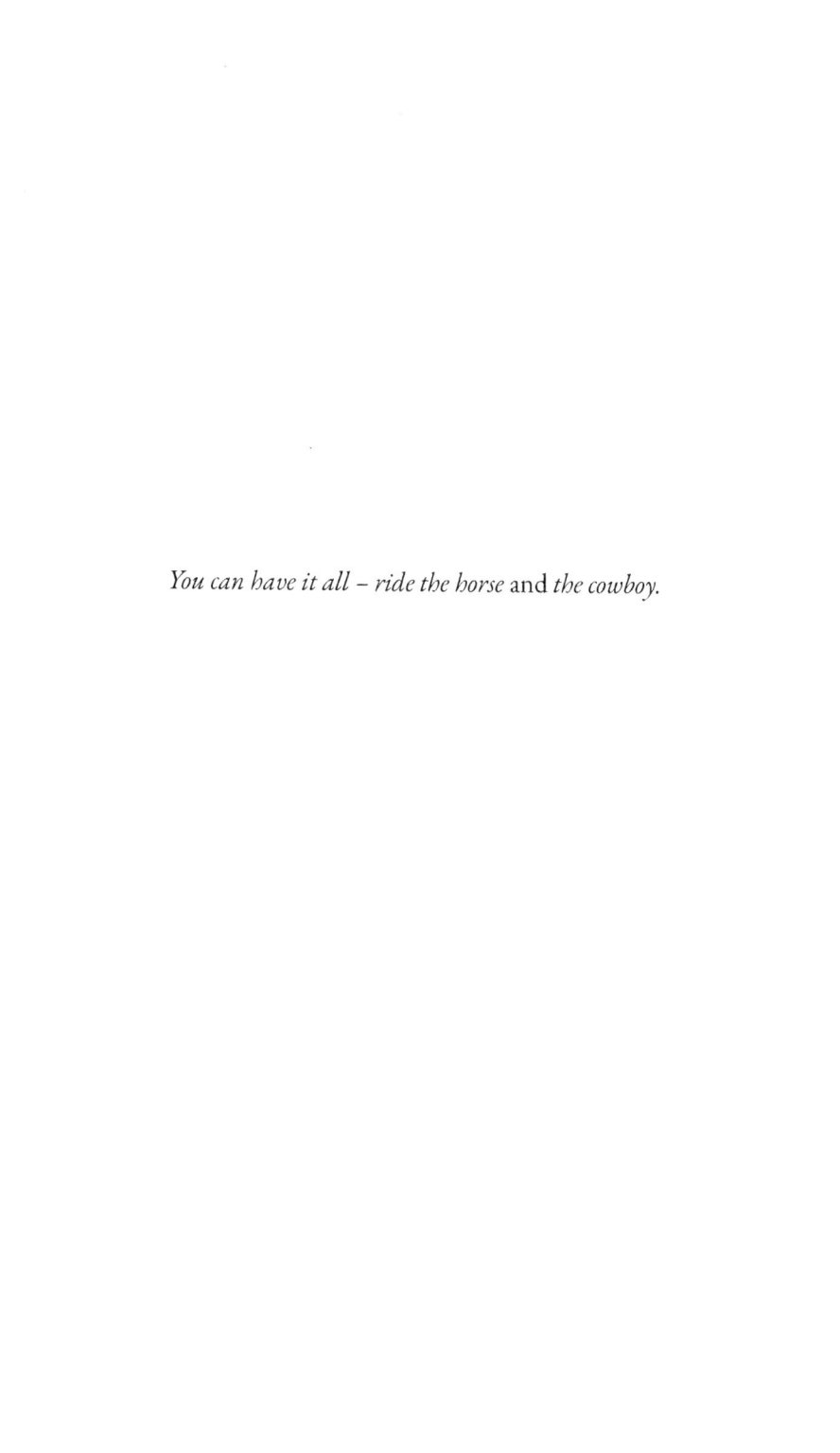

Important Note

Dear reader,

Throughout these pages, our main character, Lettie, deals and struggles with anemia. It is my hope that this was handled with the care it deserves. Please also note that this novel contains strong language and sexually explicit content.

Happy reading,
Karley

"It ain't dying I'm talking about, it's living. I doubt it matters where you die, but it matters where you live."
– Gus McCrae

1

Lettie

"He did what?!" Brandy managed to say through her fit of laughter.

"He threw up all over my boots! I'm telling you - the guy had you topped on the lightweight scale."

I brought the hammer down again, slamming it into the head of the nail to secure the board in place. Brandy was working on replacing boards on the stall doors inside the old barn while I balanced on a ladder, replacing rotting wood in the rafters.

"And you dated him? I'm surprised, Lettie. Your standards dropped after you left."

I rolled my eyes, grabbing another nail from the bucket perched on top of the ladder. "Not much into city boys. I had slim pickings to choose from."

"Tell me about it. It's the same deal here in town. You didn't miss much." Her voice carried up through the wooden structure as we worked in the blistering heat.

I'd only been back in town for two days before my dad put me to work, tasking me with repairing the old barn on the property so we could use it as a quarantine area for incoming rescue horses. Brandy was helping in between working with the horses. Partly to be nice, but mostly to catch up.

We'd been best friends since kindergarten, never apart for more than a couple days at a time. When I left for college, there was a huge void in my life without her. We still Facetimed daily, but it wasn't the same. She decided to stay in Bell Buckle to pursue horse training, and I went off to college in Boise to get a degree that wasn't getting me anywhere.

The rumble of a truck engine sounded from the dirt road as I hammered. Why didn't we have a nail gun? The hardware store would be my first stop when I drove into town this week.

"Oh, shit," Brandy said below me.

"What?" I swiveled on the ladder to try to see who was coming up the driveway. Standing on my toes, I arched my neck, but the peak of the barn shielded my view.

"Lettie! Watch out!" Brandy yelled right when I felt the ladder shake. The bucket of nails toppled over, the contents pouring out as the tin clanked down the rungs of the ladder before landing on the ground with a bang alongside the nails.

My sudden movement from twisting must have thrown it off balance because it was going down and there was no righting it. I held onto one of the rungs, but my hand slipped as it fell backward in slow motion. Slamming my eyes shut, I pushed off to the side to avoid it landing on me and braced for impact as my body propelled toward the dirt.

But instead of the hard ground, strong arms wrapped around me, cradling me like a damn baby. My heart raced as I tried to catch my breath. My eyes stayed shut, disbelief coursing through me that I wasn't a heap of broken bones on the dirt right now.

"Long time no see, Huckleberry."

There was only one man who called me that. One man's voice who made all my senses perk up on high alert. The man I was trying to avoid since coming back to town.

Embarrassment flooded my cheeks as I peeked up at him through one eye. I knew my cheeks were as red as they felt as he stared down at me with that damn grin on his face, his dimples on full display.

"Hi, Bailey."

His eyes stayed trained on me, like everything around us disappeared into the background. Damn it if I didn't stare right back, getting lost in those green eyes that had a hint of hazel around the pupils, dark lashes making the galaxy of colors pop.

I cleared my throat. "You can set me down now."

He seemed to snap himself out of whatever trance we were stuck in and positioned me upright, keeping his hand on the small of my back as I righted myself. I brushed my hands on my jeans, blowing my hair out of my face.

Bailey was my brother's best friend. Though all four of my brothers hung out with him and treated him like he was part of the family, Reed and Bailey were the closest. Growing up, they were always pulling pranks on me, hence the nickname Bailey gave me.

When I left Bell Buckle, I didn't say goodbye to Bailey. I didn't know if he'd understand why I was moving so far away for school, or any of the other reasons I wanted to get the hell out of Dodge.

He wasn't the type of guy to take education seriously, so once he graduated high school, he dove into working on his parents ranch and helping out with my family's nonprofit, Bottom of the Buckle Horse Rescue.

Looking at him now, I realized five years was a long time to be away. He'd matured, and in the best way possible. The muscles in his arms caused the material on the sleeves of his shirt to stretch. The fabric stretched over his abdomen, leaving little to the imagination. His skin was sun kissed from long hours working on the ranches, his cowboy hat angled down slightly to shield his green eyes. He was all man, no longer the boy I grew up with.

From the corner of my eye, I saw a blur of red fur right before it jumped on Bailey, barking with excitement.

I blinked, trying to believe what I was seeing. I must have hit my head when I fell.

"Rouge likes males now?" I asked.

Bailey caught the fifty-five pound Australian Shepherd in his arms when he jumped up again, licking at his chin. "Well, given the only woman in his life abandoned him, he didn't have much of a choice with all us guys around."

My jaw dropped. "I did not abandon him! I had to go to school. Dorms don't allow dogs. Especially crazy ranch dogs."

"Shouldn't have gone to school, then," Brandy mumbled from where she stood in the door to the barn.

"Don't make me kick you off this ranch, Brandy," Reed said as he came around the corner of the barn wearing leather chaps and his beaten-up straw cowboy hat.

Brandy rolled her eyes, crossing her arms. "Kiss my ass, Reed."

Bailey set Rouge down and he ran off, kicking up dust with his paws.

Ignoring Brandy, Reed came over to stand by Bailey. "You bring the hay?"

Bailey nodded, finally taking his eyes off me to face Reed, hiking his thumb in the direction of his Chevy. "Got it all loaded up if you want to help me stack it."

"Why'd you bring hay? Don't we still grow our own?" I asked.

He turned back to face me, his eyes assessing me before he spoke. "Your dad needs more. Guess you guys are bringing in too many rescues to keep up."

"Yeah, someone needs to be taken off recruiting duty." Reed pointed a glare at Brandy, who was leaning against a wood support beam.

"What can I say? I have a hard time saying no," Brandy said, a smirk pulling at the corner of her mouth.

Reed grunted. "That's been obvious in the past." He turned to head toward Bailey's black Chevy K10.

Brandy scowled at him as he stalked off.

I raised my eyebrows, turning back to Bailey. "Some things never change, do they?"

He nodded once, turning on the heel of his boot to follow Reed. I watched him walk away, then made my way over to the fallen ladder. "What's his problem?"

Brandy pushed off the post she was leaning against to help me pick it up. "I think he's butthurt you didn't tell him you were back in town."

"Why would I?"

She arched an eyebrow at me.

"What?" We hauled the ladder up, propping it back up against the side of the barn.

"You seem to forget you two were best friends before you left."

"We most definitely were *not* best friends. We were barely friends, if that." I kneeled down and began collecting the nails that littered the ground, tossing them into the bucket.

"So, you've been helping my mom find rescues?" I asked her, changing the subject.

"I was for a bit. We went a little overboard, if you couldn't tell. Your dad capped us and now makes us run all the possible rescues by him first."

I snorted out a laugh. That sounded like something my dad would do. He ran a tight ship around here, but he loved the work. He did it to make sure the rescue stayed afloat, and we all appreciated it.

I finished collecting all the nails on the ground and stood up with the handle of the bucket in my hand.

"No way in hell are you getting back on that ladder, Lettie," Reed shouted over to me from where he was stacking bales of hay with Bailey under the carport.

I stood up, placing my hands on my hips. "Dad wants me to rebuild the barn, so I don't have a choice."

Reed shook his head. "Bailey can do the roof."

I gaped at him from where I stood. "You think I'm incapable?"

"Didn't say that, Lettie. I just know you're a klutz. Ladders aren't your friend, and Bailey won't always be there to come to your rescue."

Bailey chuckled, tossing another bale over the side of the truck bed onto the ground.

"I don't need his saving." I'd be damned if I had to work with Bailey during my stay in Bell Buckle.

Bailey bent over to grab another bale by the baling twine with gloved hands. "Doesn't look that way, Huckleberry."

"Stop calling me that! I was fifteen!"

Brandy laughed from where she stood in the shade, spinning a screwdriver in her hands.

I shot her a glare as Bailey laughed right along with her. "Fifteen or not, your ass still landed in that bucket of huckleberries. You were stained red for days."

Refusing to relive the embarrassment, I turned on my heel and aimed for the main house.

My parents lived in the original house on the property. Reed had built his own house on the opposite side of the ranch. It made sense to build here rather than move away since he trimmed all the horses' hooves here. He got a majority of his work from the rescue.

They'd renovated the old farmhouse when I was younger, knocking down some of the walls to make it more of an open floor plan. They'd kept the bones of the structure, but the entire interior was redone. My dad let my mom design it all, from the flooring to the kitchen cabinets. The house had a decent sized porch in the front, but it was dwarfed in comparison to the back porch. There was a built-in barbeque, a hot tub, and an outdoor dining set that could seat twelve. Since I've been back, my mother had added a smaller dining table to the front porch that matched the rocking chairs.

"Going to get Dad?" Reed yelled after me.

"I won't let you force me to work with him!" I stomped off, hating how I let my emotions take over where Bailey was concerned. He knew how to get under my skin without even trying. Reed was doing this on purpose to force us to talk out what

I refused to speak with him about. He was trying to meddle where meddling didn't need to be done.

When my brothers found out I didn't tell Bailey I was leaving, they were nothing short of pissed. They considered Bailey a brother, so when I treated him like he was nothing to me, they couldn't believe it. The truth was, I didn't think I could have left if I saw the look on his face when I told him. I knew he'd be hurt, and that's what I was trying to prevent by keeping quiet about my plans.

I had just turned eighteen, and the day I did, Bailey started looking at me differently. He was four years older than me, so the possibility of us ever acting on an attraction towards each other was moot until I was legal.

But that day, something changed. He started looking at me less like his best friend's sister and more like he was finally starting to see me. Really *see* me. How I looked, how I acted, what I wore.

Those looks were the exact thing I didn't want. He knew me, inside and out, and I hated that. He could use anything against me if he wanted to, so I had to do the only thing I could. Leave and not look back. At least, until coming back to Bell Buckle was my only option.

Now, I was forced to face him and see just what my leaving did to him.

2

BAILEY

"I don't mind helping with the barn, but I don't want to piss her off, man," I said to Reed after jumping off the tailgate of the truck to help him stack the bales.

Reed waved me off. "Don't worry about her, she'll get over it."

Little did he know, I always worried about her.

When Lettie left without saying goodbye, it felt like a small piece of me left with her. I was hurt that after all the time we'd spent together, all the laughs and memories we shared, I didn't so much as get a farewell. Not even a damn text.

I had to find out through her brother, Lennon, when I was picking up grain at the feed store in town. He'd been talking about how Brandy was in the store just before me, moping around with nothing else to do. I'd asked why she was upset, and that's when it dawned on Lennon that I didn't know. It'd been a week since Lettie left town when I found out.

I didn't even attempt to call or text her. I figured since she left without saying a word to me, she didn't want to hear from me after, either. Hell, she disappeared without saying goodbye, why *would* she want to talk? Clearly I wasn't important enough in her life to be privy to her plans.

I heard the ladder settle against the red barn when Reed and I both looked over to see Brandy climbing the rungs. He narrowed his eyes.

"I'm not taking your ass to the hospital if you fall, too," Reed yelled over at her.

He'd had a problem with Brandy since the day Lettie brought her home from kindergarten. They were always getting into trouble together, whether it was playing too close to the untouched horses, or sliding down into the creek bed on flimsy sheets of metal roofing. Whatever plans Brandy had, Lettie followed right along with her, no matter how dangerous.

Reed was the most protective of the four brothers growing up, always asking where Lettie was when she wasn't in sight. She was diagnosed with anemia when she was nine after she almost passed out when she dismounted her horse. Ever since, her brothers hounded her like hawks. Reed may act like a hard-ass sometimes, but he had the biggest heart of all of them.

It was obvious that their love suffocated her at times, but I wouldn't act like it didn't concern me either. One of my first thoughts when I found out she left was that I hoped she remembered to take her iron supplements.

After being hounded most of her life, I didn't blame her if she wanted to move to the other side of Idaho to get away from her family. They worried about her because they loved her, but that didn't stop the concern from becoming overwhelming at times.

"I wouldn't get in the same car with you if you paid me," Brandy shouted back from where she was perched at the top of the ladder, hammer in hand.

I shook my head, stacking another bale.

"Good thing I have a *truck*, then," he yelled across the driveway before turning back to me. "Stubborn woman," Reed muttered under his breath.

Their bickering was pretty comical, but more often than not, they took it too far, slinging insults that would hurt anyone's feelings. But it was Reed and Brandy. They'd battle all night if you let them. Reed may say he hated her, but I knew he sought out those battles. One could think it was because he liked her attention, negative or not. I wouldn't be caught dead saying that to either of them, though.

"You can say that twice," I mumbled in agreeance.

"If it makes you feel any better, she let Brandy know she was heading home before telling any of us."

"Best friend privileges!" Brandy yelled over at us, clearly eavesdropping on our conversation.

Reed rolled his eyes as he stacked the last bale. I pulled my gloves off, my hands already clammy from the heat. I shoved the deerskin gloves in my back pocket before taking a piece of straw from one of the bales, sticking it in my mouth.

Reed sat on one of the bales, his elbows resting on his knees with his arms hanging in front of him. "She won't tell us why she came back."

"Sounds like Lettie." Her obstinate ways hadn't changed since she'd been gone. That much was clear.

I chewed on the piece of straw, watching the horses gather by the water trough under the shade of a pine tree.

Reed eyed the straw in between my teeth. "How is that shit enjoyable?"

I shrugged. "Cowboy's gum."

"Pretty sure you mean farmer's gum."

I waved a hand at him. "Semantics."

"Maybe she'll tell you," he said, getting back to the topic at hand.

I chuckled, shaking my head before kicking at the dirt with my boot. "Doubt that. She didn't even tell me she was home. This is the first I've seen of her."

"She damn sure loves her secrets. But it couldn't hurt to ask."

"She'd tell Brandy before she'd tell me, Reed. Why don't you ask her?"

"You mean ask a favor of Brandy? Hard pass."

I turned to find him watching Brandy where she hammered atop the ladder, her brunette hair tied in a high ponytail atop her head, swinging with the movement. "Why? It's not like you guys don't talk. You've been bickering back and forth since I pulled up."

He drew his gaze away from her and stood, changing the subject. "Better go see what chaos Lettie created with Dad."

He brushed past me as Rouge came out from around the side of the barn with feathers hanging out of his mouth. He ran up to me, panting as he sat next to my boot. I stroked his ears, shaking my head. "Always getting into trouble, you and your mom."

I followed after Reed, Rouge at my heels as we made our way to the main house.

3

Lettie

"No one told you to go to college, Lettie." My dad's rough voice grumbled from where he sat at the table, the newspaper he'd been reading laying flat in front of him.

I stood in the entryway to the house, not having made it more than a few feet inside before I let my frustration be heard. "No one needs to *tell* me to do anything, Dad. I made the choice to leave because I had nothing for me here."

"And now you do - fixing the old barn up for me."

"Replacing rotting wood isn't a purpose, Dad. It's a chore."

He folded his arms across his chest, his graying mustache doing little to hide the frown on his face. "It's a ranch, Lettie. Those are the things that need to get done."

"I can get it done, but not with him. Let me help with the rescue."

"Not happening."

I wasn't going to back down from this battle. I was capable of taking on more with the rescue, I just wished he'd see it. "Those horses need to be cared for, too. I've always been good with them."

"I'm well aware." My dad hated dealing with difficult subjects like this. He wished everyone would get along and stick to their tasks. I was the rebel child when it came to that, always pushing back. That's why my mom and I got along so well. She was the same way when she was growing up.

I took a steadying breath. "I'm not fragile."

He simply gave me a look, his eyes telling me what he didn't need to voice. He thought I couldn't handle the unruly horses or the stress of the rescue.

I threw my hands out, my attempt at getting a grip on my emotions failing once again. "I'm not some little girl anymore, Dad. Eventually you're going to have to realize that I've grown up and can handle more than just replacing old beams on a dilapidated barn."

He regarded me from where he sat, his posture making it clear he wanted to be done with this conversation. "They're rescues, Lettie. They can be unpredictable. What if you get hurt?"

"What if Brandy gets hurt, or Reed? They're around them every day."

"It's different," he clipped.

I pulled my hand through my hair, shoving the caramel-colored strands out of my face. It wasn't the smartest idea to be around untouched horses when you had the risk of minor dizzy spells, but if moving away taught me anything, it was that I was tired of living my life on the safe side. "Just give me something. Some kind of responsibility that doesn't make me feel incapable. Reed doesn't trust me on the ladder, and I will *not* let Bailey supervise me like I'm some sort of child."

"You sure about that?" I jumped at Bailey's voice behind me, twisting around only to come face to face with him. Well, more like my face to his chest.

I tilted my head up and narrowed my eyes at him as he stood there, filling the small entryway. "Am I sure I'm not a child? Yes."

He chewed on the straw sticking out of his mouth, the stubble on his jaw moving with the act. He tossed his head back and forth like he was contemplating what I said. I tried not to stare at the way his lips moved around the single piece of hay.

Stop it, Lettie. Get a grip on yourself.

"Mm, I think even children have enough sense to communicate their whereabouts to others," he said.

My mouth popped open. Was he seriously going to bring that up right now? This just added to my case that I wouldn't accept his help in any capacity. Not when he just made it clear that he hadn't let go of the past.

Ignoring his passive-aggressive comment, I turned back to my dad, who had resumed reading the newspaper as if we weren't standing here. "Please. I'm begging."

"I do have one errand you could do for me," he said before laying the newspaper back on the table.

For a man who ran a ranch and a horse rescue, he sure had a lot of time to read the newspaper. He always told us to have a healthy work-life balance, but you wouldn't catch me reading the newspaper in my free time. I'd rather ride Red or get lost in a romantic suspense novel.

"Anything."

He looked behind me to where Bailey still stood before drifting his eyes back to me. I felt his presence at my back, the smell of dirt and sweet grass enveloping my senses like a fog. Not many people liked the smell of cowboy, but Bailey wore it like expensive cologne. The scent was almost intoxicating.

Reason number one hundred as to why I didn't want to be around him.

I couldn't cross that line with him, and if I had to be around that addicting smell and see his stupid handsome face every day, I didn't know how long that line could hold me back.

"There's an auction in Billings coming up. Heard they have a few neglect cases coming through. I can't make it due to chores here on the ranch, but I'd be willing to let you go in my place on one condition," my dad said.

"What's that?"

He paused, intertwining his fingers on the table. "You bring someone with you to drive the trailer and load the horses."

A smile crept up the corners of my mouth. My choice was obvious. "Brandy can come."

He shook his head. "I need her here for training."

I'd suggest Reed, but he was busy with horseshoeing, his schedule too full to take the time to drive up to Billings. Lennon, my oldest brother, managed the feed store, so he was out of the question, and with it being the summer, riding lessons were in full swing, making Callan too busy. Beckham wasn't even in Bell Buckle right now - he was busy touring on the rodeo circuit. With all my brothers being busy, that left me with...

"No way."

My dad shrugged, his usual frown still plastered on his face. "I don't know what to tell you, Lettie. Everyone else is busy, and I'm not letting you go alone."

"The whole reason I want away from the barn project is because of Bailey! Now you want me to go spend *days* with him up in Montana?" Not to mention being alone in the truck with him for the drive north.

"Afraid of a little one on one time, Huckleberry?" Bailey said from behind me, his voice too damn close to my ear as I felt his breath on the back of my neck.

Trying to act like he didn't affect me was impossible. It wasn't that I didn't want to spend time with him. Don't get me wrong,

I enjoyed our time together - pre-college. Now I wanted to stay as far away from him as possible.

Shouldn't he have dropped my leaving without a goodbye after five years?

"It's either that, or the barn, Lettie. You don't get to pick and choose what needs to get done around here," my dad grumbled.

I gnawed on the inside of my cheek, not wanting to admit defeat on the matter. He was right. I needed to suck it up and get shit done. "Maybe I shouldn't have come back."

I knew it was the wrong thing to say before the words even passed my lips. Bailey tensed behind me before he turned around and walked out of the house, the door slamming behind him. My dad stared at me with concern in his eyes as he let what I said sink in.

During the time I spent in Boise, I think a big part of me knew I'd end up back in Bell Buckle. Even though my dad's intent was always to leave the ranch to one of my brothers, my heart belonged here. I genuinely wanted to go to college, and afterward, I tried to stay in that city, but I wasn't happy. I ignored the pull in my gut for as long as I could before I packed up and drove back to Bell Buckle. The moment I crossed the county line, it felt like I could breathe again.

College was not for me, but I made it through. After growing up on the ranch, always having new volunteers around and different horses coming through the rescue, I hated how I was suddenly stuck in a grueling routine of studying and hour-long lectures. I didn't want to be stuck in textbooks. Instead, I wanted to feel the wind in my hair as I rode through the open fields at a full gallop.

There was nothing more grounding than being on the back of a thousand pound animal - every movement your body made, every emotion you felt, casting into them.

Red was the only horse my dad felt comfortable with me riding. He'd never bucked, kicked, or gone sour. Red took care of me, no matter how I felt that day.

I needed to go see him. But first, I needed to prove to my dad I could handle what he threw at me, no matter what it was or who it was with.

"I'll do the barn, and the trip, but I'm buying a nail gun."

He raised a bushy eyebrow, seemingly surprised at my change of attitude. "Should I warn Bailey?"

I rolled my eyes at his attempt at a joke. "For the barn, Dad."

"That should work out. The rest of the wood should be delivered by the time you get back from Montana. Sounds like you're staying for a while then?"

Was I? When I made the drive back to Bell Buckle, I didn't have a long term plan. I just knew that I needed to be here. After Boise, I wasn't sure if I wanted to try out another place, but I also didn't want to subject myself to staying in my hometown just because that's where I felt comfortable.

I lived my whole life doing things that were comfortable, thanks to my helicopter family. But was it comfort that Bell Buckle brought me, or a safety net knowing I had people I could lean on here? A sense of home that no other place could provide?

"I haven't thought that far ahead."

He nodded once, picking up his newspaper to resume what he'd been doing before I stormed in here. Satisfied with the conversation, I turned to head outside to get back to work.

"Oh, and Lettie?"

Pausing with my hand on the door handle, I looked over my shoulder at my dad. "Yeah?"

Without taking his eyes off the newspaper, he said, "Be nice to the poor guy. Life didn't pause here when you drove away."

I looked down at my boots and the dirt clinging to the hem of my jeans. I was well aware that things kept moving when I left. I didn't expect anyone to wait around for me in the hopes that I'd come back someday.

I had to make amends with the people I hurt. And that included Bailey.

4

BAILEY

Six Years Earlier...

"You gonna grab me a beer, too?" I asked Reed, who was heading inside from the front porch where we'd been sitting for the past hour, waiting for Lettie to get home.

"You're not twenty-one yet, genius," he called over his shoulder as he disappeared through the door.

I jumped out of my chair, following him inside. "My birthday is in three days. I'm basically already twenty-one."

He closed the fridge, only one beer in his hand. Popping the top off onto the counter, he took a long swig. "*Basically* isn't the same thing as *actually*. Not in the eyes of the law, at least."

I rolled my eyes, opening the fridge to grab a beer anyway. We'd been drinking beers together since I was thirteen and Reed was sixteen. Though my liver and *the law* hated it, I wasn't going to stop three days before I was actually legal.

"You're a buzzkill, you know that?" I said as I popped the top off my bottle using the edge of the counter.

He shrugged. "You still hang around me."

"I've been questioning the *why* behind that for ages now."

He punched me in the shoulder and I cracked a smile, leaning back against the counter. Right as I was bringing the bottle up to my lips, Lettie came storming through the front door.

Without taking a sip, I lowered the bottle to the counter beside me as she glanced up, briefly making eye contact with me before beelining it down the hall to her bedroom. The door to her room clicked shut, and Reed sighed, looking down at the toe of his boots as he adjusted his black cowboy hat.

"If that fucker did something," he started.

"We'll have to kill him," I filled in. "I know."

We wouldn't *actually* kill him, of course. Just rough him up a bit. We always had a plan in place for Reed's little sister if shit ever went south with a guy she was with. Not that it had ever happened before, but we all protected Lettie.

"I'll go see what's up," Reed said, taking a step before I stopped him with a hand to his chest.

"I'll go," I offered. I wanted to be the one to hear it from her lips before I grabbed my shotgun.

I was exaggerating. Okay, maybe I wasn't. The point is, no one fucks with Lettie and gets away with it. Not on my watch.

He eyed me. "You sure? She can get a little snappy with you."

I raised an eyebrow, dropping my hand from the center of his chest. "As if she doesn't do the same to you?"

"You're right. You better talk to her. I'll probably say the wrong thing, then she'll go get Dad, and it'll be a whole thing." He grabbed his beer and walked past me, heading for the couch.

I let out a small snort at his comment. Lettie was always using the "dad" card on Reed because she knew he was always doing his best to live up to his high expectations. He loved all his kids, and me, but that didn't mean he didn't have high standards for all of us.

I hated thinking of Lettie out with some guy, even if I knew who he was. She was worth more than some lowlife from school who played tennis. I mean, really, *tennis*, Lettie? On top of that, the guy was thinner than a toothpick. She could probably lift more with her pinky than he could using both arms.

Lettie was the most beautiful woman I'd ever seen - aside from my mother, of course - and I'd always had this unwavering attraction for her. She could trip me in the mud at the creek and I'd still worship the shin that made me fall. *That's* how fucking gone for her I was.

Would I ever admit that to her, though?

I didn't know.

It felt weird thinking of crossing that line with her no matter how much I wanted to cross it. Lettie and I had this relationship that was like an unspoken truce. We were always there for each other when we needed someone, but only ever just as friends.

Did she even want more than that with me?

Leaving my beer on the counter, I made my way down the hall, coming to a stop at Lettie's door. I went to reach for the handle, but stopped myself. What if she was indecent?

Tapping my knuckles lightly on the door, I heard her bed shift, then light footsteps padding on the hardwood. Setting a hand on the door frame above my head, I waited for her to peak out.

It slowly swung open a few inches, and Lettie tilted her chin back to look up at me. "May I come in?"

She crossed her arms, narrowing her eyes. "It depends."

The corner of my mouth lifted slightly. "On?"

"Are you going to ask how my date went?"

"Why would I care about how your date went?" I asked innocently.

"So you're telling me that you and Reed weren't waiting for me to get home just now?"

"Nope." She was pinning me with those baby blues, making it so fucking hard to lie to her.

"You guys are always out doing stuff on the ranch when you hang out. You really think I believe that?"

I shrugged, adjusting my grip on the doorframe to lean down a bit closer to her. "Now why would I lie to you, Huckleberry?"

She rolled her eyes. The nickname got her to break every time. "Fine. You can come in."

I smiled, dropping my hand from the door frame and walking past her. She closed her door, which she only ever did with me. Any other guy and she'd keep it cracked.

I walked over to her dresser, noticing the lack of dust on the surface, and eyed the photo of her and Brandy on their horses. "So how was your date?"

"Bailey Cooper!" she squeaked.

I couldn't help the smirk on my face as I turned to face her. "Call a guy curious."

"I don't need you meddling in my relationships," she huffed.

I arched my brow. "Is it a relationship, though?"

She pursed her lips, plopping herself on the edge of her bed. After a moment of trying to keep up her hard exterior, she broke, looking down at her hands tangled together in her lap. "No," she admitted softly.

She'd changed after she got home and was now wearing pink shorts and an oversized t-shirt, which covered the shorts. The shirt stopped mid-thigh, exposing her long, tan legs down to her bare feet.

Forcing my eyes to stop trailing down her body, I sat down next to her on the edge of the bed, our shoulders touching. "You want to talk about it?"

"No," she said through a sniffle.

"Alright." I laid back on her white comforter, grabbing her pillow and setting it behind my head.

"That's my pillow!" She grabbed it from me, my head plopping to the blanket.

"I was using that," I pointed out.

She set the pillow right above my stomach, laying her head on it. I resisted the urge to stroke her hair or rest my hand on her arm.

After a few moments of listening to her breathing, she said, "He didn't want to be in a relationship with me."

My eyes stayed trained on the ceiling, which was basked in an orange glow from the sun setting outside her bedroom window. The entire room was the color of a flame as day slowly turned to night.

"Lettie?" I said after a few minutes.

"Yeah?"

"He doesn't deserve you. You know that, right?"

She gave a poor attempt at a shrug with her current position. "Will anyone deserve me in your eyes?"

"Honestly, no." Not even me. But fuck, I'd work my damned hardest to become the man she did deserve. I didn't know if that'd be in one year or ten, but I'd earn Lettie Bronson one day, and I'd treat her better than any man could.

Once I was sure she'd fallen asleep, I slipped out from under the pillow, hating that I couldn't stay. If Reed found me asleep in here on her bed, he'd flip.

Slowly standing up, careful to not jostle the bed, I looked down at her. Her chest was rising and falling with her steady breaths, her lips slightly parted.

She looked so peaceful.

So damn beautiful.

I crouched down, my fingers just barely touching her as I pushed a strand of hair out of her face. Before I did anything stupid, I stood, then made my way to the door.

I twisted the handle slowly, knowing that if you twisted it too fast, it'd make a small squeak, and I didn't want to wake her.

Before slipping out of her room, I took one last look at her sleeping on her bed, one arm curled under her cheek and the other draped across her stomach. I committed the image to memory, never wanting to forget how she looked in this moment.

5

LETTIE

I closed the door to the house behind me and found Reed sitting on the porch, beer in hand. He regarded me from where he sat, then looked back out at the ranch, taking a swig from his beer. I took the seat next to him, leaning forward with my elbows on my knees. I knew Reed had things he wanted to say, but he'd keep quiet, his silence speaking louder than his words could.

He didn't understand what changed to make me close myself off from everyone. How could he? He wasn't the youngest sibling with a medical condition who couldn't get a break from people hovering over her.

Out of the corner of my eye, I saw him lift the beer again. I snatched it out of his hand and took a long pull, the cool liquid pooling in my belly, feeling damn good on this hot day. I reluctantly held it back out to him after I took a second sip. He grabbed it, sitting back in his chair.

"Dad's right, you know. Give Bailey a break."

I kept my eyes trained on the horses out in the pasture as I spoke. "Why's everyone so concerned about Bailey?"

"He did a lot while you were gone. More than you may think."

I sighed. Life didn't pause for anyone, no matter how much you wanted it to. I didn't think my leaving would have affected the people I loved so much, but I was coming to find that I shouldn't have been so selfish in my decision to leave.

Though I regretted it now, back when I came to the conclusion that leaving was the best option for me, it seemed like a good idea. Feeling like a burden being passed around between the people in my life was mentally draining.

"I'm not blind to the hard work he does. I just don't know how to talk to him anymore. He seems so…"

"Different?" Reed filled in.

"Yeah."

He paused, finishing off his beer. "That's because people change over the course of five years, Lettie. Did you expect to come back and things would be the same?"

"No, but I didn't expect everyone to hate me."

In my peripheral, I saw Reed was looking at me. I sat back in my chair, facing him. "No one hates you. We just missed you, and now that you're back and not telling anyone why, we're confused."

"Trust me, you're not the only ones."

"Why did you come back, Lettie? Why now?"

"I guess I just missed you guys, too."

***

I found Bailey in the white barn, cleaning out Red's stall. He had a wheelbarrow blocking the entrance to the stall as he scooped the soiled flakes off the ground. Rouge was sprawled out on the ground beside the wheelbarrow taking a nap.

"You know we have volunteers for that, right?"

He had his back to me as he worked. "They do the rescues, not the personal horses."

I opened the stall door a few inches more, squeezing past the wheelbarrow. Red let out a snort when he saw me, his ears perking up. "Hey, old man. I missed you." I closed the distance, rubbing my hand up his muzzle to itch between his ears. He lowered his head slightly to give me a better angle.

Bailey turned with his pitchfork, tossing a load into the wheelbarrow. He stabbed it into the growing pile and set his hands on his hips as he turned to look at me. I ignored him and came up on Red's shoulder to reach below his neck, scratching him where he loved it most. His top lip lifted as he arched his neck, enjoying the attention.

"I've kept him exercised while you've been gone."

I looked at Bailey, patting Red's neck after I stopped scratching him. "Thank you."

He gave me a single nod but made no move to continue cleaning.

I bit the inside of my cheek before turning away from Bailey, running my hands across Red's flank, my fingers combing through his roan coat with my back to Bailey. "I'll go to Montana."

"I can go on my own if you don't want to."

Taking a deep breath, I faced him. "I want to go with you."

His eyes bored into me like he was trying to read my thoughts. "That's not what it sounded like ten minutes ago."

"Well, I had a change of heart."

He turned around, grabbing the handles of the wheelbarrow to push it out of the stall. "Don't go getting soft on me now, Huckleberry."

I'd always been soft for Bailey, as much as I didn't want to admit it. Between the four year age difference and him being friends with all of my brothers, he was off-limits growing up.

I pushed any and all feelings away when it came to Bailey, but it was nearly impossible to do that once I turned eighteen. I'd been planning to go to college anyway, but it ended up serving as my getaway without having to be upfront about running from him.

I didn't want anything coming between us that could ruin our friendship, and I was scared that if we gave into those feelings, there were too many possibilities for things to go south. I couldn't handle the rejection if it came to that.

"Looks to me like you're the one getting soft. Taking care of my horse all these years?"

I patted Red on the neck before making my way out of his stall. Bailey closed the sliding door behind me.

"Took care of your dog, too."

Turning around, I came face to chest with him again. "You didn't have to do that."

His eyes held mine for ten seconds too long before he grabbed the handles of the wheelbarrow and walked down the aisle with it. The only sounds were the squeak of the wheel and our boots on the rubber mats as I walked a few steps behind him.

Following him outside the barn, the afternoon sun blazed down on us. He walked over to the manure pile, dumping the contents of the wheelbarrow on top. When he set it back down, he turned to me, taking his cowboy hat off to rub the sweat off his brow. His brunette hair curled around his ears and at the nape of his neck, stray strands plastered to his forehead.

"You going to be ready to go in three days?" he asked as he put the hat back on.

"Most of my clothes are still packed, so yeah."

"And the barn?"

I glanced over at the red building, the paint peeling off in more places than not. "My dad said the wood should be here by the time we get back. I'll just need your help on the roof, if you're okay with that."

He licked his lips, contemplating. He took his time before replying, gazing down at his boots, kicking a rock in the dirt, angling his hat down further so the brim covered more of his eyes. I wished he'd wear it higher and not cover his eyes so much.

His gaze landed back on me before he spoke. "Couldn't think of a better way to spend my time."

I raised an eyebrow. "Really?"

"What's a summer without some trouble? Just like the good ol' days, huh?" He grabbed the wheelbarrow and walked past me with it, leaving me standing there.

"No trouble, Bailey Cooper!" I called after him.

He waved a hand in the air, dismissing me and not bothering to look back. I couldn't help my eyes from landing on his Wrangler clad ass and the gloves dangling out of his back pocket.

God, help me.

6

BAILEY

The heat was unforgiving as I worked my way through the stalls, despite it being seven in the morning. I'd been getting up earlier the past couple weeks to get started before the worst temperatures set in, but lately, the time of day didn't seem to matter.

Callan's voice echoed in the distance as he gave a riding lesson to a little boy. I shoved the pitchfork through the flakes, scooping the last bit out before shoving the wheelbarrow through the door and shutting the stall. I wheeled it to the next one, expecting to be greeted by Red, but found his stall was empty. Lettie probably took him out this morning for a ride, so I wasn't too worried about his whereabouts.

That horse took care of her, that was for damn sure. People say horses can feed off your energy, which I wholly believe, but it was like he knew she needed the extra care. His eyes always softened when she was around. Their bond was unmistakable.

I got to work cleaning his stall, stopping to rub the sweat away from my forehead with my bandana halfway through. I had my own chores to take care of at my parents' ranch, but I balanced my time between the horse rescue and there as best I could.

The Bronson family was stretched thin on hands, despite being a family of seven with Lettie back home. Brandy helped with handling and training the new rescues. But as for the Bronson family, the second oldest son, Reed, was a farrier both for the rescue and his other clients at local ranches, Beckham was busy with rodeo most of the year, Lennon managed the feed store in town, and Callan instructed horse riding lessons here for youth to young adults. Travis and Charlotte, their parents, took care of the loose ends and managed the rescue, which left little time for other tasks like cleaning stalls and turning out horses.

They kept telling me the volunteers could muck the stalls in the white barn, but I refused, taking the chore on myself. The volunteers had their work cut out for them with the rescue horses. Cleaning their stalls took longer, as they had to be extra careful with sudden movements around the more frightened horses.

I didn't mind mucking stalls. It caused me to slow down and be with my own thoughts. Reed already agreed to take over while I was in Montana. I knew he'd have to wake up extra early to get it done, but I'd be back in a few days to relieve him.

I finished up, pulling the wheelbarrow out of the stall to close and latch the door. Rouge barked in the distance, probably chasing after another ground squirrel.

As I was moving onto the next stall, he shot past the barn door, his red merle coat a blur. His barks didn't cease as he kept running, the sound echoing from the pasture now.

I left the wheelbarrow in the aisle and headed for the opening of the barn to look out in the direction he was headed, trying to find where he took off to. His barking quieted and I shook my head, turning to go back inside.

Before I made it back through the door, my eyes caught on the horse standing out in the field. I narrowed my eyes, focusing in on Red saddled up with no Lettie.

That was never a good sign.

I ran back into the barn, grabbing Nova from his stall at the end. I slipped his halter on and jumped on him bareback, looping the lead rope around his neck and tying it in a quick knot. I squeezed my legs, urging him into a gallop.

Nova belonged to the Bronsons, but I was the only one who rode him nowadays. He wasn't fit to be a lesson horse and he didn't do well with different people riding him. He needed consistency, and I gave that to him.

The gate to the pasture was open due to all the horses being in the stalls today. When it got too hot, we kept them inside to track their water intake and keep fans on for them. Nova flew through the opening, aiming straight for Red without me having to point him in the direction. His jet black mane flew in the wind, his ears alert. I felt his muscles work underneath me as I leaned forward to let him fly.

Nova slowed as we approached Red, my vision landing on Lettie laying on the ground next to him. I cursed, pulling back on the lead rope to slow Nova enough for me to jump off. I landed, taking off at a run the rest of the way to Lettie.

I crouched next to her, afraid to touch her in case she was injured. "Lettie?"

"Mmh?" she hummed without opening her eyes.

"Lettie? Are you okay?" I tried to catch my breath despite my heart racing a mile a minute.

"Why wouldn't I be?"

My brows furrowed. "Did you hit your head?"

Her eyes popped open, landing on me. A smile crept up her lips as I scanned her, visually checking for injuries. "You thought I fell off?"

"You didn't?"

She shook her head, her hair splayed across the grass. That damn smile of hers shined up at me. "No."

"Then why the fuck are you on the ground?"

"Trying to take a nap." She laced her fingers together on her stomach.

"In the middle of a field?"

"What better place?"

I shook my head, falling back on my ass to sit next to her. She was crazy, always keeping me on my toes. I looked up at Red who still stood there, not a care in the world. "You've got that horse wrapped around your little finger, you know that, right?"

She smiled again, her eyes closed. "I know."

Nova grazed a few feet from us. You couldn't guess the beast just ran full gallop across a field with his cool demeanor as he munched on grass. I dangled my arms across my knees as I looked back at Lettie.

I watched the rise of her chest as she breathed, oblivious to the fact that I thought she was injured, or worse. Growing up, scares like this were normal. With everyone treating her like a child incapable of taking care of herself, any wrong move made her brothers worry, which in turn, made me worry. But she was an adult now, no longer the little girl I used to tease, and that had to count for something. Even her dad wasn't giving her a break, and I was concerned it would only scare her off and make her leave again.

My gaze moved to her neck when she swallowed, then up to her face to land on her lips. Her bottom lip was just a bit fuller than the top one, giving her a natural pouty look.

Shaking my head, I moved to lay down with my head next to hers, my body on the opposite side, causing me to see her upside down. I kept my eyes on her, noticing the way her nostrils flared slightly as she breathed, how her dark eyelashes laid against her skin with her eyes closed.

She was silent as she turned her head toward me, those baby blues making an appearance. "You watching me, Bailey Cooper?"

"Some sights deserve to be admired."

Her eyes darted back and forth between mine before she pushed off the ground, standing up. I heard her boots shuffle through the grass as she walked over to Red.

I sat up, twisting to face her. "You're leaving?"

I watched as she grabbed the reins, set her foot in the stirrup, and hefted herself into the saddle. Holding the reins in one hand, she turned Red to face me. "Nap time's over."

She clicked her tongue and Red took off in a relaxed lope, her wavy hair bouncing against her back as they rode toward the barn. I didn't take my eyes off of them until she dismounted and led him into the barn. I sighed, standing up to grab Nova from where he'd wandered to.

Fisting the lead rope still looped around his neck, I positioned myself beside him, grabbing his mane before swinging my leg over his back. I patted his neck before turning him around to walk in the direction of the barn.

"She's going to be the death of me, buddy."

7

LETTIE

Fourteen Years Earlier...

"Are you doing FFA again this year?" Lennon asked me from where he was perched on a chestnut horse to my left.

Lennon, Callan, Beckham, Reed, and I had gone on a long trail ride to savor the last bit of summer. Thirteen miles total, about six hours in the saddle. We'd taken turns racing each other on the trail, everything naturally turning into a competition for my brothers.

"I think so. Dad said I can do it with one of our calves again," I replied. Last year, I had shown one of our calves in my school's Future Farmers of America program.

"You gonna get all sad again at the end?" Beckham teased from ahead of us on his bay.

I shot a glare at his back. "No."

Reed burst into laughter next to Beck. "She's such a liar."

"Am not!" I shouted. I was so tired of them trying to get a rise out of me. "Mom said I just have a big heart."

Callan, who was on the other side of me riding a palomino, said, "It's okay to have a big heart, Lettie."

"I know! But Reed and Beck always make fun of me for it," I complained.

Lennon reached over, patting my tiny knee. "Just ignore them. Brothers always make fun of each other, you just get caught in the crossfire sometimes."

"Sometimes?" I huffed. "It feels like all the time."

Lennon shrugged. "We love you even if sometimes it doesn't feel like it, little sis."

Callan nodded in agreement. "Always."

Beck looked over his shoulder at the three of us. "I didn't ask to go on a sappy trail ride."

"Race you to the barn?" Reed challenged Beck.

"You're on," Beck said right before kicking his horse into a gallop.

"Hey!" Reed yelled before following in his dust.

"Do you think they'll ever grow up?" I asked Len and Cal.

Lennon smiled. "Lettie, you're nine years old."

"Yeah, but even *I* know they act like boys," I stated. *Childish* boys.

"That's because they *are* boys," Cal pointed out.

"You guys don't act like they do," I said.

Cal nodded. "Fair."

"They'll mature one day, Lettie. Just gotta deal with them until then," Lennon said.

Callan had never acted like Beck and Reed. He was always mature in his own way, always offering to help our mom clean or take on extra chores.

Reed and Beck were the two who were crazy, always causing problems and getting into trouble by our dad. Then add Bailey into the mix, and they were really stirring up trouble.

Lennon was a lot like Callan, less interested in causing havoc and more into taking on responsibilities. It's funny how a ranch can mold people differently. The ranch matured Len and Cal, teaching them important life lessons, while Reed and Beck used it as their playground.

That wouldn't be the case for long though.

Reed was four years older than Beckham, and it was slowly starting to show. While Beck still thought their childhood games were fun, Reed was beginning to grow up more, becoming the respectable teen our dad urged him to be.

We approached the barn, Reed and Beck's voices drifting out from inside. Len, Cal, and I pulled our horses to a stop beside the pasture fence. The two of them dismounted as I took my time, looking out at the cows, wondering which mama's calf would end up being mine in the spring.

They were busy taking the bridles off their horses when I dismounted, and the second my feet hit the ground, the world spun. It felt like I was tilting backwards, so I clamped my eyes shut to stop the sky from turning into the ground. My mind felt like a cloud, my fingers going warm and cold at the same time.

"Lettie?" I heard who I think was Lennon say, but then my back slammed into something hard and metal, and I struggled to catch my breath.

Something fell to the ground - *a bridle, maybe?* - and a hand wrapped around my arm, pulling me upright and into what had to be a chest. "Lettie, what's wrong?"

Lennon. That was Lennon's voice.

My hands pressed against his chest like an anchor, trying to keep the boat that was my mind from rocking against the waves.

I was so dizzy.

"Did she eat this morning?" Callan asked.

I managed a nod, but it made my head swim faster.

"Reed! Beck! Get out here!" Cal yelled.

I heard boots pounding on dirt as Lennon grabbed my chin, making me look up at him. My eyes were open now, but there were two of him. "Are you hurt?"

"No," I croaked.

"Dizzy?"

I nodded, and the tidal wave came back, turning me upside down. I clamped my eyes shut again as Lennon dropped his hand from my chin. My forehead slammed down into his chest. I didn't mean to drop my head so fast.

"What's wrong with her?" Beck asked at the same time Reed spoke. "Is she okay?"

There were too many voices coming from my brothers, echoing in my head.

"Beck, get Mom," Cal instructed him.

Boots faded into the distance, a door slammed, and my mind righted itself.

"Lettie, do you think you're going to pass out?" Lennon asked me.

I shook my head, and this time I didn't spin. But honestly, I wasn't really sure what was happening.

"Keep her against you," Cal said. "I don't know what's going on with her."

Join the party, Cal.

I lifted my head, looking around us. There was no more spinning, but I felt tingly.

"Your lips," Reed muttered, looking at me like he saw a ghost.

One of my hands on Lennon's chest reached back to touch my lip, unsure what Reed was seeing.

"I think she's going to pass out," Cal said, staring at me with wide eyes.

Lennon shook his head, keeping his eyes on me. "She's okay."

Was I?

Lennon just didn't want to freak me out.

The door to the house swung open and I turned to look. Our parents were running out ahead of Beck, down the porch steps and over to us.

"What happened?" Mom asked, frantic.

"She got off her horse and fell into the fence," Lennon said.

"She said she was dizzy," Cal added right after.

"Her lips, Mom." Reed hadn't taken his eyes off me.

What was wrong with my lips?

Mom reached for me, cupping my face in her hands. "You're white as a ghost, Lettie. Do you feel okay?"

"I don't know," I replied honestly. I really didn't know what I was feeling other than tired and dizzy.

"I'm going to take her in," Mom said to Dad.

"The hospital?" Lennon questioned.

Hospital?

Mom nodded. "Something could be wrong."

"It was a long ride," Beck pointed out.

Callan shook his head, looking almost mad at Beck. "You don't just pass out after a ride, idiot."

"Boys," Dad warned. "Go inside."

They shook their heads. "No. We want to go with them."

Dad pinned them with his *I'm-not-fucking-around* face. "Go inside, and your mother will update us once they know something. She doesn't need four boys running around a hospital while Lettie is being taken care of."

What if I didn't want to go?

Hospitals were scary. Hospitals were the place you went before you died.

"Am I dying?" I asked no one in particular.

Mom pulled me to her chest, hugging me tight. Lennon stayed close by our side. "No, sweetie. We're just going to make sure you're okay. We'll be home in no time."

A hand rubbed up and down my back, but it wasn't Mom's hand.

"We'll be right here waiting for you, Lettie," Dad said.

My bottom lip trembled, and I turned from Mom's arms into Dad's. He wrapped himself around me, pressing his lips to the top of my head. "Everything's okay, sweetheart."

But I got the feeling my entire life wouldn't be the same from this point forward.

8

LETTIE

The next day, I woke up early to meet Lennon in town for coffee at Bell Buckle Brews before he opened the feed store for the day. I drove Reed's truck to town since I had to pick up grain for the horses. When I left, Bailey's Chevy was already parked out front of the white barn.

As teens, he was always busying himself with chores around the ranch instead of doing homework or extracurricular activities at school. He preferred working with his hands and getting things done around the two ranches he split his time between.

I'd only been back a few days, but I could already tell he spent more time here than he used to. I hoped he left time for himself and didn't lose himself in the work. Dealing with one ranch was hard enough, but dividing your time between two, *and* helping out with a rescue? I didn't know how he did it, but just like everything else, he made it look easy.

I pulled into the parking lot of the feed store, opting to walk the short distance to the café. Lennon's old truck was already parked in the corner of the lot when I got here. The men in my life loved their early mornings, that much was certain.

Less than five minutes later, I opened the door to Bell Buckle Brews. The smell of freshly brewed coffee and warm pastries filled my nose. I found Lennon sitting at a small table and made my way over to him. He stood up when he saw me, a smile lighting up his face before he pulled me in for a hug.

"Hey, sis. Long time no see."

I relaxed against him, the realization of how much time passed hitting me like a truck. He looked so different, his dirty blond hair longer, light scruff lining his jawline. I pulled back and he motioned for me to sit.

"Got you a vanilla latte. Hope that's okay," Lennon said to me.

I nodded as I sat down across from him. "Thank you. So, how have you been? Anything new?"

He took a sip of his coffee. Black, just like all my brothers drank it.

"Besides the store, not much. I'm hoping to buy the building from the guy who owns it. Now that I manage the employees and keep up with everything else, I don't see the point in leasing the space anymore."

"That'll be so good for you. I'm glad you love management enough to take it over."

He chuckled. "I don't know if anyone really *loves* management, but it keeps me busy. Something to do that's my own. Plus, it gets me away from Dad's grumpy ass on the ranch."

The corners of my lips tipped up at the memories of Dad bossing us all around when we'd help out with the horses or cattle.

I cupped my hands around my coffee, running my thumbs up the sides. "I've been trying to find something like that for a long time."

"College didn't do it for you, I take it."

I shook my head, letting out a sigh. "Despite popular belief, they don't hand out jobs or tell you what you're meant to do in life."

"Do you know what you want to do?"

"Honestly, no. You guys have it all figured out and I feel like I'm the only one still lost."

"You'll figure it out, Lettie. You always do."

I stared down at my coffee. "I hope so. It's frustrating to have spent all that time at school and still have no path."

"It'll come to you one day. When I started working at the feed store, I never once thought I'd own the place, and now look at me. Don't try to force it. You'll know it when the work starts feeling less like a job and more like a passion."

I sipped my drink, the caffeine making its way through my system. "I'll let you know when that happens."

He sat back in his chair, studying me. "So, do you know how long you're staying?"

"I'm not sure. I'm going to Montana for the auction in Billings. Dad has some horses he's got his eye on that I'm picking up."

"You're driving six hours with a trailer alone?"

I pursed my lips. "I'm going with Bailey."

He tried to hide his smile behind his coffee.

"What?" I asked.

"Nothing. Enjoy your trip."

I rolled my eyes at the smile that stayed plastered to his face. If Lennon thought there was something going on between me and Bailey, he was sorely mistaken.

***

Bailey was leading an elderly rescue horse to the pasture when I pulled up to the ranch. I parked Reed's truck outside of the white barn and was getting out of the truck when I saw Bailey gently pulling the halter off of the chestnut horse. Once free, the horse turned and took off at a gallop through the field, his tail sticking up behind him. There was something moving about watching a once-neglected horse have all the freedom it ever dreamed of.

I rounded the truck to open the tailgate and grabbed a bag of grain, turning with it to find Bailey standing directly behind me.

He grabbed the bag from me and set it on top of two other bags in the truck bed before picking up all three of them together.

"Do you ever take a break?" I asked as I grabbed another bag.

He carried them into the barn, setting them on the floor in the room where we kept all our medicine, supplements, and feed. I followed, setting my one bag on top of his three.

"Yep."

"Really? When?"

He brushed past me as he headed back to the truck to grab the rest of the bags. "Took a water break earlier."

I followed, watching the muscles in his back move as he walked, his white shirt stretched across his form. "For what, two minutes?"

"Something like that," he said as he grabbed the remaining three bags, tossing them onto his shoulder to close the tailgate with his other hand.

"I could have closed that."

He ignored me, making his way back to the feed room. I didn't bother to follow him this time. Instead, I walked over to the fence surrounding the pasture. I laid my arms across the metal fence, resting my chin on top of them to watch the horses graze. The only sounds were a distant whinny and the breeze blowing through the fields.

I deserved the cold shoulder from Bailey. He didn't have to ask for me to know he wanted answers. I just didn't want to give them. I was scared that the answers I had would change our relationship, but a part of me felt that the way I'd been neglecting to be honest was changing us already.

I heard Bailey's boots a second before he showed up at my side, resting a knee on the fence and dangling his arms over the top. We both stared out at the field, feeling tranquil with the silence and peace this ranch brought. This is what I missed; what I had longed to come back to.

"I'd like to leave at sunrise tomorrow. Get to Billings early so we can get our hotel situated," he said, keeping his eyes on the land.

"That's fine." I straightened, grabbing hold of the dusty fence. I was silent a few moments before asking, "Do you hold it against me?"

His body tensed. He knew what I was referring to. "No."

"Then what is it, Bailey?"

He let out a sigh and brought his gaze to me. "Just trying to figure you out, Huckleberry."

He could join the club. I felt like I wasted all those years being away when I could have been trying to figure out my life here, with the support of friends and family.

Instead, I ran. From Bailey's feelings and my own, from this small town that I thought had nothing to offer me. But maybe I wasn't meant for bigger and better. Maybe Bell Buckle was the place I was meant to be. Being back here, that was starting to feel more true every day.

9

BAILEY

"You want to help me hook up the trailer?"

Lettie looked over at me, the early afternoon sun lighting up the faint smile on her lips. "You do remember what happened the last time, right?"

I smiled, remembering all too well. "How could I forget? You made me dent my bumper. Waving your hands to keep going when I was well past the ball."

She laughed, the sound almost taking me to my knees. "I was waving at you to stop!"

I pushed away from the fence, dusting my hands on my dirt-stained jeans. "That's not what it looked like to me."

She shoved my shoulder and *fuck*, if I didn't want her hand back the moment she took it away. This was the Lettie I missed

- the Lettie I could joke with and poke fun at. I'd get the old Lettie back, no matter how long it took.

We walked over to the dually Travis owned. He'd bought it primarily for the rescue. They'd needed a bigger rig after the previous truck crapped out on us while we were hauling horses back from Texas.

"Another Ford?" Lettie asked as we approached the vehicle.

I shrugged, pulling the key out of my pocket. "You know your dad."

She rolled her eyes as I got behind the wheel. I rolled the windows down and watched out the rearview mirror as she walked over to the gooseneck trailer, her ass perfectly shaped in her Kimes Ranch jeans. I set my hand on top of the steering wheel as I took her in. I'd stolen a look or two growing up with her, but five years did a lot to a person, and she came back looking downright mouthwatering.

She turned around by the trailer and must've seen my face in the mirror because she frowned. I shot her a smile and reached for the shifter to put the truck in reverse. I eased my foot off the brake, letting the truck roll back on its own.

As I got closer, I looked back out the mirror to find her standing there, waving me backwards. She motioned to the left, so I turned the wheel, following her direction. Almost immediately after I turned the wheel, she changed her hands to point right. Spinning the wheel slightly, the truck's back end drifted to the right.

And this was when she started being unclear.

She kept waving her hands, the direction looking right but the more I kept right, the more frantic her hands got. Seconds later, she threw her hands out, and I tapped the brake, the truck rolling to a stop. I put it in park and got out, walking along the side to check if it was lined up with the ball. I frowned and turned to her.

"Lettie, I'm like four inches off."

She put her hands on her hips. "I tried to tell you to go left."

"Your hands were pointing right."

She rolled her eyes. "Maybe I should get behind the wheel."

I chuckled, turning around to get back in the truck. I put it in drive, pulling forward a few feet, then shifted it back to reverse and didn't bother looking out my side mirror. I looked through my center mirror, lining the truck up with the trailer.

I didn't *need* her help, but I did want to spend time with her, despite us going to Montana for a few days alone. She was pretty cute when she got frustrated, and there was no way she wasn't going to get frustrated trying to line up the trailer. Her mental measurements of distance were shit.

I put the truck back in park after I felt satisfied with where the ball was lined up. Killing the engine, I got out, double checking the position.

She crossed her arms. "I saw that."

I got busy hooking the trailer up to the truck. "Saw what?"

"You lined it up perfectly yourself."

"Had to get good at doing it alone without you here."

She was silent for so long that I paused, looking over my shoulder at her. She was biting the inside of her cheek, staring at her boots with her hands now shoved in the back pockets of her jeans.

"Lettie-"

"I'm sorry," she said softly, her eyes cast down.

I turned to face her but kept my distance. "Don't be sorry."

She looked up then, her eyes slightly glassy. "Well, I am, Bailey. I'm sorry I left."

I stood there staring at her like an idiot. After about a minute of silence, she turned and walked away. I debated going after her, but thought better of it. We'd have plenty of time to talk during our trip. I didn't want to start it out on a bad note, so for today, I'd drop it.

I finished hooking the trailer up and locked the truck before heading to my own truck to go home. I still had to pack and wrap up my chores on my parents' ranch before leaving tomorrow.

Hopefully, the sixteen hours between now and when we left was enough time to let things cool down. Otherwise, this was going to be the longest three days of my life.

10

LETTIE

It felt like I had just fallen asleep when my alarm went off. I tossed and turned all night with the anticipation of going on this trip for the rescue and being alone with Bailey for three consecutive days, causing my mind to race. I didn't pack anything last night since the majority of my clothes were still in duffel bags. I grabbed one that I knew had my summer clothes, pulling some out to lighten the load since we wouldn't be gone too long.

After getting dressed, I slung the bag over my shoulder and headed for the kitchen. Grabbing a banana off the counter, I turned to find my dad starting a pot of coffee.

"The sun's not even up yet," I said.

He grunted, pouring the ground beans into the top of the machine.

"You'd think after waking up at the crack of dawn for so long, you'd be a morning person at this point," I mumbled.

He stabbed at a button on the machine before opening one of the cabinets and pulling two mugs out. One for him, and one for my mom, who I knew was still in bed.

"Don't forget to send me updates. Bailey knows what horses to bid on, and I don't want one more than what's on that list." He eyed me, his typical frown plastered to his face. "I mean it, Lettie."

I rolled my eyes, peeling away at my banana. "Yeah, yeah. Only the horses you say. I've got it, Dad. You can trust me."

He grunted again as Bailey's truck lights lit up the driveway through the kitchen window as he pulled in next to the house. "That's my cue. Love you, Dad."

"Love you, too. Be safe."

I tossed the remnants of my banana in the trash after taking a few bites and headed out the front door, making it down the porch steps as Bailey unlocked the dually. I opened the back door, tossing my bag in, then got in on the passenger side.

He opened the driver side door, the rising sun just barely illuminating the sky behind him. "Good morning," he said as Rouge jumped in the truck, hopping into the back seat.

I reached back to scratch the top of his head. He was already panting, anxious for adventure.

"Morning. You gonna keep my dog forever?"

He closed his door. "Not my fault he likes me better."

I scoffed. "He does not."

Bailey twisted in his seat to look back at Rouge. "Me, or Ms. Huckleberry-ass over here?"

"Hey!" I smacked him on the arm.

Rouge barked, coming to Bailey's protection. I rolled my eyes at the grin on his face. "That means nothing."

"Whatever you say, Huckleberry."

I was glad the mood was lighter than how we left things yesterday. When I left Bell Buckle, everything I did around the ranch and the rescue was pushed off onto someone else. Bailey took care of Rouge and Red, adding them to his already overflowing plate. Any chores I used to do were shoved off to Brandy and various volunteers.

I felt guilty for abandoning them. The more I thought about it, the more it sunk in. My brothers didn't leave, Brandy and Bailey didn't leave, and they were all doing better than I was.

Bailey started the truck, letting it warm up for a minute before heading out. I felt the truck jolt with every bump the trailer hit on the dirt road. Thankfully, once we hit pavement, it smoothed out. Bailey turned on a country playlist on his phone, Colter Wall's deep voice filling the cab.

After thirty minutes on the road, Rouge finally stopped pacing in the back seat and laid down, his panting quieting as he fell asleep stretched out. I stared out the window, laying my head against the headrest as Bailey drove silently. The only sound in the cab was the music and the faint hum of the tires.

***

I woke up to Bailey putting the truck in park and lifted my head off the window where my forehead had been resting to take in our surroundings. We were parked at a gas station, the pumps full of tourists and truck drivers.

"I'm going to check the trailer and let Rouge out to pee," Bailey said.

"I'm going to use the restroom, if that's alright."

He nodded and grabbed Rouge's leash as he got out. He opened the back and attached it to the dog's collar. As soon as his paws hit the ground, he was tugging at Bailey. He was used to running free and hated being tethered to a person by a six foot rope. I couldn't blame him. Sometimes, I felt like I was on a tight leash with my family too.

"Call me if you need me," Bailey said before closing the door.

I grabbed the handle and got out. My body felt stiff from my nap, my legs already aching. Despite the extra bit of sleep, I still felt exhausted. I headed inside the gas station, finding the restrooms tucked in the back corner.

After relieving myself, I wandered the aisles for a specific item, my eyes lighting up when I found it. I grabbed the bag and headed to the counter to check out. Walking back to the truck, I found Bailey loading Rouge up and unhooking the leash. I got in the passenger side and buckled myself in.

"Looks like there's a thunderstorm up ahead that we're going to hit. Shouldn't be too bad, though," he stated as he started the truck.

Looking at the dash, I saw I'd been asleep for three hours. That meant we were halfway to Montana. It wasn't uncommon for summer thunderstorms in the west, but hopefully, Bailey was right in that it'd be light. Driving a trailer in a storm could be dangerous, depending on the conditions.

"It's a good thing we left early then."

He nodded as he turned up the music, "Fast Hand" by Cody Jinks coming through the speakers. Rouge barked as we pulled back out on the highway, a protest to being stuck in the vehicle. I twisted in my seat to scratch behind his ear. "I know, bud. We'll be there soon."

He stared out the window, watching as cars passed us. I faced forward again, pulling the snack I bought from the gas station out of the pocket in the door. Bailey heard the crinkle, briefly glancing over at it.

A smile reached the corners of his mouth. "Sunflower seeds."

I opened the bag, holding it out to him. He stuck his hand in and grabbed a fistful, tossing his head back as he popped them in his mouth. I set the bag in my lap, staring down at the seeds. "Remember when we used to shove our cheeks full of them as kids, see how many we could fit?"

He chuckled before grabbing the empty water bottle from the cupholder, twisting the cap off and spitting a shell in the hole. "I remember you stuffed so many in your cheeks you almost choked to death."

I laughed, grabbing a few from the bag and dropping them in my mouth. "But I won."

"It was disgusting that we counted them afterward, saliva and all."

I grabbed the open water bottle, spitting a cracked shell in. "It was so gross."

He was grinning from ear to ear, one hand on the wheel, the other arm leaning on the center console as his eyes stayed focused on the road. "And you tried to *plant* them."

"I watered them every day and they never grew."

"No shit they didn't. They were shells."

"I was a kid! I didn't know."

"Callan and I didn't want to spoil your fun so we never told you."

He grabbed the bottle again, bringing it to his lips.

"You guys probably made fun of me behind my back."

He laughed again, handing the bottle back to me. "Oh, we definitely did."

Raindrops landed on the windshield, quickly turning into a downpour. With the land so flat in this area, I could see lightning in the distance, miles in front of us.

I reached forward to turn down the music after finishing off the last of the sunflower seeds in my cheek. I rolled the top of the bag and shoved it back in the pocket of my door.

Anxiety crept in as we drove further into the storm, my palms getting clammy. When I was thirteen, there'd been one of the biggest storms we'd seen pass by. Through all the chaos of the high winds and downpour of rain, lightning had hit the tree directly outside my bedroom window. I screamed so loud, the entire house woke up. They'd all stormed into my room to find the tree on fire through the window.

I'd ran outside with my brothers and dad wearing my flannel pajamas when Bailey and his dad sped into our driveway, having seen the fire from their house. One look at me and Bailey could tell I was terrified. While his dad helped the guys put out the fire in the storm, Bailey had held me to his chest in the driveway, rubbing circles on my back. I never would have thought the tree could have lit up so fast with all the rain, but the flames were relentless. Thankfully, there was no damage to the house, and soon after, the fire department showed up to help battle the fire. The entire time, I could tell Bailey wanted to help, but he'd stayed right with me.

I wiped my hands on my denim-clad thighs, trying to wipe the memory away. Bailey caught the movement from the corner of his eye, and I knew he was thinking of the same night.

"Forgot you hate thunderstorms," he said.

I turned to check on Rouge behind my seat to find him sleeping. He wasn't a fan of storms either, but at least he could sleep through them. I was thankful for the little bit of sleep I got earlier because until we got out of this weather, I wouldn't be able to relax.

I faced forward in time to see lightning strike the open field out the passenger window. I flinched as thunder rolled around us.

"Look at me."

My hands fisted on my seatbelt, holding onto it as I looked at Bailey. His green eyes landed on me before turning back to the road. "We're going to be okay. It's just a little rain."

As if the sky heard him, another lightning strike hit. The light illuminated the cab, and seconds later, thunder boomed. The rain pelted the windshield and Bailey turned up the speed of the wipers, their efforts doing little against the battering of rain.

I took a deep breath, attempting to calm my nerves. I leaned the back of my head against the headrest, clamping my eyes shut. I knew we'd be okay, but that didn't stop my fear from taking over. I probably looked pathetic sitting here while the storm did nothing to jar Bailey, even driving the trailer through this. I admired his ability to keep calm in stressful situations.

When I was ten and he was fourteen, I twisted my ankle trying to balance on rocks to cross the creek on my parents' property. Reed had freaked, running back to the house to get my dad. Bailey stayed with me on the shore of the creek bed, talking to me about the new rescues my dad had brought in. We'd sat there, my ankle elevated in his lap, and named each horse. He'd distracted me from the pain effortlessly.

That's just who Bailey was.

I hated the feelings that came up with the memories of us growing up. No amount of time away could keep those at bay.

"I bought the twenty acres next to my parents' ranch so we can grow more hay."

I gnawed on my cheek, the nervous tick doing little to ease me. "Really?"

"Yep. Bought it shortly after you left for college. We've upped our profit. Any bales not going to Lennon's store go to our horses and Bottom of the Buckle. Saves a hell of a lot on feed."

"That's really good."

"I heard that property next to your dad's might be up for sale soon. Billy passed away about a year ago and his kids have been trying to figure out what to do with it."

"Let me guess - you want to buy that one, too."

"I've thought about it. If I did, we could expand the rescue and have more space to take in more horses."

"My dad would like that. He's stretched thin on space. I can't believe he's seriously limiting how many horses we bring back."

Bailey chuckled. "Can't bring back a whole trailer full of 'em if we don't have the space, Huckleberry. You can't save them all, as much as we all want to."

"If we had more space, we could damn sure try," I said.

"You trying to convince me to buy Billy's land?"

I looked over at him. "Don't you want to save as many as you can?"

"Of course I do. I'd also like to get out of my parents' in-law unit. As convenient as it is living on their property, I need a place of my own."

I nodded, tapping my finger on the outside of my thigh.

"Reed won't ever leave my parents' ranch."

"You think?" He must've seen my anxious tapping because he reached over and set his hand on mine, his fingers resting on my thigh. My hand froze as all of my awareness focused on his touch.

"I mean, why would he? Cheap rent, and all his work is close."

"Yeah, maybe. I think he's hoping he can take over the ranch someday. Horseshoeing is hard on the body as you get older."

A breathy laugh escaped my lips. "He is getting a bit of a hunchback, huh?"

Bailey chuckled. "That's exactly why I didn't go into that field."

"Oh? Not because you have a million other things on your plate?"

He slowly slid his hand away from mine. "Had to keep my mind busy these past few years."

No doubt because of me. There was that guilt creeping in again.

He was silent for a moment before he spoke again. "Lettie."

"Yeah?"

"You can open your eyes now."

I hadn't even realized they were still clamped shut. I looked out the windshield to see the rain had slowed to a light trickle. I was so lost in his voice that I didn't notice when the sound of the wipers slowed and the thunder stopped. I brought my gaze to him and saw a faint rainbow painting the cloudy sky out his driver side window.

He glanced at me. "I'd save every single one of them if I could."

I studied him as he drove, his eyes not straying from the road in front of him for a while after our conversation. His cowboy hat was sitting on the dash against the windshield. His hair was messy but his jaw was free of the stubble that was there yesterday. He must've shaved this morning, but I knew by the end of our trip, his usual five o'clock shadow would be back.

Damn him and his big heart and his jawline and his hair and every word he spoke that made me forget every reservation I had when it came to the possibility of me and him.

We were barely a few hours into our trip and I was already falling back into old routines.

11

Bailey

I flicked on the blinker, turning into the hotel parking lot. The lot was packed, so I drove around the back and found an empty row to pull the truck and trailer into.

It took up a few spots, but I didn't have any other options. Hotels really needed to offer trailer parking. I couldn't keep track of how many dirty looks I'd gotten in the past for parking like this.

The clock on the dash showed it was half past one p.m. Though we left at the crack of dawn, the storm we passed through slowed us down quite a bit, but regardless, we made good time.

Beside me, Lettie unbuckled and opened her door before I had the chance to get out and do it for her. Heaving a sigh, I got out and opened the back door to grab our luggage. Rouge jumped past me, flying over my shoulder. I looked behind me to see him taking off in the direction of the grass.

"That dog is crazy," I said when Lettie opened the back door on her side. She reached in to grab his leash from where it sat on the floor.

"I call it full-of-life."

She closed the door, whistling for Rouge as she came around the hood of the truck. Pulling the luggage out, I turned in time to see him running at Lettie full speed. When he made it to her, he jumped up on her, his front paws almost reaching her chest.

She hooked the leash on his collar and he let out a whimper. "Sorry, bud. Can't have you running around the place."

She rubbed the top of his head as he tried to lick her, failing to reach her face. I closed the door to the truck and we headed inside, Rouge pulling on the leash in an attempt to get Lettie to walk faster.

As we approached the hotel lobby, I quickened my pace to get ahead of her and shoved the door open with my shoulder. She walked past me, Rouge right ahead of her. I guess the dog didn't understand *ladies first*.

Following after them, I came up beside Lettie at the front desk. The woman sitting behind the computer looked up, a bright smile on her face. "Do you two have a reservation?"

I nodded. "Yes, ma'am. Under the last name Cooper."

She typed on her keyboard briefly before turning to the printer right as a piece of paper slid out. She grabbed it and leaned forward in her chair to set it in front of me, placing a pen on top. "I just need you to sign and provide me with a credit card. It won't be charged until you check out."

I shifted the luggage to one hand and grabbed the pen, signing on the bottom line, then slid the pen and paper back to her. Pulling my wallet out of my back pocket, I handed her my card and ID. She typed the information into the computer and handed it back, then set a room key on the counter in front of me. "Room eighteen, up the stairs and to the left."

"Thank you."

Lettie grabbed the room key before I had the chance and brushed past me. I followed after her, failing miserably to keep my eyes off her ass as we climbed the stairs. I willed myself to think of anything but her ass. It was extremely difficult when it was so damn perfect-looking in her light wash boot cut jeans. I imagined leaning over her in bed, her on all fours with her ass on display before burying myself inside her.

I cleared my throat as we got to our floor, casting my eyes to the ceiling to rid myself of any dirty thoughts about Lettie. I was a goner for her and she didn't even know it.

Lettie inserted the key, the handle making a soft click before she turned it. The door swung open and she let go of Rouge's leash as he bolted inside, immediately jumping onto one of the beds.

I closed the door behind me, setting our bags on the small desk against the wall. The smell of lemon disinfectant and Windex filled my nose as I turned the AC down. Two queen-sized beds took up a majority of the space, a small TV sitting atop an oak dresser in front of them. Lettie pulled open the curtain, gazing out at the hills in the distance.

I ruffled the fur on Rouge's head where he was perched on the bed. "You can take a nap if you'd like. You seem tired."

She stayed silent for a minute before turning to face me, coming to sit on the edge of the bed next to Rouge. He rolled over, exposing his belly to her. She ran her hand along his chest as his tongue hung out the side of his mouth.

"I'm okay, I napped in the car."

I pulled out the chair that was tucked under the desk, taking a seat a few feet from her.

"You want to go to the restaurant next door for dinner in a bit?"

She turned to check the digital clock on the nightstand, then faced me. "At two in the afternoon?"

I frowned. "In a few hours, then."

"Sure." She reached over to grab the remote and turned on the TV. She flipped through the channels, each one progressively louder than the last. After a commercial blasted through the speakers, she muted it as she searched for something to watch. I stayed seated in the chair, watching as she settled on a History Channel show about ancient aliens.

I kept my focus on the TV, but every so often, I felt her eyes drift to me. Rouge slept on the bed next to her as we both pretended to be immersed in the show.

The only thing I was engrossed with was thoughts of her.
Questions.

Fantasies.

Why did she leave Bell Buckle? She went to college, sure, but that couldn't have been the only reason. Unless it was, and I was overthinking it. I had a hard time believing Lettie was so involved in her studies that she couldn't even send a text. There was something else she ran from, and I hoped that something wasn't me.

12

BAILEY

I paid the dinner bill despite Lettie's protests to split it. She came back from the restroom to find her cash still sitting on the table.

"I'll just leave it as a tip then," she snarked as she grabbed her cowhide wallet.

I smiled, rolling my eyes. We made our way through the restaurant, the space cramped with the amount of people dining here tonight. A kid ran out in front of Lettie and she stumbled back to miss colliding with him. I shot my arm out, my hand instinctively going to her waist to steady her. She leaned back into me slightly and I didn't miss when she briefly squeezed her eyes shut.

"Lettie?"

She righted herself, pushing my hand away. I reluctantly let go of her. "I'm fine."

She continued out of the restaurant and I followed, concern flowing through me. Whatever that was in there didn't seem like just a small stumble.

She stood on the sidewalk out front of the doors, taking a deep breath. "Just hot in there."

I didn't buy it, but I wouldn't push her. It'd only cause her to retaliate, and I didn't want to piss her off on our trip.

She turned to face me, a devious smile on her lips. "Want to go to the bar?"

"We've got a big day-"

She interrupted me. "Oh, c'mon, Bailey, we're supposed to be having fun. Trouble, remember?"

I did say that, didn't I? I guess there was no harm in a drink or two. The auction didn't start until the afternoon, anyway.

"Sure, but only for an hour." If Lettie had it her way, we'd be out all damn night.

"Rules? That's not the Bailey I know."

I rolled my eyes as she aimed for the dive bar next door. Once again, I followed. I was a lost puppy with Lettie, hopelessly wishing she'd throw me a bone.

At some point, I'd get around to getting answers out of her. Answers as to what made her go radio silent with me for five years before all of a sudden deciding to come back. But for now, I'd enjoy her being here, with me. I had five years to make up for. I'd better make it count.

***

Three shots and two beers later, I was pretty fucking buzzed, and not just off the alcohol. I was drunk off Lettie's laugh, her smile, her eyes. I couldn't keep my eyes off her ass every time she wandered to the jukebox, queuing up yet another Zach Bryan song. The woman was obsessed, but I wasn't holding it against her. The guy knew how to write a damn good song.

She made her way back to our table full of glasses, sliding into her chair and taking a long pull from her beer before speaking. "So, Bailey, tell me what I missed."

"Over the last five years?"

She nodded. "Mmhm."

"Well, your dad adopted out around eighty horses in the last two years. I lost track of the number before then. Callan's been getting good business as more people sign up for lessons. Beck has no problem staying on broncs for longer than eight-"

"No," she interrupted.

I cocked my head. "No?"

"I don't want to hear about *them*. I mean *you*. What have I missed with you?"

I rolled my lips together after I took a sip of beer. "You haven't missed much."

She grabbed the edge of the table, leaning forward. "Oh, c'mon! Give me something."

"I've just been doing what I've always done. Balancing the workload on my parents' ranch and helping out with the rescue."

"You're telling me *nothing* has changed with you since I left?"

I reached up to shove my cowboy hat lower, angling the brim down. The axis in which my world sat stopped spinning the moment Lettie crossed the county line.

I shrugged. "I help out where I can. I'm content."

She reached across the table and grabbed my hat, pulling it off and setting it on her own head. I frowned as she adjusted it.

"Stop covering those eyes," she said.

A smile pulled at the corners of my mouth. "Why?"

She sat back in her chair, shrugging as she crossed her arms. "They're beautiful, is all."

I leaned forward, the table small enough to where I was more than halfway across as I laid my arms on the sticky surface, folding my fingers together. "You think my eyes are beautiful?"

Her eyes were glued to mine as her features softened, her voice quieter than before. "I always have, Bailey."

I searched her eyes as the realization of what she said sunk in. She stared at me, my hat looking damn good on her despite it being many sizes too big, causing it to tilt slightly. Though her comment was innocent enough, I couldn't help but think further into it and what her admission had revealed.

She'd looked at me, *really* looked at me. As more than a friend, I was sure.

I didn't miss when she watched me walk away that day on the ranch, her face displaying her feelings, or all those times we'd swam at the creek as kids, her eyes lingering on me when I'd wear nothing but boxers. I didn't imagine any of it, I knew that now. No matter how long it took, I'd get her to open up and admit those feelings. Even if she did all she could to hide them. Even if those feelings were part of the reason she left.

Snapping us out of the trance we were in, she pushed back from the table and stood, a smile that meant she was up to no good pasted on her lips. "Let's do a shot."

I raised an eyebrow. "Another one?"

She crossed her arms in challenge. "You quitting on me early, Bailey Cooper?"

I stood up, shaking my head. "Wouldn't dream of it."

She made her way over to the bar, and again, I followed. This time, I was better at keeping my eyes on the back of her head instead of her round ass. That was, until I was practically face to face with it when she put her knee on a bar stool with her hands on the bar.

"What are you doing?" I hovered my hands beside her hips in case she fell. She *had* to be buzzed at this point.

She sat her pretty ass on the bar, facing me with her boots planted on the stool and her hands gripping the edge. Her hair fell around her face as she spoke.

"I dare you to do a belly shot."

A nervous laugh escaped me. "This isn't truth or dare, Huckleberry."

She raised an eyebrow, challenging me again. Lettie was going to be the death of me - my ruin, my damnation - but I didn't mind. She'd ruined me before, when she left all those years ago. At least this time, she was within reach. As long as that was the case, I'd go down willingly.

Taking a deep breath, I gestured to the bar. "Fine. Lay flat." She thought I'd back down, but I was determined as hell when it came to her.

Shock passed over her features briefly before she took my hat off, setting it on the bar beside her. She obeyed, her back resting on the top of the bar with her hair falling around her shoulders to rest on the wood. She didn't lift her shirt, so I took the initiative before she could take the opportunity from me.

Her hands laid at her sides as I stood over her, my fingers slipping under the hem of her shirt. When my fingers made contact with her skin, her breath hitched. I slid the material up, only enough to expose her belly button. I swallowed as I saw the rise and fall of her stomach, looking over to her face to see her eyes glued to me.

The bartender came over and handed me the bottle of whiskey, assumingly not wanting to come off as disrespectful by pouring it himself. I grabbed the bottle, hovering it over her before I broke eye contact and poured the amber liquid, the liquid pooling on her belly.

Setting the bottle on the bar, I grazed my fingertips over her jean-clad thigh as I bent down. Instead of getting it over with, I took my time. If this was the only opportunity I got to put my mouth on her, I was going to enjoy it.

I kissed the smooth skin next to her belly button, my breath hot on her skin as my tongue slipped out, lapping at her stomach. I felt her breath hitch again as I moved my tongue lower, right below where the whiskey sat. I felt her fingers twitch against my chest and I ached to feel them on my body and in my hair.

My hand on her thigh inched upward, but I stopped before I could get ahead of myself. I kissed her skin again before pulling away an inch, only to come back down, closing my mouth over her belly button. I sucked the rich liquid up. The burn down my throat was nothing compared to the pressure in my dick. I lapped out, licking up any missed alcohol, making sure to clean her of the substance entirely before pulling back to stand up straight.

I moved my hand from her thigh to grab the bottom of her shirt, pulling it back down to cover her stomach. She gazed at me a moment before she came to her senses, finally moving her arms to push up off the bar. Before she could jump down, I stepped in between her legs, setting my hands on her waist. Her eyes flicked down to my lips before they shot back up to my eyes. Setting my hat back on her head, I lifted her effortlessly and took a step back, setting her on the ground.

"Quittin' time?" I asked her, our bodies mere inches from each other.

Her gulp was audible as she nodded her head. I stepped out of her way, gesturing for her to go first. She walked by me, her shoulder brushing my chest. I grabbed my wallet, pulling out cash to put it on the bar. I slapped the wood twice, the bartender glancing over. I waved my thanks and followed after Lettie, slipping my wallet back in my jeans.

I could blame what just happened between us on the alcohol, but as the saying goes, drunk words are sober thoughts. There was no denying the way our bodies just reacted to each other. I could practically feel her holding back as my mouth came in contact with her skin.

If she was tamping down her body's response because of that small moment, I could only imagine how it would be if I had the chance to explore her entire body.

Thank goodness we were heading back to separate beds because I wouldn't be able to keep my hands to myself if I tried after getting a taste of her.

13

Lettie

I woke up alone, Bailey and Rouge nowhere in sight. I should be thankful I didn't have to face him bright and early after last night. In a way, I'd tested him by making him take a shot off of me. The way his mouth brushed my skin, the feel of his tongue on me, it only confirmed what I'd suspected. He thought of me as more than just his friend.

I guess I'd also tested myself. After having his mouth on me, I couldn't deny the feelings I'd been trying to keep at bay. I *enjoyed* the feel of his tongue on my skin, and that's what scared me. Sober me was too scared to cross that line with Bailey, but tipsy me wanted nothing but to destroy that invisible line and give in to all the urges I'd been trying to push away for so long.

Did I really rob myself of those years with him, trying to ignore the growing feelings between us, all because I was terrified of ruining our life long friendship? It was a pathetic reason.

I wished I was able to say I went away to college just for the education. The unknown of what would happen if we took that next step kept me from entertaining the possibility of more between us. He was twenty-two at the time, I was eighteen. He had far more experience in that field yet his eyes were always on me. He never brought girls around the ranch and the guys never talked about their flings, at least not around me, but it was no secret they had them.

Pushing away any thoughts of Bailey with another woman, I opted for a cold shower. Pulling the covers off, I grabbed my phone and headed for the bathroom, turning the water on as cold as it would go. Before getting in, I checked my notifications, finding two unread texts from Brandy. They were sent ten minutes apart from each other.

> **Brandy:** Have you given in and ridden that cowboy yet?

> **Brandy:** You must be busy. Don't forget to wear the hat.

The corners of my mouth ticked up as I typed my response.

> **Lettie:** No riding has happened, but his tongue was places it's never been before.

Three dots appeared as she instantly replied.

Brandy: Are you insinuating that his tongue has been places before?

Brandy: Forget I asked that. What do you mean his tongue was "places"?!

Lettie: I'll tell you when I get home.

Brandy: I have to wait?! This is so not best friend behavior. I'm replacing you while you're gone.

Lettie: You'd never. You're too obsessed with me.

Brandy: This is true. And also why I need to know why his tongue was on you, where his tongue was on you, and how his tongue was on you!

Lettie: I guess you'll have to wait.

Brandy: Does Bailey know you're such a tease?

I sent the middle finger emoji back and set my phone on the counter. Stripping from my pajama shorts and oversized t-shirt, I stepped into the shower, bracing against the stream that hit my skin like tiny needles. I pulled the door to the shower closed and fully immersed myself under the spray, soaking my hair.

I washed my hair, then moved to my body, grabbing the bar of soap from the wall. I forgot all my toiletries at home. I must've grabbed the wrong bag when I left because my bathroom bag was nowhere to be found. I'd have to get over-the-counter iron supplements at some point, and soon, because I'd already neglected to take them since I arrived home. My head was somewhere else these past few days, causing me to stray from my daily routine.

I ran the soap over my belly, remembering the feel of Bailey's mouth on me. I hated that I wanted it back. One hit of Bailey and I was addicted.

Setting the soap back on the tiny shelf, I stood under the shower head to rinse off, but as I did, the door to the bathroom swung open, slamming against the wall. I yelped, moving to cover myself as I faced the wall. Rouge ran over to the toilet and proceeded to drink from it.

"Get out!" I yelled at my dog.

"Rouge!" I heard Bailey shout right after the door to our room clicked shut. He came around the corner, eyes widening when they landed on me through the glass door of the shower before slapping a hand over his eyes. "Fuck! Sorry, Lettie. Rouge, get out here!"

Embarrassment flooded over me as my skin turned pink despite the freezing water rolling down my body. Rouge was a blur as he ran back out of the bathroom. Bailey blindly reached for the door handle. Once he found it, he swung the door shut as I stood frozen, still attempting to cover my body with my hands.

Standing there for a few more minutes, I gathered myself, turning off the water. I stepped out, grabbing a towel and wrapping it around myself. I looked in the mirror, giving myself a mental pep talk. He probably didn't see anything. I could go out there, grab my clothes, get dressed in here, and everything would be fine.

Mustering the strength, I took a deep breath and headed into the room. I avoided looking at Bailey, but it was hard when he sat at the desk chair, right in front of where our bags were. Rouge was perched on the end of my bed, panting as he watched me.

I walked the four steps to my bag, unzipping it with one hand while holding my towel shut with the other. God forbid it fall open.

Bailey's back was to me as I rummaged through the bag, grabbing an ivory and peach striped Wrangler button-up, my jeans, underwear, and bra. The hook on my bra snagged on the zipper to my luggage as I tried to pull it out. *My luck.* I yanked on it, the motion causing my hair to hit the back of Bailey's neck.

"Cold shower?" he asked, then took a casual sip of his coffee.

Fuck my life.

I didn't have to look to know he had a shit-eating grin on his face.

"Water heater must not work," I lied.

My bra now free, I held the wad of clothes to my chest as I made my way back to the bathroom. I closed the door, making sure it clicked this time. I locked it, too, for safe measure. I dressed, then used my fingers to comb through my hair in a meager attempt to work the knots out.

I walked out of the bathroom after hanging up my towel.

"I got you a spinach and egg breakfast burrito, and a coffee," Bailey said, not turning to look at me.

"Thanks," I replied before sitting on the bed, grabbing the coffee from where he set it on the nightstand.

"You're welcome."

I unwrapped the foil on my burrito, the smell of food making my stomach growl. Even though I drank more last night than I typically did, I didn't feel very hungover. I hoped it stayed that way throughout today.

"So, how do horse auctions work?" I'd never been to one before even though my parents had started the rescue well before I was born. They didn't bring me along on any of their trips, usually opting to take one of my brothers instead if they needed an extra hand.

He finished chewing his bite of food before he spoke. "Once we're inside, we'll get a bidding number from the window. Depending how early we get there, we can walk around the stables to see the horses. Travis already knows which ones he wants, though, so once the auction officially starts, we'll bid on them. If we're the highest bid, we'll sign some paperwork after the auction is over, and tomorrow morning we can pick them up."

I nodded as I chewed. He made it sound so simple, as if their lives weren't in our hands.

We sat in silence for a while, enjoying our small breakfast. Even after finishing off the burrito, I had the craving to eat ice, but settled on a sip of coffee. Growing up, I always loved bringing a bowl of ice to my room and crunching on it as I watched movies. Some people snack on chips, I snack on ice.

If all went to plan, we'd be on the road tomorrow, heading back to the ranch. Before leaving on this trip, I wanted to stay far away from Bailey in the hopes of not bringing up the past. Being in Montana alone with him, I had no choice but to confront my feelings about him.

I missed him, not just right now, but every day that passed in the last half a decade. I couldn't count the number of times I'd pulled up his contact in my phone, my finger hovering over the call button before I'd think better of it and put the phone down.

After all this time, I'd assumed he'd moved on. I never asked my brothers about him because I didn't want to hear that he was dating someone or that he was happy without me there. It was cruel, really, to wish he was missing me as much as I was him.

I was the one who left, knowing the damage it could cause, and yet I still made my choice. I'd have to live with that for the rest of my life regardless of what ended up happening between me and Bailey. I didn't deserve it, but I hoped he forgave me. I wasn't sure if he already had, but the only way I'd get my answer would be to ask him myself.

That was exactly what I'd been avoiding since I'd gotten back, and soon, I'd have to face it head on.

14

LETTIE

After parking in the dirt lot, we headed inside the auction house. The building looked like an oversized old barn from the outside. Saddles were stacked on racks directly inside the doors, and as we continued on our way, halters of every color, bits, stirrups, and spurs lined the rows of tables. Behind the tables were wooden bleachers that formed a U around the dirt sales ring, which had a tall structure on the other side of it that looked sort of like a lookout tower. There were large openings on either side of it, and through them, I could see horses corralled in small pens outside, people walking about as they viewed them.

We approached the long line of people waiting to get their bidding numbers from the elderly lady at the window.

"I'm going to go out back while you get our number," I said to Bailey.

He surveyed the crowd before looking down at me. "Just be careful, alright? I'll come find you after."

"No promises," I said with a wink.

He rolled his eyes as I turned to walk down the narrow hallway, squeezing against the wall when people brushed by to avoid shoulders clashing. I blinked against the sun when I made it out of the dimly-lit hall, walking down the ramp beside the building.

A few feet away, a man gripped a lead rope, pulling it to try to encourage the horse attached to it to walk. Seeing that he was clearly struggling, I approached with caution before swinging my arms up, clicking my tongue. The horse eyed me before stepping a few feet to the side, tossing his head up in the air and swishing his gray tail.

"Be careful, little lady, he's a wild one."

Ignoring the name, I swung my arm closest to the horse's rear, clicking my tongue again. After a few tries, the horse took my direction and stepped forward, lowering his head slightly, his flea-bitten coat taut over his muscles as the man took advantage and led him away.

The horse's ears were pinned back as they walked through the rows of pens before he stopped in front of one, swinging the gate open. He led the horse into the pen, closing the gate behind him and unhooking the lead rope, but keeping the halter fastened. The man climbed through the metal fence before disappearing inside the auction house.

I walked down the aisle in front of me, feeling my throat tighten at the sight of all these horses awaiting an unknown fate. Some would get homes, work on ranches, maybe become some little girl's dream, but some wouldn't get so lucky.

I knew that lower bids were typically from kill buyers. Some kill buyers would try to resell them privately at a higher price, but most shipped them off to Canada or Mexico for slaughter. Hate was too nice of a word to describe how I felt about them. Growing up with the rescue and knowing too many horror stories, I wished we could own the whole state of Idaho and take them all there for sanctuary.

I wasn't oblivious to the fact that sometimes, euthanasia was the best route. I never wanted an animal to suffer, but if there was a chance we could help them without letting them go to a kill pen, I wanted to do all I could to make it happen.

My parents had been doing this for years before my brothers and I were born. They started Bottom of the Buckle Horse Rescue after attending their first horse auction and seeing all the malnourished horses going for cheap, knowing what that meant.

My mom had the biggest heart and I liked to think I got that from her. Charlotte Bronson wanted to save them all, and that rubbed off on me growing up when I'd hear my parents arguing after a long trip, my mom heartbroken over the ones left behind. My dad would comfort her, like he always did when she was upset. He'd become her punching bag for the emotional toll animal rescue took on her. It was hard, but it was worth it. Saving even one life may seem like such a small act, but to that one life, you were changing their entire world. I couldn't help but hope that gray horse the man just locked away was on my dad's list to come home.

In all my life of being around horses, I came to quickly find that you can't force a horse to do anything. You have to emotionally connect with them, reason with them so they understand why you're asking them to do something. Horses were more like us than a lot of people might think.

I came up to a pen where a bay filly was nursing on her mother, then made my way to the one beside it to an older chestnut gelding who was basically skin and bones. I set my hands on the metal fencing, emotion swelling as he stood there, looking defeated. I already knew he was on the list. My mom had direct contact to this auction house, and the owner always called her when they got ones like this.

"You'll be safe soon, buddy," I whispered to him, his ear twitching as a fly landed on it.

Continuing on my way through the pens, I stopped to admire a palomino mare, her muscles indicating she was most likely used on a ranch most of her life.

"Pretty one, ain't she?" a male voice said as a figure came up beside me, leaning his elbow on the fence to face me.

"Yep." I didn't bother looking at him, hoping he'd take the hint and continue on his way.

"You'd look good riding her." Though he was talking about the horse, I knew what he was insinuating with the comment. I pushed away from the fence and moved to the other side of the aisle, not giving him the reaction he wanted.

"What's your name?" Of course, he followed.

I kept my body facing the pen as I looked at him. He was wearing a faded baseball cap, stained jeans, and an old Bud Light shirt.

"Wouldn't you care to know?"

He flashed a smile that he must've thought got him all the ladies. "Wouldn't be asking if I didn't."

Turning back to face the horse in front of me, I grabbed the dusty metal. He took a step closer, my shoulder almost brushing his chest. "That's not very lady-like, now is it?"

"You're not being much of a gentleman yourself," I retorted.

He grabbed the fence above my head, caging me in from the side. I bit the inside of my cheek. "That's alright, we don't gotta know each other's names to have a good time."

Barf in my mouth.

"Back the fuck up."

Looking to my left, I saw Bailey standing behind the guy, smoke practically coming out of his ears as he took in how the guy had me caged. The man threw his hands up in mock surrender, taking a step back and turning to come face to face with Bailey.

"My bad, man. Didn't know she was taken."

Bailey stared him down, his fists flexing at his sides as he clearly tried to contain the rage building inside of him. Not wanting to be a part of it if they made a scene, I turned to my right and headed further down the aisle, dust kicking up behind my boots as I went. I turned the corner, my arms crossed against my chest.

"Lettie, hold up," I heard Bailey say somewhere behind me.

Ignoring him, I continued walking, seeming interested in the horses I passed.

"Lettie." He grabbed my elbow, his grip gentle before I shook him off, spinning on him.

"What was that?"

He blinked, shaking his head before gesturing to where we were standing moments ago. "That guy was making you uncomfortable."

"I had it handled."

"Sure looked like it."

I pursed my lips together and turned on my heel, but before I could walk away, he grabbed my elbow again. "I'm sorry. I just, I saw that look on your face and-"

"I don't need saving." I whirled on him, but he didn't flinch.

"I'm just looking out for you, Lettie."

My fingers dug into my arms as I stared at him. "Well, I don't need that, either."

He dropped his hand, pulling his hat off and running a hand through his hair. "It's hard not to overstep around you."

"What's that supposed to mean?"

He set the cowboy hat back on his head, then grabbed the fence beside him. "It means my whole life, I've watched you whither under your brothers' concern for you. I've seen the way you tense when you think someone sees something wrong, or the look on your face when your parents tell you that you can't do some reckless shit they wouldn't think twice about letting your brothers do. I've had to tiptoe around my feelings for you since we were kids. Every time I worry about you, I have to hide it, Lettie, and even more so since you got back, because I'm scared that if you see it written on my face, you'll disappear again."

I dropped my hands to my sides, gnawing on the inside of my cheek. He was right. He was the only one who didn't try to shelter me, and he paid the most for it when I left. It wasn't fair to him.

"I'm sorry." All I could do was apologize.

He looked down at his boots, dropping his hand from the fence. "You don't have to be sorry."

"I am, Bailey. I'm sorry I made you feel like you couldn't care about me."

He looked back up at me, his green eyes full of emotions he'd been holding captive since I got back. But I knew he wouldn't voice them because of the fear I had instilled in him. This was the same way he'd looked at me when I'd made the decision to leave and not say a word.

"Even if you push me away, Lettie, I'll always care about you."

"I know." And he'd proved that the moment he'd caught me from falling off that ladder.

He visibly swallowed and his expression changed in a flash, a slight smile spreading on his face. "Let's go save some horses."

I gave a closed-lip smile, thankful he didn't push the subject further.

15

BAILEY

"Tag twenty-seven, six-year-old quarter horse, sorrel gelding." The auctioneer's voice echoed through the building as a cowboy about my age mounted the horse. He looked sound from where I sat, his body toned from years of work. The guy trotted the horse in the small space, then stopped him to back him up. The horse obeyed with no problems, the price on him going up with each fancy maneuver.

Minutes later, the horse was led out of the building. He sold for forty-six hundred dollars to a family in the corner. Their little boy beamed as he jumped from his seat, eager to see his new horse in the back. Another horse was shooed into the ring, this one with no tack.

"Tag twenty-eight, three-year-old quarter horse, gray gelding."

Beside me, Lettie leaned forward, planting her hands on her knees as the horse trotted around the enclosed area, tail sticking straight out, his movements frantic. I glanced between her and the horse in the pit as the crowd began their bidding, the auctioneer rattling off numbers.

After a few back and forths, the highest bid landed on two hundred. "Two hundred going once," the auctioneer boomed over the mic.

Lettie gnawed on her bottom lip as her grip on her knees tightened.

"Two hundred going twice."

I watched her arm flex right before she threw it up in the air. The auctioneer added one hundred dollars to the bid. *This* was exactly why her dad didn't let her go to the auctions. She was just like her mom. I stayed quiet, knowing if I fought her on it, it'd only piss her off. She could be the one to explain this extra horse to her dad, not me.

The man across the way kept his hand down, not upping the bid any higher. He sat back on his bench, ready for the next horse to come in. While it wasn't always the case, low bidders typically indicated they were kill buyers. From the looks of this guy, I didn't doubt it.

Before I knew it, the auctioneer was shouting "Sold!" and the horse was being ushered out the back by a man swinging a lead rope behind him. The horse galloped out the door and disappeared. I leaned forward to look at Lettie's face and found a massive grin plastered on her mouth.

She looked over at me like she almost forgot I was sitting beside her.

Without a word, I shook my head, fighting the smile that threatened to bloom. Thankfully, Travis had sent a few hundred extra dollars in case something like this happened. He knew what kind of trouble his wife could get into and had the good sense that Lettie would follow in her steps.

***

Three hours later, the last horse came through the pen, selling for sixteen hundred dollars. We'd won each bid we put out on Travis's list, but instead of four horses coming home, there'd be five, thanks to Lettie.

I didn't know what she thought she'd do with a green three-year-old that looked ready to stampede every person in this building. She was crazy if she thought her dad or brothers would let her near the gelding once she got him home.

Satisfied with how the night went, I stood from the bench, my ass sore from the wood. Lettie followed suit, speaking up for the first time since that gray horse came out.

"Now we go to the window?" she asked.

I nodded, seeing the excitement overshadowing the emotional toll the last few hours took on her. I saw her eyes brim with tears at some points as bids stayed low on a few horses. She knew their fate just as much as I did. We did the best we could, but it still hurt to see the ones that didn't get so lucky.

We headed down the bleachers to the line in front of the window. Four people later, we approached the woman.

"Bidding number?" she asked, her voice scratchy.

"Forty-four," I replied.

She wrote it down. "Tags?"

"Three, sixteen, thirty-seven, thirty-nine." My eyes drifted to the number jotted on the bottom of the paper, then to Lettie before continuing. "And twenty-eight."

Lettie beamed at me, and I couldn't help but stare. Her smile, her heart, everything about her drew me in like a fish to bait. She sure had her hook sunk deep in me.

Maybe her dad never brought her to these things because he knew he couldn't say no to her. If that was the case, I was in the same boat. There was no way I could've told her not to bid on that horse, not when I saw how passionate she was about getting that highest bid, the way her eyes narrowed in challenge at the guy bidding against her. She was dead set on getting that horse well before he ran through, that much was clear.

I handed the woman the money after signing paperwork, signing over the rights of the horses to the rescue.

"See you tomorrow morning, ma'am." I dipped my chin, then turned, Lettie beside me as we walked toward the exit.

"So, that gray," I started.

"Please don't be mad at me." From the corner of my eye, I saw her gaze locked on her boots as we walked through the dirt parking lot.

"I'm not mad, but you know your dad will be once we get home."

"I'm going to pay the rescue back for him."

I looked at her, drawing my brows together. "What?"

"He'll be my personal horse."

"What about Red?"

She shrugged, her eyes still downcast. "He's getting older."

"You can't break a three-year-old, Lettie."

Her lips twitched. "I'm not. Brandy is."

"How do you know she'll do it?"

She looked up at me then as we approached the truck, frowning. "She's my best friend. Plus, she's broken half the horses on the ranch herself. She'll do it."

I reached around her to open the passenger door. "I'm sure she'll love one more horse on her plate."

Lettie rolled her eyes, then turned to reach up for the handle. Instead of grabbing it, her hand missed, bracing on the frame of the door while her other hand landed on the leather seat.

"Lettie?"

From the side of her face, I could see her lips pale, her face draining of color before she hung her head. I grabbed her waist, steadying her as she swayed.

"Lettie, what's wrong?" My voice was laced with concern as she stood there, quiet.

She swallowed audibly, noticeably trying to catch her breath. After a few moments, she shook her head, straightening her back and releasing the seat. I kept my hand on her waist in case she lost her balance again.

Her voice was barely above a whisper as she spoke. "Just got a little dizzy."

"Have you been taking your iron?"

"Forgot them at the ranch. I was going to get some."

She lifted her leg and set it on the step before pulling herself up into the truck. I took a step forward. "Are you going to be okay?"

She avoided eye contact with me, gnawing on her cheek as she nodded.

I reached to grab the seat belt and pulled it around her, buckling her in. I rested my hand on her thigh, gazing up at her. She stared straight ahead, refusing to meet my eyes.

I reluctantly pulled my hand away and closed her door before coming around the hood of the truck to get in on the driver's side.

Lettie was quiet the entire drive back to the hotel. She made no move to get out when I parked, allowing me to come around to her side and open the door for her. I held my hand out to help her out of the truck and she took it, accepting my help. Her hand was soft from years at college, but that was surface level compared to what her time away from the ranch had done.

She let go of my hand as soon as she had both feet on the ground and walked off in the direction of the hotel as I closed her door and locked the truck. I rushed to catch up with her as she opened the door for herself this time. I slipped in behind her, staying close in case she got another dizzy spell.

I was trying to be there for her without overstepping. I saw firsthand in the past how she resented the way her brothers would baby her if anything seemed off. I could still care for her and respect her boundaries at the same time.

Unlocking the door to our room, she ignored Rouge's pleas for attention as he jumped at her legs and beelined for the bathroom, closing the door behind her. I patted Rouge's head and sighed. If space was what she wanted right now, I'd give it to her.

"I'm going to take Rouge out," I said to her through the door. She gave no indication she heard me as the shower turned on.

Grabbing the leash, I hooked it to Rouge's collar and grabbed the room key from where she tossed it on the desk, then headed outside.

I knew she didn't want to talk about it and I wouldn't force her, at least not right now. We had a good night and I wasn't going to ruin it by bombarding her. Questioning her a million times about why she didn't go to the pharmacy the moment she realized she forgot her pills wouldn't do anything but start a heated argument.

Instead, I'd do the only thing I could right now. I'd show her I cared through my actions.

16

LETTIE

Six Years Earlier...

Red's back was sweating under my thighs as we trudged up the trail in the summer heat. With it being over ninety degrees and Callan, Reed, Beckham, and Bailey done with their chores for the day, we decided to go to the swimming hole.

It was a two mile trail ride to get there, and though I was used to riding bareback, my thighs were burning with the strain to stay on Red going uphill. Rouge was jogging alongside me, panting with excitement. He knew where this trail led and was blissfully aware that after baking in the afternoon sun, he'd be swimming in no time.

"I can't wait to go back on the circuit next week and kick some ass," Beck exclaimed. He, along with my other brothers and Bailey, had shed his shirt before we took off.

"You referring to kicking some bronc's asses or opponents?" Bailey questioned.

"Both," Beck said with a nod.

Beckham was on his sorrel gelding, Butters. We'd taken the horse in from an auction years ago, and Beck claimed him as his own. Even though he was traveling most of the year now, we kept him here for when he was home. Butters still got worked regardless if Beck was home or not. Some of Callan's more experienced students got to ride him around the arena from time to time.

"Should've been a farrier. You don't have to deal with any ass kicking," Reed muttered.

Beck looked at Reed next to him. "I'd rather fuck up my back having fun."

Reed rolled his eyes at him, scooting up on his gray horse's sweat-slicked back.

Bailey and Callan were ahead of me, placing me at the back of the bunch with Rouge. Bailey was a bit behind Callan though, placing Nova's black butt almost at Red's shoulder.

Bailey glanced back at me like he was checking to make sure I was still there. As we crested the hill, Rouge let out a bark and took off, diving straight into the deep blue water.

The grass was tall around the pond, shaded by the pine trees surrounding the water. Beckham clicked his tongue, urging

Butters into a trot. They headed straight into the water, splashing it high above the horse's head.

"You taking Red in?" Bailey asked me.

I nodded. "I didn't come all this way not to."

I passed Bailey at a fast walk, heading into the water behind Beck. Callan was on a four-year-old bay, and it was clear the horse was still green. Cal was always so gentle with them, but he preferred training people how to ride the horses, not the other way around with teaching the horses how to be ridden. He nudged his sides, easing him closer to the water.

Reed led his horse into the water with no problems. It was like the beast knew Reed wouldn't take any bullshit and did everything he asked. Some cowboys just had that touch.

As Callan continued working with the bay, I urged Red deeper so the water was up past my knees. The horses settled while Rouge splashed around on the shore, his red fur covered in mud and water.

Closing my eyes, I took in the silence of nature, listening only to the sounds of the birds and the water. A slight breeze rustled the leaves of the trees around us, cooling us off even more.

All of a sudden, a huge wave of water washed over me. I rubbed my eyes, shoving my hair out of my face to find Bailey grinning at me from ear to ear.

"You're going to pay for that," I said in a cool tone.

"Oh, yeah?" he challenged.

"Yeah." Without hesitation, I twisted Red toward him, then I shoved as much water as I could manage at Bailey.

"Children, please keep it civil," Reed pleaded.

"Yeah, some of us have chickenshit horses," Callan complained, having managed to get the bay's front two hooves in the water. The horse was eyeing the ripples of water like they were going to eat him.

"Scaredy cats," Beck joked before splashing Reed.

Rouge barked at the excitement, swimming over to us to join in. He came over to me and I helped him climb onto Red's butt.

I turned to splash Reed, Beck and I ambushing him with as much water as we could shove his way.

Another wave washed over me and I screamed, turning to find Bailey rushing Nova to the shore.

"You're not going to get away with that!" I yelled after him, clicking my tongue at Red to follow him. Rouge jumped off his back, swimming to shore next to us.

Bailey and Nova emerged from the water as Red and I approached fast. Bailey jumped down, leaving Nova with his lead rope looped around his neck. I followed suit, dismounting from Red and leaving him to graze.

I picked up a fistful of mud, chucking it at Bailey.

"Hey! There could be rocks in there!" he yelled as he tried to dodge the flying mud. It landed right on his toned stomach, splattering his skin.

"Should've thought of that before soaking me!"

I bent to pick up another fistful of mud, but before I had the chance to throw it, strong arms were grabbing my hips and hoisting me up. Then the world turned upside down. I screamed, slapping at Bailey's back. "Put me down!"

"No way, Huckleberry. I'm not getting more globs of mud chucked at me."

"Globs?" I squeaked right before he was flipping me back over, landing me ass first in the water.

He turned to head back to Nova, but he wouldn't get away that easy. I fisted the sandy mud under the water and threw it, the chunks splattering against his back. He froze, then slowly turned.

"You're going to pay for that," he repeated my words.

I squealed as he came running at me, trying to get to my feet before he reached me. Before I had the chance to get up, he was scooping me up into his arms, holding me like a baby.

"Hold your breath, Huckleberry," he instructed with a smile.

"What?" I squeaked.

He didn't answer. Instead, he lifted me higher, then tossed me deeper in the water like I weighed nothing. My head went under, and when I came up to the surface and wiped the water from my eyes, he was standing there with his arms crossed, smiling down at me.

"That was so mean!" I yelped.

"You kind of deserved it," Callan pointed out from the shore where he'd given up on getting the bay in the water with all the splashing.

"He's got a point!" Beck yelled from behind me.

My feet found the bottom of the pond and I stood, the water coming up to my breasts. From where Bailey stood a few feet from me, he was a lot taller than he typically was with the angle of the ground below us. The sun was glistening off the water droplets clinging to his chest, and my eyes trailed one sliding down his stomach to his shorts.

He smirked, and I tore my eyes away. It was hard not to look at Bailey when he was standing there like that, all of his attention on me. But it wasn't fair to myself to imagine him as anything other than my brother's best friend.

Plus, I still wasn't sure where I'd be going to college, and I only had a couple months to decide. There'd be no point in getting into anything with anyone here if I'd just be leaving, especially with Bailey.

I saw the way he looked at me sometimes, the hint of something more than friendship shining in his green eyes. He'd always cared about me, always made sure I was okay, but that was where I drew the line with us.

There couldn't be a Bailey and Lettie without complicated feelings mixed in, and the last thing I wanted to do was complicate his life.

After a couple hours of basking in the sun in between swimming in the water, we led the horses back to my parents' ranch. We were all starving and ready to dig into whatever dinner my mom had prepped.

I had already put Red away by the time Bailey was done hosing the sand off of Nova's body. The horse had decided to roll on the shore, which in turn coated Bailey's shorts in sand on the ride home.

I stood in the doorway to the barn, watching as Bailey walked down the aisle to Nova's stall.

"Enjoying the view?" Callan popped up beside me.

I jumped, shoving at his shoulder. "There's no view."

He raised an eyebrow, the corners of his lips twitching. "Really? I swear I see some drool…" He reached out like he was going to wipe the drool away with his thumb.

I shoved his hand away, turning around and stomping off in the direction of the house. I couldn't help the slight smile that pulled at the corner of my mouth.

There wasn't a better view than Bailey Cooper, but I wouldn't admit that out loud.

17

LETTIE

Turning off the steaming water, I stepped out of the shower and toweled off. Despite the scorching water, I still felt cold. My skin wasn't cold to the touch, but I felt it in my bones. I didn't have to look in the mirror to know my complexion was dull and my lips were still drained of color. Usually, I could go a few days without my supplements and be fine, but with all of the excitement, I got ahead of myself.

I was embarrassed, even though I shouldn't be. Bailey probably thought I was the same helpless little girl, not being able to take care of myself. Having lived with this condition for the better part of my life, you'd think I'd have this down pat, but I didn't. I hated it, and sometimes, I let that hate get the best of me and would purposefully not take my prescription; just to see if it had magically gone away. I should know by now that it didn't. I should also know that it wasn't the smartest way to go about being anemic, but like most things in life, I didn't like to be bound by rules.

My family knew this about me. Reed even blamed my growing up around Brandy, as if that was the reason I rebelled against this diagnosis every so often.

Unlocking the bathroom door, I headed into our empty room. I heard Bailey when he left, but I was too humiliated to respond to him. He had to practically hold me up when the wave crashed into me as I was about to get in the truck. If that didn't raise alarm bells, I didn't know what did.

I left Bell Buckle to get out from underneath everyone's overbearing umbrella. I was barely back a week and already showing that there was every reason for them to worry.

Bailey was never the overcrowding type, which I was thankful for, but I hoped he didn't tell my brothers about what happened. I knew he cared about me, and if he did tell them, I knew it'd be coming from the kindest parts of his heart. How could I hold that against him if he did? My loathing of everyone close to me caring about me was a problem, but growing up, it got to the point that I couldn't even muck a stall without someone around the corner listening for me. I rarely had alone time because of it. After so many years of dealing with it, I started to detest their worry for me. I should appreciate them looking out for me, but instead, I tried to push everyone away. For five years, it worked. But now that I was back, I could see how moving away wasn't the best course of action.

I grabbed my shorts and oversized shirt from my duffel bag, slipping them on and crawling under the covers. Clicking on the TV, I flipped through the channels until I settled on a home renovation show.

The next episode had just started when the door opened. Rouge ran over to the bed after Bailey unhooked his leash, immediately welcoming me with a lick to my cheek before circling twice to lay at my side. I draped my arm over him, scratching his shoulder as he rested his snout on my stomach.

Bailey rummaged through a plastic bag before walking over to my nightstand, setting a water and bottle of pills down. Without a word, he went back to the desk, working to untie the knot on another bag.

I sat up, leaning my back against the headboard. Rouge moved his head to my thigh, letting out a sigh as he got settled again. I reached for the bottle, shaking out two iron pills before uncapping the water and swallowing them. I held the water in between my thighs, watching Bailey pull two containers out of the bag.

The TV was the only sound in the room as he set the containers in the middle of my bed and sat next to me, kicking off his boots before crossing his legs.

He reached over to open my to-go box, a steak, mashed potatoes, and a side of green beans on display.

All of those were rich in iron.

He opened his to reveal the same meal, then laid a knife and fork next to my box before cutting into his steak.

"It's rare, just how you like it." He gestured to my steak with his knife before taking a bite of his own.

I looked at him as he chewed. Once he swallowed his bite, he met my gaze.

"Thank you," I said.

He nodded before turning back to his dinner, acting interested in the show as he ate.

We didn't talk as we ate, the TV blasting commercials every few minutes. Once we were both finished, he grabbed the boxes, discarding them in the trash before pulling off his jeans and shirt, leaving him in boxers as he crawled into his own bed. I'd seen him in boxers before when we'd go swimming on a whim in the creeks and lakes. It was nothing new, but I averted my eyes anyway. Something about being in this hotel room felt more intimate than all those times in nature.

Taking that as his sign that he wanted to sleep, I clicked off the bedside lamp before turning the TV down to the point it was barely audible. I liked sleeping with the TV on. Brandy always hated that when we had sleepovers growing up. More times than not, I'd wake up to her sleeping in a different room.

Rouge moved to the end of my bed as I got myself situated, laying on my side facing toward Bailey, bringing the comforter up to my neck. Through the dim light of the TV, I could see his eyes on me from where he was laying on his side.

"You didn't have to do that," I said quietly.

"I did."

I paused, then asked, "Why?"

"Because I care about you," he said matter-of-fact, and while I already knew he did, it felt like it was the first time that it held any weight, and that weight didn't scare me. Not this time. Not when it came from Bailey.

Sometime later, sleep claimed me and I dreamt of what the last five years would have looked like if I had stayed in Bell Buckle instead of running from the man that my heart never stopped beating for.

18

BAILEY

After loading the truck with our bags, I headed back inside the hotel to check out. Lettie was in the shower when I'd started bringing our things down. She already looked better today, even having just woken up. I'd brought Rouge out to pee after feeding him, then picked up two coffees and breakfast burritos from the buffet downstairs, and when I came back with them, she was still in the bathroom.

Not wanting to impose on her privacy, I went downstairs to let the desk attendant know we'd be leaving soon, then took my time heading back to our room. Swiping the key to let myself in, I found Lettie's back facing me from where she sat at the small desk, eating her burrito and sipping on her coffee.

"Good shower?" I asked.

She jumped, swiveling in the chair with her cheeks full of food. She nodded as she managed to swallow.

"Truck's all loaded whenever you're ready. We just have to pick up the horses and then we can get on the road."

"Hopefully, there's no storm to slow us down this time," she said before taking another bite.

"Mm, I don't know. It was looking a little cloudy out there."

She stopped midchew, her eyes big saucers.

I chuckled. "I'm kidding, Huckleberry. How'd you grow up in the West being this damn scared of a little rain?"

She resumed her chewing, swallowing before she spoke. "Have you *seen* the storms out here?"

I nodded, leaning my shoulder against the wall beside the bathroom door. "Well, I did grow up here, so..."

She set what was left of her burrito on the desk before taking a sip of her coffee, rolling her eyes. "Men," she said, making it sound almost like an insult.

"What about men?" I asked, putting up air quotes around the word.

"You guys act like you're not scared of anything," she griped.

"That's not true."

Her brows inched up her forehead. "Oh, yeah? Then what are you scared of?"

There was only one thing I knew for sure that I was scared of, and that fear didn't creep in until the day Lettie fell off that ladder. "Losing you again."

Her eyes scanned my face before she stood up, throwing the remnants of her breakfast in the trash and grabbing Rouge's leash from the end of the bed.

"Don't shut me out," I pleaded.

She faced me from where she stood feet away, leash gripped in her fist. "I didn't mean to hurt you by leaving. I just..." She trailed off.

"Just what?"

"I just needed space."

"From me?" I would have given her space if she had just asked. Moving hundreds of miles away was not the only way to get space from someone.

She let out a frustrated sigh, her hands slapping against the sides of her thighs. "No." She shook her head. "Yes. From everyone."

Something like pain filled her eyes, like she regretted saying it.

"I'm not leaving. Not again," she added after I didn't respond.

"How do I know that, Lettie? How do I know you're not going to run off again the second things become too real for you?"

"*Too real*? Bailey, my entire life, I've been bombarded by the people who care about me. I love them for it as much as I hate *myself* for it."

I shook my head, closing the distance between us. With my height, she had to crane her neck back to look up at me. "The last thing I want to hear is that you blame yourself for this. I know every damn bad thing about you, Lettie, and I still think you're the purest fucking woman I've ever met. Do not for one second blame yourself for your condition."

She broke our eye contact, looking down at the floor as she whispered, "You can't say that."

Refusing to let her hide from my words, I grabbed her chin, tilting her head up to look at me again. "Why?"

Tears welled in her eyes. "Because *that's* too real."

I pursed my lips, searching her eyes for any indication that she didn't mean that, but all I found was an ocean of agony. Frustrated, I dropped her chin, taking a step back from her.

I lowered my voice. "If I get close to you and lose you again, I don't know if I can handle it."

"Then stop trying to get close to me!"

As if it was that easy. What made this woman so damn adamant that pushing everyone close to her away was going to solve her problems?

"Is this your way of trying to show your family you can take care of yourself?"

She blinked, confusion clear on her face. "What?"

"This." I waved my hands in between us. "Pushing me away. *Everyone* away."

"I didn't push *everyone* away."

"Oh, so what? It's just me? I'm the problem?"

She shook her head, taking a step toward me, the toes of our boots touching. "No, Bailey, you were never the problem."

"Then what was it?"

She set her palms on my stomach, looking down at where she connected with me. "Can we talk about this later?"

Tell me about beating around the damn bush, and I'll tell you Lettie was the reason behind the invention of that idiom.

"Sure," I clipped. I grabbed the leash from where it was looped around her hand and moved around her to hook it on Rouge's collar where he sat by the AC.

Lettie was jamming a pin in this conversation, and I didn't have to be an idiot to know it wouldn't be brought up again. She might as well have put a lock on it and thrown away the damn key. She didn't owe me an explanation, but for my sanity, I selfishly wanted one.

If she really left because of me, I'd have no choice but to become a stranger to her again. I wasn't sure how that would affect my work on their ranch, but I'd figure it out when we got back to Bell Buckle. As much as I hated the idea of losing her so soon after just getting her back, I'd force myself to do it if that's what would make her happy.

19

BAILEY

We were five minutes away from the auction house when Travis called my cell phone, his voice coming through the speakers of the truck.

"Did I catch you two before you checked out of the hotel?" he asked.

"Just left. Why? What's up?"

"If you're up for it, I need you to head over to a kill pen today."

Lettie straightened in her seat, breaking her silence. "A kill pen?"

"I just got off the phone with Beckham. He said he saw an old bronc posted on their Facebook group. Guess he's been bucked off of him a time or two and wants him to retire here."

Though he didn't show it, Bekcham had a heart of gold just like Lettie and their mother. It came with the territory of being around these thousand-pound animals. They knew how to tug at your heart strings.

"He wants a crazy old bronc retiring on our ranch?"

Taking note of the way she said *our* ranch, I glanced at Lettie. Maybe she really did intend to stay in Bell Buckle.

"They're only crazy if you make 'em so," Travis said.

"We can stay another night, it's no problem," I interrupted, already knowing Lettie would be up for it. Just like her mother, she never could say no to a horse, regardless of its background.

"Great. I already called the auction house, told them you'll be coming tomorrow to pick up the other four."

"Five," Lettie corrected.

Travis was silent for a beat before his sigh filled the cab. "I figured that would happen. Keep me updated. And Lettie, no more horses. You're lucky that's a stock trailer."

Knowing Lettie, she'd walk the damn horse from Billings all the way to Bell Buckle if there was no room in the trailer. Her dad should know her by now. Nothing stopped her if she set her mind to it.

"No promises," she said as she leaned back in her seat.

"We'll be ready to help unload the *six*," he overemphasized the number, "horses when you get here tomorrow evening. Char's barbecuing, so come hungry. I'll text you the address. Though his job is shitty, the guy is nice, so I expect you two to be respectful."

My mouth instantly started watering at the thought of Mrs. Bronson's cooking.

"We will. See you then," I said.

Before I hung up, I heard Travis grumble, "Like mother, like daughter."

Lips twitching, I pulled into a parking lot to turn around. Since we already checked out of the hotel, we'd have to reserve another room for one night. Getting back on the road, I headed toward the hotel in the hopes we could reserve the same room. With the limited available parking this morning, I had a feeling there was a slim chance of any rooms being empty, but it was worth a shot.

"I'm surprised Beck keeps up with a kill pen's Facebook group," I said.

I didn't miss the slight lift of Lettie's lips out of the corner of my eye. It was pretty damn funny that he was even on Facebook.

"He tried his best to take part in the rescue. My mom wouldn't let him have it any other way."

"Yeah, but now that he's some big rodeo guy?" I shook my head. "A bronc rider with a big ol' heart. Imagine that," I joked.

"What'd my mom used to call it? Silent compassion?" She held up air quotes.

We both laughed at the memory, remembering all too well. "That was your mom's way of coping with the fact that he was the least interested out of all of us."

"He gets brownie points for trying. I think you being involved made up for it when he was out of town for weeks on end."

I shrugged. "Rescue never stops. Neither does ranching. He's got other things on his plate, but I'm not holding it against him."

She looked out the window at the large expanse of green hills and mountains peaking up in the distance. "He found what he was passionate about, so I'm happy for him, regardless of the fact that it takes him away from family."

"Yeah, I sure do miss him when he's gone."

"Just makes you appreciate the moments he's here a little more," she said.

I looked over at her to find her eyes on me, sympathy shining in them.

I nodded, swallowing the emotion building in my throat. "Yeah. It does."

If she thought for a second I didn't appreciate every moment I'd been able to spend by her side, she was crazy. Lettie Bronson was the only woman on this planet I wanted to spend my time with. I didn't give a fuck what we were doing. As long as we were in each other's presence, that was enough for me.

***

Pulling the truck up along the curb on the street since every spot in the parking lot was taken, I killed the engine, getting out to come around the hood to open Lettie's door for her.

"Thank you," she said before slipping past me.

I nodded, closing the door. I grabbed Rouge from the back seat before we headed inside the hotel lobby. The eating area was packed with families, kids' shouts filling the small area as people dined on their late breakfast.

We walked up to the front desk, the woman's face lighting up as she recognized us. "Hey! Forget something?"

"Actually, I was hoping you might have a room available for one more night?" I asked.

Lettie picked a brochure about wildlife in Montana up off the counter, flipping it open and acting interested in the information.

"Let me check. We're pretty packed tonight." A few clicks later, she took her eyes off the screen, looking up at me from her swivel chair. "We have a king-sized bed available, but it's only one."

Suddenly not deeply invested in the words on the paper, Lettie flipped the brochure shut. "You're sure there's nothing else?"

The blonde looked back at her computer for a moment, scrolling on her mouse, then back up, her eyes glancing between the two of us. "No, I'm sorry."

I turned to Lettie, tightening my hold on Rouge's leash as two kids ran behind us. "We can check a different hotel if you want."

She visibly gnawed on her cheek before shaking her head, plastering on a smile as she faced the woman behind the desk. "No, that's fine. We'll take it."

The blonde smiled back, oblivious to the tension rolling off Lettie. "Great. I'll just charge the same card you used the last two nights?"

I nodded. "That'd be great. Thank you, ma'am."

"My pleasure." She typed something on her computer, then handed another room key over. Lettie grabbed it before I had the chance, spinning on the heel of her boot and walking toward the exit of the hotel instead of in the direction of our room. Granted, we had no reason to go up to our room yet. I offered my best apology smile to the woman behind the counter and took off after Lettie.

She was halfway to the truck by the time I caught up to her, Rouge panting beside my leg as the afternoon heat beat down on us.

"My dad send you the address yet?" she asked.

"Yep. Looks like it's about thirty minutes away."

"Great," she clipped as we approached the truck. I opened the back door for Rouge to jump in as she pulled the passenger door handle.

"Are you mad about the room? I can sleep in the truck if it's that big of a deal."

She faced me. "No."

"No about the room, or no to the truck?"

"No to both. It's fine. It's just one night. What's the harm in sleeping next to each other?"

I arched an eyebrow. Lettie wasn't ignorant. A lot could happen in one night.

But I'd be a gentleman, keep my hands off of her. I could do that for one night.

Right?

20

BAILEY

I parked the truck and trailer behind the large metal shop where the pens were set up on the property.

"It looks like a normal ranch," Lettie observed as she took in our surroundings.

Killing the engine, I asked, "What were you expecting?"

"Not this."

Unhooking my seat belt, I got out of the truck, leaving Rouge in the back seat. Lettie met me by the hood, crossing her arms as she surveyed the area. Her gray tank top hugged her curves, and my eyes landed on her breasts being put on display by the position.

"You here for Travis?" a voice interrupted. Clearing my throat, I turned my attention to the ordinary looking guy. I guess when you think of someone who runs a kill pen business, you think of some old, ugly brute. This guy was anything but that. Hell, if I didn't know better, I'd think he worked in some office out in Missoula.

The smirk on his lips told me he definitely saw where I was looking seconds before.

"Yep. Here for the bay bronc," I said.

He nodded, gesturing for us to follow him. Lettie walked ahead of me and my eyes fell to the Kimes Ranch logo etched onto the back pockets of her jeans. I was a goner for everything Lettie Bronson. I couldn't keep my damn eyes off her. It was like I needed to make up for all the lost time. Or my brain was trying to ingrain her image in my head in case she took off again.

She may say she was staying for good, but there would always be that little part of me that feared she wouldn't be here when the sun rose.

He led us to the pen at the end of the row, the horse standing in the corner with his head hung low, his tail swishing to bat away a fly.

"Every so often we get a retired rodeo star in here. Hate to see it," the man said as he leaned his forearms on the fence. "Glad you guys are getting him out of here."

Lettie's face was pure confusion and disbelief, but she kept her comments to herself as she turned to the horse.

He held his hand out to me, and I shook it with a firm grip. "Austin."

"I'm Bailey. This is Lettie." I gestured to Lettie after dropping his hand.

He nodded at the two of us. "Nice to meet you both."

"So, why do you do it?" And there she went, her thoughts coming out in full force.

He turned back to the horse, his posture softening as sadness crept into his voice. "Got to pay the bills somehow."

"Can't work a different job, like everyone else?"

I pursed my lips at her bold question.

Austin kicked at the dirt. "You're right. I could. But then these horses would end up in the same situation, but with a monster who doesn't care about them. At least I feed 'em, water 'em, give them a little bit of peace before they head off."

As much as I hated the reality of this, he had a point.

"Well, we can load him up if you're ready," I said before Lettie could ask any more questions.

Austin nodded, reaching for the halter on the gate.

"I'll open the trailer," Lettie mumbled before turning on her boot and stalking off.

Once out of ear shot, I said, "Sorry about her. She's a little sensitive about all this."

Austin unlatched the gate and stepped inside the pen. "No biggie. Everyone is. I don't blame her. Seems like she's got a big heart."

On instinct, I reached up to tilt my hat down, but stopped myself, remembering what Lettie said at the bar. I turned to see her swinging the door to the trailer open without a glance in our direction. "She's somethin' alright."

Austin led the horse past me, heading in the direction of the trailer. Though retired, the horse's muscles still rippled with each step, his bulky frame evidence to the years of hard work he put in. He loaded him in the trailer with no problem, the horse clearly having done it a million times.

"Travis has my number. If you guys ever see any come through here that you'd like, just let me know. I'll hold 'em for you."

He stepped out of the trailer and Lettie swung the door, latching it shut.

"Thanks, Austin. We appreciate it," I said.

He tipped his chin. "'Course. You two make it home safe."

"Will do," I replied.

Lettie was silent as she got in the truck. I double checked the door to the trailer and the hookup on the hitch to make sure everything was secure. Satisfied, I got in the truck to find Lettie watching Austin walk back to his double-wide.

She may have been babied her whole life, but Lettie sure held her own, regardless of the situation. She was soft on the outside, fucking beautiful, but that mind of hers was harder than steel, never afraid to voice its thoughts. I guess that could take people off guard and make them uncomfortable, but not me. My Lettie was a force to be reckoned with, and I was damn proud that she never let anyone dim that side of her.

She was a little firecracker, and I was bound to get blown away, but for some damn reason, I wanted to play with fire. It was time to show her just how much she lit up my world.

21

LETTIE

After dinner, we checked on Bucky in the trailer, feeding him a few flakes of hay and making sure he had a bucket full of clean water before heading to our room. Beckham had called to check in on how the pickup went, and that's when we learned the horse's nickname.

A typical bay, his coat was a rich, dark brown with black accents on his legs, ears, mane, and tail. He had a little white star between his eyes that oddly looked like the shape of Texas.

Our room was drastically smaller than the last one, putting emphasis on just how close Bailey and I would be in that bed tonight. We'd gone camping so many times over the years that we were no strangers to sleeping close to each other, but we were never alone. My brothers were always there, acting their usual obnoxious selves and pulling pranks. One year, Brandy and I woke up with our tent in a damn tree. We'd stolen some of my parents' liquor to take on that trip. It was our first time getting drunk as teens, so we slept right through them moving our sleeping bags and tent. We'd get them back for that one day, I'd make sure of it.

Bailey was in the shower as I changed, opting for my oversized t-shirt and shorts again. I laid them out on the bed, stripping my clothes from the day. I pulled on my shirt when Rouge shot off the bed, his paw snagging on the hole of my shorts, unintentionally taking them with him.

"Rouge!" I chased after him, my heart picking up speed as I heard the water in the bathroom shut off.

"Rouge," I hissed at my dog. Thinking it was a game, he spun, chasing his non-existent tail, my shorts hanging on for the ride. Australian Shepherds typically had docked tails, but that never stopped Rouge from trying to reach the little nub. I bent over, grabbing at his fur to try to get him to stay still so I could unhook my shorts from his back leg.

As I got a hold of him, the bathroom door opened behind me. Rouge and I both froze, knowing who stood there.

There was silence, and then Bailey cleared his throat. "Lettie..."

Perfectly aware that my underwear did little to hide my ass, I straightened, yanking the shorts with me. Rouge darted past me as I turned to come face to face with Bailey, his chest glistening with water just inches from mine.

"Rouge stole my shorts," I said as a way of explaining my mooning him. My cheeks heated as he studied me, something like hunger shining in his eyes.

I inhaled deeply. It was just my ass. I'm sure Bailey had seen plenty of those in his lifetime. He took a step forward, and in response, I took a step back. He took notice of the space I left between our bodies, then brought his forest green eyes back up to mine.

"I trained him well while you were gone."

"You trained him to take women's pants?"

His lips twitched, and he took another step forward. I was all too aware of the fact that he wore nothing but a towel draped low around his waist.

"No, but I should have."

Attempting to keep the space, I took one more step backwards when my back hit the wall. His wet hair hung over his forehead, drops of water falling between us off the chocolate strands.

"You're too scared to do it yourself, you have to make the dog do it?" My voice was too breathy, and he took one last step forward, his hands coming up to the wall on either side of my head. He caged me in, and it should be suffocating, but in this moment, I never felt more alive, every hair on my body standing on end with anticipation.

"Kind of hard to take your pants off when you were three hundred miles away, but now that you're right in front of me, I'm not waiting any longer."

It was useless to try to hide the effect he was having on me right now, but that didn't stop me. "It's a good thing my pants aren't on then."

He smirked. "Ripping this shirt off of you will more than make up for it."

I gasped as he did just that, his hands coming to the neckline of my ratty t-shirt and yanking it, the material tearing easily. I stood there as it slid down my arms to the floor. The only thing left covering me was my lacey underwear. His eyes roamed my body as he kneeled down. I watched him as he hooked his fingers in the waistband of my panties before looking up at me.

"I've dreamt of what you would look like standing before me like this for as long as I can remember. What you would taste like when you finally let me devour you. How you would feel when you let me in for the first time."

I bit my lip as he slowly tugged my underwear down, the gentleness of it a contrast to how he removed my shirt.

He took me in, and fuck, if his starved expression didn't make my thighs clamp together, my body begging for any kind of pressure. He slid his hands in between my legs, pulling my thighs apart.

He brought his gaze back up to mine. "No more hiding, Lettie. No more running. I'm taking what I've craved, and the only way I'm stopping is if you tell me to."

The thought didn't even cross my mind as I let my body sag against the wall to spread my legs just an inch wider, showing him I wanted it just as much as he did.

His lips lifted as he slid his hands around to the backs of my thighs. "Hold on," he commanded.

I laced my hands through his wet hair a second before he lifted me with little effort, settling my legs over his shoulders. All that ranch work paid off, if not for the simple pleasure of him manhandling me.

I gasped, my body at his mercy as he licked back to front, his tongue buried in my pussy. A groan escaped him as he discovered how wet I already was.

"You taste better than I ever could have imagined, Huckleberry."

I pulled at his hair in response to the nickname. Now was not the time for childish names.

He looked up at me, his head still between my legs. "Two can play the punishment game, Lettie." He lifted his right hand and brought it back down with a hard slap, gripping my ass in both hands. Pleasure surged through me at the sting his palm left, the slight pain coursing through my body as I ached for his tongue back on me. A smirk crested his lips before he brought his mouth back to my center, his tongue easily finding my clit and lapping at it.

I moaned, leaning my head back against the wall as he anchored me in place. "You like that, Lettie?"

"Yes," I breathed.

With my legs still wrapped around his shoulders, he brought one hand around to slide one finger into me, curling it just right as he pumped it in and out. My mouth popped open, the sensation eliciting another moan from my lips.

His mouth worked me as he added a second finger. I ground my hips against his face as he sucked on my clit, his tongue flicking against the bundle of nerves. I always had fantasies of being with Bailey, but never expected them to come true. Now that it was happening, my body couldn't hold back at how it reacted to him. All-consuming, taking over every thought in my head, every nerve in my body. I was at Bailey's mercy, and there wasn't a single place on this planet I'd rather be.

His other hand was still gripped on my ass, encouraging my hips as I ground against his mouth. He released my clit, his breath hot on my skin.

"You tell me when you're going to come, Lettie." His slight stubble blissfully scratched against my thighs as he spoke.

I managed a nod as his fingers pumped in and out of me, his mouth closing back over my clit. He added a third finger, and the fullness of them inside me caused pressure to build low in my belly. His tongue lapped at my clit hungrily, sending sparks to my vision.

"Bailey," I breathed.

"Yes, sweetheart?" His voice vibrated through my center and I closed my eyes, my head arched back against the wall. He could call me anything he wanted as long as he didn't stop.

"Now." I managed to get out. He moved his tongue down to my opening as his fingers worked me.

"That's my good girl." His voice was all I needed to send me over the edge.

I exploded, stars erupting in my vision as I tried to quiet my scream, gasping at the orgasm that rippled through my entire body. He kept fingering me, his rhythm never slowing as I clenched around him. My hands fisted in his hair, keeping his head between my legs as I came down off my high. As I relaxed against him, he slowly removed his fingers, his tongue licking me clean.

Slowly, he set me back on my feet, then stood up, his hand trailing up my body to land on my neck, his fingers closing around it, but adding no pressure.

"Open," he commanded.

I parted my lips and he slipped one of his fingers that had been inside me in my mouth. I closed my lips around the digit, sucking on it. My tongue swirled his finger, licking it clean the same way he did between my legs. He groaned as he watched my mouth work his finger. Just that simple action had me getting wet again.

He slowly pulled it out of my mouth, causing a popping noise to sound when it was freed.

"The next time you feel like running, Lettie, think of my tongue between your legs, lavishing up every last drop of you. You may hate how everyone cares about you, but I know for a fact you didn't hate how I just made you feel."

I nodded, at a loss for words.

"Now we're going to go to bed together and sleep, and you're not going to overthink what just happened. Got it?"

I nodded again. I was in complete awe of what had just transpired between us and the man Bailey became when he got a hold of me.

"Oh, and Lettie?"

"Hmm?"

"Don't hold back those screams. I want to hear my name on those lips the next time I make you come on my tongue, and the same goes for my cock. Because mark my words, Lettie Bronson, I will be inside that sweet pussy of yours. Got it?"

I gulped audibly, my core heating all over again as he released my neck. Bailey could make me fall to my knees with just a few words.

I felt bad for every woman that's never had a cowboy between her legs. They were a different breed when they were hungry.

22

BAILEY

"Come on," I said, still tasting her on my tongue.

Folding my hand around hers, I led her over to the bed and pulled back the covers. She got in and I brought the covers up over her, then came around to the other side and laid beside her on my back, staring at the ceiling.

I'd wanted to hear her unravel, and while I'd felt every twitch along with the tightening of her core, my name on her lips was the best part of the entire moment. I'd dreamt of my name coming from those pink lips on a moan too many times to count.

I was determined to hear it again.

There wasn't a hint of sarcasm when I'd told her I'd be inside her. Knowing I made her come undone with just my mouth made my cock twitch under the blankets. It was so fucking hard not to roll over right now and take what was mine.

"Are you awake?" she asked.

"We just laid down."

She was quiet a minute, the darkness swallowing up the space around us. "Can we turn the TV on?"

Right. Lettie fell asleep to the TV.

"Sure." I blindly reached for the remote on the nightstand, my hand knocking the corded phone a few inches before finding it. My thumb clicked random buttons until finally the TV lit up.

"Do you want to find a movie to watch?" I asked her.

She was curled on her side facing me, her arms folded under the pillow. "You're not going to sleep?"

I shook my head, finding her blue eyes in the dim light. "Not really tired yet."

"Oh."

"If you fall asleep during it, that's fine," I assured her.

"Okay. Put on whatever you want then." By the tone of her voice, I could tell she felt awkward. I didn't blame her, but I had no regrets. Though a part of me still felt betrayed at her leaving all those years ago, the more rational part of me was trying to do anything I could to convince Lettie that she belonged here.

If giving her orgasms was the key to making her stay, consider my tongue a new full-time employee to the Lettie bus.

I flipped through the channels, settling on *The Notebook*. I figured she liked the movie. I was more of an action kind of guy, but I already knew I'd be focusing little of my attention on the movie while Lettie was lying next to me.

"Flip over," I instructed.

Her eyes moved from the TV to me. "Why?"

I rolled my eyes. Always so skeptical. "Just do it."

She shuffled, rolling to her other side and angling her head so she could still see the TV. I scooted closer to her, her back to my chest, and wrapped an arm over her waist. Her all-consuming smell invaded my senses, taking over every part of my brain.

My cock pressed against her ass, and while it made me all the more hard, I didn't try to reposition myself. I wasn't going to do anything other than cuddle with her tonight.

"Is this okay?" I asked, my voice hoarse. My breath moved the little pieces of hair near her ear, and I felt a slight shiver from her.

She nodded and I reached up, pulling her hair back from her neck. In the dim light, I could see her pulse fluttering. The urge to press my lips to her smooth skin was too strong to fight.

Brushing my mouth across her neck, she inhaled sharply as my tongue darted out for a taste. I was addicted to her taste like an alcoholic was to whiskey.

"I thought we were watching a movie," she whispered, finally exhaling.

"You are." But I just needed another hit.

She looked over her shoulder at me, meeting my gaze. Our mouths were so close, it'd take one small movement and I'd be right where I wanted to be.

"As much as I loved...earlier," she said awkwardly, like she didn't know what to call it, "I don't think I can go for round two tonight. I'm really tired and we have a long drive tomorrow."

"Not even a little neck kissing?" I teased. "I know, Huckleberry. Get some rest. I'll see you in the morning." I pressed my lips to her forehead, then laid my head back on the pillow, keeping my arm around her waist.

Lettie and I fit together like two pieces of a puzzle. We were always made for each other, but we were just waiting to be put together. And now that we were? I'd never let anything break us apart.

23

LETTIE

When I woke up the next morning, Bailey was gone. He'd scribbled "Took Rouge out to check on Bucky" on the tiny hotel notepad that sat on the nightstand. I laid on my back, unable to keep my thoughts from straying to last night.

After he gave me another orgasm while *The Notebook* credits rolled by in the background, we watched an episode of *Family Guy* and fell asleep. I'd meant it when I said I was tired, but something about his cock pressed against my ass made me unable to sleep. Sensing that, he'd disappeared under the covers and used his tongue in more ways than I could count.

Sometime in the middle of the night, I'd woken to his arm wrapped around me, his chest to my back with Rouge at our feet. I couldn't help the smile on my face at how that moment felt. Almost like nothing changed between us, yet everything did. Like there wasn't a big chunk of our lives without each other in them.

Since my shirt was destroyed, he'd let me sleep in his, and as I got dressed in an old Coors Banquet t-shirt and high waisted Kimes Ranch jeans, I debated stuffing it in my duffel bag to keep it forever. He smelled like cinnamon and the sun and I wanted to fall asleep to that scent every night. I tucked my shirt into my jeans and slid on my boots just in time for Bailey and Rouge to come back into the room.

Knowing he'd notice if his shirt was gone, I left it out of my bag and zipped it up. As amazing as last night was, I didn't think it'd happen again, and if that was the case, stealing his shirt would just be weird.

As if he read my thoughts, he said, "You can keep that if you want."

I stopped with the shirt in my fist, hovering over his open luggage. "What?"

"My shirt. You look good in it."

I set the shirt in his bag. "I don't want to take your clothes..."

He stopped in front of me, picking the shirt up and holding it in between our chests. "I want you to."

I shook my head, my gaze dropping to the clothing in his fist. "It was a mistake Bailey. I don't-"

"Want to ruin things between us? Tell me, Lettie, what would giving in to what we both want ruin?"

He was right. God, why was he always right?

He gently grabbed my chin with his other hand, guiding me to meet his eyes. "I don't want to ever hear you say that what we do is a mistake. You leaving for five fucking years was a mistake. Me not chasing after your ass was a mistake. But us? That will *never* be a mistake."

"I'm sorry, Bailey, I a-"

He shook his head, his thumb running over my jaw. "Don't apologize to me, Lettie. That's in the past now."

I nodded and he let go of my jaw, waiting until I grabbed the shirt from his hold to zip up his bag.

"We can hit the road if you're ready."

I nodded again, not trusting myself to speak through the lump of emotion stuck in my throat. He may not *want* me to be sorry, but I was. I'd never stop apologizing for my selfishness that caused us to be apart for half a decade. Where would we be now if I had stayed? If I had given in to him instead of running three hundred miles away?

I silently followed him out of the room as he held our bags and Rouge's leash, my hands empty, but my mind loaded heavy with regret.

***

After grabbing a quick bite to eat and loading up the five horses from the auction house, we started the long drive home. Every hour, we stopped to check on the horses to make sure they were all getting along and none of them looked visibly ill. The stress of the past few days could catch up on them quickly, and the last thing we wanted to deal with on this drive was colic.

We listened to my country playlist up until the fourth hour when I turned the volume down.

"I feel bad," I confessed.

Bailey glanced at me before bringing his eyes back to the road. "Why's that?"

"Well, you got me to... And you didn't get to... So I don't think that's fair."

He chuckled, shaking his head. "You mean orgasm?"

I nodded, facing forward to look out the windshield. "Yeah."

I watched as we passed wide open fields that stretched for miles, no end in sight. The West was truly breathtaking. Montana especially. Once you crossed over the state line, it was like the blue sky opened up and you felt free, like you could slow down, take a deep breath of air, close your eyes, and enjoy the sun beating down on your skin without the stress of life wearing down on your shoulders. It was a place of serenity like no other.

"I don't mind, Huckleberry."

I crossed my arms. "Don't you want, like, I don't know, road head or something?"

He snorted as he burst out laughing. When I didn't join in on the laughter, he looked at me. "You're serious?"

I widened my eyes as I raised my eyebrows in a way that screamed "duh."

"If that'll make you feel better about it, Huckleberry, have at it. I won't stop you."

I frowned at the center console. These damn new trucks had them in permanently with no ability to lift them out of the way.

"Well, I can't even if I wanted to." I gestured to the leather dividing us.

He shrugged. "Guess it'll have to wait until we're in my truck." He drove an older vehicle, so the front was a bench seat. It made road head easy. Not that I'd know.

I narrowed my eyes at him, pressing my lips into a thin line. "I guess it will."

I gnawed on the inside of my cheek, turning my attention out the window.

"You're gonna chew your cheek clean off if you keep at it."

Swallowing my nerves, I said, "It was the way you looked at me."

His brows furrowed with confusion. "What?"

"The day I turned eighteen, something changed between us. I knew if I told you I was leaving, you'd try to change my mind."

He nodded. "I would have."

"At the time, I didn't want my mind changed. But now, looking back at all this lost time, I wish you did."

"Like I said, Lettie, that's in the past."

"I know. I just wanted you to know that I noticed it."

"Huckleberry, if you noticed it, you would've seen I've been looking at you like that since the first day I laid eyes on you when we were kids. It was you who looked at me differently that day, not the other way around."

I didn't respond as I sat there thinking back to my eighteenth birthday when Bailey showed up with a vanilla cake coated in homemade huckleberry frosting. He'd made it from scratch, and if I knew anything about Bailey, it was that he didn't bake. But he did it for me, and it was the best cake I'd ever had.

My lips twitched with a smile at the memory. "You want to give me the recipe to that cake you made me?"

He shook his head. "I'd rather make it myself for every birthday you have from this point forward."

I rolled my eyes at him. "Since when did you become such a romantic?"

He flashed his teeth with a smile as he clicked on his blinker to pull over since we were approaching our fifth hour in the truck. Shifting to park, he got out to check on the horses and the trailer. I wondered if my family would see that something changed between us on this trip when we got home, and how my brothers would feel about it if they found out.

24

BAILEY

We pulled into the ranch a couple of hours before sunset. Everyone's vehicles were parked in front of the ranch-style home, every Bronson, aside from Beckham, here to help unload the horses and get them situated. No matter the circumstances, rain or shine, the Bronsons showed up.

Lettie hopped out of the truck as soon as the tires stopped spinning, Rouge taking off after her. Brandy was talking to Callan when Lettie approached her, a smile lighting up their faces.

I got out of the truck after killing the engine, meeting up with Reed, who had made his way around the side of the trailer.

"Six horses, huh?" He stepped up on the wheel well, peeking in the trailer.

I chuckled. "Blame Beck and Lettie."

After getting a good look at them, he stepped down. "I figured that would happen. Though I was surprised when Beckham called my dad. He practically begged him to call the kill pen. I'm sure if Travis said no, he'd be on his way there right now."

"I'm sure your mom would've had Travis's head if he said no to him."

"That's why we're packed full. My mom can't turn down a sob story."

Callan came over to us, his cowboy hat tilted low with his sandy hair curling at the nape of his neck. "I need the covered arena tomorrow so we've got to let 'em loose in the pasture. It'll be harder to catch them but Brandy's confident she can handle it."

Reed crossed his arms. "That won't work. She'll never get a halter on them out there."

Callan's hands shot up, palms out. "I don't argue with the ladies. You can be the one to fight her on it."

Reed's eyes found Brandy standing with Lettie and Charlotte, narrowing before he took off in her direction.

I leaned my shoulder against the trailer, directing my attention to Callan. "You get any new students?"

"Two. I could fit some more into my schedule, though, so I posted a flier on the board at Lennon's store."

"I don't know how you deal with it - teaching so many new riders. I could do it a few times, but after that?" I shook my head.

He shrugged. "I love kids, so I don't mind. I think of it as giving them the confidence to keep with it, not let the snobby people in the horse community get to them."

I let out a small chuckle. "There's plenty of those to go around. Gotta toughen those kids up."

He nodded once before Travis whistled to get everyone's attention. We ambled over to him, joining the others and forming a circle. Lettie stood on the opposite side from me. I shot her a wink and her cheeks flushed before she looked away.

"I know we don't usually leave halters on them, but since they're going out in the pasture, I want to make it easier on us to catch them." Reed shot a look at Brandy, which she promptly ignored, her chin held high. "We're going to use some of the cattle fences to corral them toward the gate, but if any spook, you drop the gate. Don't need anyone getting hurt. Got it?" We all nodded in agreement. "We've done this over a hundred times at this point. You think something's going south, you tell someone. You all know the drill. Let's get 'em out and get 'em fed."

Callan, Lennon, Reed, Travis, and Brandy each grabbed a fence panel, bringing them over to the trailer forming a sort of path in the direction of the pasture gate. Charlotte opened the gate to the pasture, standing post there to close it once they were all in. I followed Lettie to the back of the trailer, where she jumped up on the wheel well to usher them all out once I had the door open.

She nodded to me, indicating she was ready, and I unlatched the door, swinging it wide. Lettie clicked her tongue, swinging her arm through the slat in the trailer to get them moving. All at once, they began shuffling, the trailer swaying with their weight. One by one, they stepped out, trotting in the direction of the pasture.

It seemed to be going smoothly until a little sorrel got turned around, his movements jerky as he pushed past the others in the opposite direction. I swung my arm before he could get back in the trailer, which caused him to spin, his back end slamming into the fence panel Brandy was holding up. The force of it caused her to stumble back but she stayed upright, bracing herself on the panel.

Once all six of the horses were in the pasture, Charlotte swung the gate shut, latching it. Seeing that all the horses were corralled, Brandy dropped the panel, bending over with her hand gripping her opposite wrist.

Reed heard the panel fall and dropped his when he saw Brandy bent over, rushing over to her. "What happened?" he demanded.

Brandy's eyes were on her hand as she pressed her lips together, a look of pain on her face.

"That horse's ass crushed her hand," Lettie answered for her as she jogged over.

"Is it broken?" Lennon asked after Callan grabbed his fence panel from him, bringing them over to the stack along the barn wall.

Reed reached for Brandy's forearm, pulling it up to look at her hand. From where I stood, I could see her finger bent at an odd angle, the skin already turning a slight shade of purple.

Reed cursed as Brandy pulled her arm out of his grip. "I'm fine."

"Don't look fucking fine, Brandy. Get in the truck," Reed demanded.

"I'm not getting in your damn truck," she spit at him.

"I can take her," Callan offered as he made his way over to us.

Reed shot daggers at Brandy, but she jumped at Callan's offer. "Thank you, Cal."

He nodded, setting his hand on the small of Brandy's back to lead her in the direction of his truck. Reed practically had fire in his eyes as he watched Callan and Brandy walk away, his gaze trained on where Callan's hand was touching her.

Travis patted Reed on the shoulder as he walked past. "Stuff like that happens, son. Come on, let's eat. She'll be back in a couple of hours. Probably only needs a splint."

Reed didn't follow his dad as he stood there watching Callan help her into the truck.

"She knows the risks, Reed. Stop being such a hard ass," Lettie said to him as she walked to the porch, climbing the steps.

He didn't move until Callan drove past us, then proceeded to stomp off in the direction of the house, his movements stiff. I didn't know what the problem between Reed and Brandy was other than Reed thought she was a bad influence, but it was starting to seem like there was something more to it.

Choosing to move past that, I joined the rest of the Bronsons on the porch, pulling out the chair beside Lettie at the table.

"Don't people usually have the table on the *back* porch?" Lennon asked as he reached for Charlotte's homemade potato salad.

"Lennon Bronson, is there a problem with the way I have things set up?"

His cheeks flushed. "No, Ma."

"Your mother wanted to see the sun set on the horizon when we ate out here. This is the best spot," Travis explained, grabbing the tongs off the plate full of ribs.

"Ain't no one around, anyway. You could put the table in the middle of the driveway, if you really wanted to," I pointed out.

Travis shot me a look that said *don't give her any ideas*.

I stifled a chuckle as Charlotte spoke up. "A little outdoor setup in the yard would be nice."

Charlotte's pretty soft-spoken but when she's passionate about something, she came at it full force. She had Travis basically eating out of the palm of her hand. The man loved her harder than I ever thought possible. Their dynamic worked for them. Hell, it had kept them happy ever since they got married straight out of high school.

"So, Lennon, how's the feed store?" I asked before taking a bite of the tender meat. Reed sat across from me, silently pushing his potato salad around on his plate.

"I lost an employee yesterday, so I listed an opening today. Hoping someone fills the spot soon. Winter will be here before we know it."

"I could help out if you need it," Lettie offered.

He waved her off. "Working with siblings is the worst idea."

I laughed as Lettie said, "We've all worked on this ranch our whole lives."

"That's different. Dad was here to delegate. You wouldn't like me as your boss."

She rolled her eyes, taking a bite of potato salad.

"Plus, you've got that barn to finish, in case you've forgotten," Travis piped in.

If Brandy's finger was broken, which I was almost positive it was with the way it looked before she left, it'd just be Lettie and me working on the beat down structure. I had a feeling Lettie would be more than willing to work with me this time around though.

"And..." Charlotte nudged Travis with her elbow.

Lettie looked between the two of them. "What?"

Travis took a bite of food, taking his sweet time before responding. "We thought you might like to learn a bit more about managing the rescue."

Lettie's fork dropped to her plate and my eyes shot to her, her mouth popping open, then closed, as she struggled to form words.

"I-I'd love that," she managed to get out.

Charlotte gave her a sweet smile. "Your father told me how you felt like you had no purpose. You've made a huge impact on this ranch, Lettie. If you're planning to stay in Bell Buckle, you're more than welcome to keep living in your old room until you figure something else out."

I smiled as Lettie nodded vigorously at her mom. What better purpose than the rescue?

"But what about our conversation before the trip, Dad?" she asked.

"I underestimated you, Lettie, and I apologize for that. You clearly handled the trip well and proved to me you could hold your own under the stress rescue can bring. With you being gone so long, I guess I forgot how capable my little girl is."

"I guess I should apologize for that extra horse, then," Lettie said to her father. Lennon had a big smile on his face while Reed rolled his eyes.

He waved his hand through the air. "Why do you think I sent Bailey with some extra money? I had a feeling you'd do that. Your mother raised you, remember? I know the effect she's had on you when it comes to rescue. But Lettie, try to keep that under control, alright? There's only so much space and money in our budget for all these horses."

She bobbed her head back and forth like she was contemplating it. "I can try."

"That's all I ask," he said.

Charlotte shot Lettie a wink before digging back into her plate of food.

An orange glow was casted over the table as the sun set in the west, light chatter filling the air as we enjoyed a family meal. Though Beck, Callan and Brandy weren't sitting here with us, it felt like we were all back together again, like the good old days.

I didn't miss the fact that Lettie was confirming her place in Bell Buckle. Deep down, I didn't think she'd leave again, especially after our trip to Montana, but it was still in the back of my head. If she had a reason to stay, something other than me, I could expect her to be around for a long time.

God knows I wasn't good enough to keep her around before.

25

Lettie

After pouring a cup of coffee that I desperately needed to fight off the exhaustion from our trip, I pulled the wad of cash from my back pocket and set it in front of my dad.

"What's this?" He eyed the cash, laying down the morning paper before looking up at me.

"For the gray. I want him to stay here at the ranch."

He took a sip of coffee. "Is this your way of saying he's yours?"

Cradling the steaming mug in my hands, I tossed my head side to side. "Yeah, basically. But I'm going to ask Brandy to help break him and everything. I'm in no rush, just couldn't stand to see him shipped off."

"Bailey told me you outbid a kill buyer. Sounds like it was pretty intense."

I rolled my eyes. "Far from it."

He chuckled. "Well, all I can ask is that you be careful."

"Since when have I ever not been careful?"

He frowned at me and I laughed in response, laying a hand on his shoulder before walking past him to make my way down the hall to my mom's office.

At dinner last night, Bailey had pressed his knee up against mine as we ate and talked, but after that, he'd simply said goodnight and headed home. I couldn't help but wonder if he regretted what happened at the hotel. As much as I felt awkward about it, I didn't wish it never happened.

Peeking my head in the door, I knocked lightly. My mom's head popped up from behind her laptop and she smiled. "Good morning, sweetie."

"Good morning." I crossed the room, taking a seat opposite of her. The walls were lined with mahogany bookshelves that were passed down from my grandparents. Not an inch of space was to be found with books crammed into every nook and cranny.

"What's on your mind?" She eyed me, closing the laptop in front of her.

"I just wanted to thank you for last night. I've always loved rescue work, you know that. If I had known that was your plan, I never would have left."

"Oh, honey. I wanted to give you the chance to pave your own path in life. I didn't want to offer it to you and make you feel like you had to say yes. Plus, you were so young. Now, you're twenty three, you've held your own through college, and proved you have what it takes to learn this side of things."

"Why didn't you offer it to any of the guys?"

She folded her hands together on the desk. "I know my boys' limits. They're good at keeping their hands busy and diving into labor-intensive work, but managing a rescue? Besides Lennon, I couldn't see any of them taking that on. They'd rather be out there," she lifted her hand to gesture behind me, "checking fence, shoeing horses, and stacking hay. Just everyday ranch chores. That's what they're good at, and I wouldn't want them to change to appease me. But you've always had a big heart, Lettie. You've worn it on your sleeve since you were little, and while that can be a dangerous thing, it can also be a really good thing. Just don't be like me and drive your father crazy with wanting to take in every neglect case under the sun."

A smile pulled at my lips. "It's a good thing I don't have anyone to make insane."

She dipped her chin, raising an eyebrow in a knowing look.

"What?" I asked.

"Lettie Bronson, I didn't raise you to be clueless."

I put a hand over my heart, feigning innocence like I didn't know what she was talking about. "Clueless?" I shook my head. "Me? Never."

She opened her laptop, shaking the mouse on the pad beside it to wake it up. "You be nice to that boy. He didn't mope around this ranch for five years for nothing."

I froze. "He did what?"

She smirked, bringing her attention to the computer screen. "Oh, yeah. Kept his hands dirty, but man, was he lost without you around."

She had to be messing with me. Bailey wouldn't have waited around for me. He had to have forgotten about me sometime in those five years, at least with mindless hookups.

"I can't tell if you're being serious," I said hesitantly.

Her eyes met mine over the computer. "Why do you think he took your dog home with him every day? Kept your horse in shape? He sure didn't do it for his own health."

I shook my head, standing from the chair with my mug in hand. "Because he's polite."

She snorted. "Your brothers are polite. Bailey? He's lovestruck. He's got that same look in his eye your father had all throughout high school."

"Please don't compare Bailey to Dad," I groaned.

She grinned, turning her attention back to the screen in front of her. I turned to head out of the room, wishing I could unhear what she said that made me realize what his actions really meant. That he did those things because of the way he felt about me, not just because he was being nice while I was gone.

We shared a moment in the hotel, but I didn't expect it to happen again, even though my body begged for it to. I'd felt bad for not returning the favor, and although we joked about it on the drive back, I wasn't actually anticipating it would happen.

This was too much to think about at seven in the morning.

***

I found Brandy in the white barn, jotting down notes on a clipboard in the room we kept our medical supplies in.

"Did Bailey bring any girls around while I was gone?"

She paused her writing and turned to me. "Well, good morning to you, too."

I closed the door behind me, closing us in the small space. "I'm serious, Brandy."

"My finger's fine, by the way. Got a splint." She held up her hand.

I was a shitty friend. "Fuck, I'm sorry. I'm glad it's okay. Did they say how long it'll take to heal?"

She set the clipboard on the counter. "Six to eight weeks, but I ain't waiting that long. And to answer your question, no. He didn't."

Not wanting to get into a battle about her broken finger, I asked, "Why not? I mean, five years, and no girls?"

She opened a cabinet above the small sink, reaching in to grab a tube of dewormer. "Maybe you should ask him. You know the ranch isn't the only place he can bring a girl, right? Maybe he was getting his dick sucked on the reg at the Watering Hole."

I cringed at the mention of our favorite bar, Outlaw's Watering Hole, and the picture her statement put in my mind. Being locals, they allowed us in when we were underage, but we never drank. We'd go to dance and hang out to get away from the ranch after a long day's work, but I hadn't been back since the night of my eighteenth birthday, and I wasn't making any plans to change that, especially after the image Brandy just put in my mind.

"Thanks for that lovely image, Brandy."

She wrote something down on her clipboard and shot me a wink. "What's a best friend for?"

"Anyway, aside from Bailey's personal life, I have another question to ask."

She set the pen and dewormer down, facing me. "What's up?"

"I'm keeping that gray we brought back, and I was wondering, after your finger is healed, would you be up for breaking him?"

She grinned, looking borderline evil. "I'd never say no to a challenge."

Unable to hide my smile, I pulled her in for a hug, squeezing her. "Thank you." I pulled back. "But only after your hand is healed."

She waved the hand with the splint in the air. "Yeah, yeah. Give it a couple weeks and I'll get to work."

I frowned, but let it go, knowing I wouldn't be able to convince her otherwise. She was as stubborn as I was, which is why we got along so well. We were unstoppable when we put our minds to something.

I followed her out of the small room, the dewormer in her hand. Reed was in the aisle bent over with a file, shaving away at a horse's hoof. The sound echoed through the barn as we walked by him.

"Good morning, Reed," I said to him.

He grunted in response, but must have seen I wasn't alone, because he gently dropped the horse's leg and straightened.

Brandy opened Nova's stall door and walked in, talking to the gelding.

"You better not be about to stick dewormer down that horse's throat," Reed warned.

She peeked her head out of the stall. "Why's that?"

He tossed the file in the bag that sat open on the floor and set his hands on his hips. "Do I need to remind you that your finger is broken?"

She rolled her eyes at him, disappearing inside the stall again. "It's a broken finger. I can still work."

He stomped over, his boots echoing on the mat. "Brandy if you so much as-" He stopped as he saw her with her hands already opening Nova's lips, emptying the tube in his mouth. His tongue darted out as he worked the green substance around in his mouth before swallowing it.

I tried to hide my smile as Reed scowled at Brandy. She wiped her hand on her jeans, the saliva leaving a wet mark on them. "See? All done." She walked past him, her hip brushing his hand. "Don't forget to close the door," she yelled back over her shoulder.

She disappeared back into the room we had come out of. Reed pulled the door to Nova's stall shut and turned to me. "What?" he snapped.

I blew air out of my nose, shaking my head. "So grumpy," I said before continuing down the aisle to head outside.

It was time to get to work on the barn despite my desire to go back to bed and crawl under the covers and never come out.

26

BAILEY

The morning air was cooler as summer began its transition into fall, so I opted for my red flannel over my white t-shirt. Once the sun warmed up, I'd shed it, but for now, I was comfortable as I headed over to Bottom of the Buckle Ranch to start my chores.

Aside from Brandy breaking her finger, last night went great. It brought up feelings of nostalgia as we all sat around the table. We'd done it plenty of times in the past few years, but without Lettie there, it always felt like something was missing. I'd been awestruck watching the sun set, the colors dancing across Lettie's features, her eyes blazing sapphires against the orange glow.

I parked my truck and hopped out, leaving it unlocked on habit. Halfway to the white barn, a whistle sounded from my left. My head swiveled toward the sound. "Over here." Lettie waved her hand in the air from where she stood bent over a pile of two-by-fours.

I made my way over, my boots kicking up dust with each step. "I've got to muck the stalls before I can get started," I said when I approached her.

"Our volunteer, Cathy, offered to do it so we could get a head start on the barn before it got too hot."

She wrapped her hands around three boards at once and I quickly bent to grab them before she hurt her back. "I can whip it out real quick. Won't take longer than thirty minutes if you'd wait."

She let me take the planks of wood from her and then bent to grab another three. "You're going to hurt your back lifting them like that," I said.

She ignored me, lifting the boards with a grunt. She headed around the side of the barn, awkwardly maneuvering the beams before tossing them down on the dirt behind the building with a loud slap.

She dusted her hands on her jeans as she said, "Things should speed up now that we have all the lumber and a nail gun."

"I don't see why we couldn't get it done before winter then."

"If you don't let the volunteers keep up with your chores, there'll be no way. Do you see this thing?" She gestured to the barn but I kept my eyes on her, already well aware of the state the structure was in.

"You doubt my ability to keep up with our project and get other work done around here?"

"No, but there's only so much one person can take on. I don't want you stretching yourself thin."

I leaned a shoulder against the outside wall of the barn, smirking at her. "You worried 'bout me, Huckleberry?"

Her cheeks heated and she looked away. "Worried about you?" She scoffed. "Please."

When she met my gaze, she saw the look in my eye before I moved. She darted in the opposite direction and I ran after her, catching her before she made it even ten steps. I wrapped my arms around her middle, lifting her feet off the ground.

She screamed, but I saw the smile on her face. "Bailey! Let me go!"

My fingers skittered around her stomach, causing a laugh to escape her lips. "Not until you admit it."

My hat fell off with her struggle, landing in the dirt. "Oh, now you've done it." I dropped to my knees, lowering her to the ground. She tried to squirm away from me, but I got her on her back, pinning her hips as I straddled her. She tried to push against my shoulders, but I grabbed her hands, bringing them above her head and holding them in the dirt.

Our chests touched as we tried to control our rapid breathing. "Admit it, Huckleberry."

She shook her head, her hair fanning out in the dirt. She pursed her lips as if to give the impression they were sealed.

I only took that as a challenge and lowered my head, our noses touching at the tip. Her eyes blazed up at me as tension crept up between us.

"You care about me." She gave no response, but I felt the slight shift in her hips.

Bringing my mouth closer to hers, my lips brushed against her skin as I spoke, my voice deeper. "Don't make me force it out of you, Lettie."

She parted her lips as her arms relaxed under my hold. I knew what I was doing to her, and I fucking loved it. She was dropping her defenses one by one.

"Why the hell would I care about you?"

I smirked, shifting to hold both her hands in one of mine. My other hand glided down her hair, trailing along her neck all the way to her hips. I watched as her eyes glazed over and brought my hand between her legs, adding a bit of pressure against the material of her jeans. "Because I know if I didn't have these skin tight jeans in between us right now, I'd feel just how soaked you are for me, and I've barely even touched you."

"I'd say you've touched me quite a lot in the past few minutes, actually," she snarked.

Drawing my hand away, I brought it up her body to wrap it around her neck, not adding any pressure. My thumb stroked her pulse point as I felt it beat rapidly. "You've got a mouth on you."

Her body arched in response, her neck pressing slightly against my palm due to the movement. I kept my hold light, letting her add any pressure if she wanted it.

"Maybe I should put it to better use than mouthing off to me, huh?"

Her eyes flamed, her cheeks turning a bright shade of red. She wanted it. She wanted *me*.

But now wasn't the time or place.

I released her in one swift movement, grabbing my hat behind me and standing up. After placing my cowboy hat on my head, I reached down to grab her hand, pulling her up. Our chests bumped each other as she stared up at me.

"We've got work to do, Lettie."

I left her standing there as I walked back around to the front of the barn to grab some tools.

As much as I tried, I couldn't control myself around her. My hands itched to touch her, even when she wasn't around.

That woman was my kryptonite, and I had to admit, I liked how weak she made me. If there was anyone on this planet that could bring me to my knees, it'd be Lettie Bronson.

***

We worked through the midday heat, making progress on replacing the old boards that used to make up the stalls. Anytime I caught Lettie watching me, she'd quickly avert her gaze, busying her hands on whatever she was working on.

It was cute, seeing her so flustered. Though we'd been intimate in the hotel, I wanted her to initiate it this time. Once she did, I'd know there was no stopping the inevitable. But until then, I'd wait.

Lettie walked behind me from where I crouched, messing with the hinge on an old stall door. The butt of her jeans was covered in dirt from where she'd been sitting on the ground, but it just made her all the more attractive.

She bent over to pick up a few slats of wood when she dropped them, letting out a hiss. I dropped the screwdriver in my hand and ran over to where she was still bent over.

"Are you okay?" I asked as she reached her hand behind her, rubbing at a spot on her back.

"Think I just pulled something," she muttered.

"Here, sit down." I wrapped my hand around her upper arm, helping to guide her onto the ground. She winced as she sat and closed her eyes.

I sat behind her, spreading my legs so they were on either side of her. I brought my hands up to her back, aiming for the area she had her hand over moments ago.

"Here?" I pressed my thumb in slightly.

"A little to the left," she directed.

I slid my hand about an inch left and felt the ball under her skin. She inhaled sharply as my thumb got to work.

"Told you to be careful."

"I don't take orders from cowboys." Her posture relaxed despite the bite in her tone.

My lips grazed the shell of her ear as I whispered, "Didn't seem that way in the hotel."

Goosebumps freckled her skin where I rubbed. "That was different."

"Oh, yeah? Bet I could make you do it again. I bet I could make you do a lot of things."

She laid back against me so my chest was pressed against her back, my fingers still working at the knot between our bodies. Her head came to lie on my shoulder and I looked down to find her blue eyes boring up at me. Taking this as my cue, I lowered my head, but as my lips brushed her mouth, she said, "In your dreams, Bailey Cooper."

With that, she pushed off me, standing up and walking her pretty ass all the way up to the damn house. She didn't so much as glance back, but if she did, she would've seen me sitting in the dirt like a damn dog.

She was right on the mark. My dreams were always about her.

27

LETTIE

The warm water washed over me, easing a bit of the ache in my muscles. All of the heavy lifting and bending over from the past week was catching up to me. Every night when I crawled into bed, my body would throb until I fell into a dead sleep, not waking until morning, when we'd do it all again.

We were on track to have the barn finished by winter thanks to Brandy's help, despite Reed trying to bully her into resting her hand. I wasn't sure if I could consider the way they treated each other as tough love. It was more like extreme torment at this point. Sometimes, it got to the point where I thought they might murder each other.

After washing my hair and body, I turned off the water, stepping out to wrap a towel around me. My mother's cooking wafted down the hall into my room, causing my stomach to growl. Leaving my hair wet, I threw on a pair of black leggings and an old t-shirt, then made my way to the kitchen.

Chatter filled the house as it usually did, but it wasn't until I heard a specific deep voice that I stopped in my tracks. I listened, unable to believe my ears. Rushing the rest of the way down the hall, I came around the corner to find Beckham standing in the kitchen, beer in hand, laughing with my brothers.

"Beckham!" I ran towards him, throwing myself at him as he turned around. He took a step back to steady himself as I wrapped my arms around his torso.

"Hey, Lettie." He wrapped his arms around me, crushing me to his chest.

"I didn't know you were coming home," I said into his shirt.

He chuckled. "Figured I'd surprise you guys."

I pulled back, releasing my grip on him.

"That's not true. He just missed my cooking," my mom piped in from the stove.

Lennon lightly punched him on the shoulder. "Mama's boy, huh?"

"Oh, shut up. As if you all aren't. I'm the only one who doesn't still live at home."

A chorus of "hey's" sprung up from Callan, Lennon, Reed, and Bailey.

I laughed. "You all act like that's true. Reed and Bailey are the only ones who still live at home."

Reed held his beer up in the air, a finger pointed at me. "No. I live on their *property.* That is entirely different."

Bailey nodded. "Yeah, same here. Our houses aren't even attached to theirs."

Callan rolled his eyes and turned away from the conversation, grabbing tongs off the counter to help my mom toss the salad she'd thrown together in a large bowl.

"Which means," Lennon announced, "that you're the only one living with your parents."

"I moved away for five years, so this doesn't count," I defended myself.

"Pretty sure it does," Beck said.

"I had nowhere else to live for the time being."

"Give her a break, guys. Lettie's just used to the special treatment, is all," Bailey joked. Yet it didn't hit me as a joke. It hit me like he knew I was babied. They all did.

"I forgot something in my room." I excused myself, walking back down the hall. Once inside, I closed the door behind me and stood in the middle of the room, counting my breaths.

Once my brothers slowly moved out of the house one by one, they'd stopped hounding me as much, but with Callan and Reed always around the ranch, they had the ability to keep an eye on me. I appreciated it at times, I really did. But other times, it was too much.

Brandy and I couldn't run off and do our own thing without one of them trying to join and make sure I was okay. Brandy was well aware of my health and the signs to look out for, but Reed didn't trust her to pay close enough attention. That's what I loved about being alone with Brandy: she could care and show her concern, but she didn't try to control the things that I did.

My parents took the protectiveness down a notch after I made it clear when I was a teenager that I could handle myself. My brothers took that as their cue to step up their game. Bailey knew this. He also knew that I hated it.

A light knock sounded on my bedroom door before it opened behind me, but I didn't bother turning around. "Please get out."

Two steps, then the click of the door, and a sigh.

"I didn't mean it like that, Huckleberry."

I whirled around, my hands fisted at my sides. "Stop calling me that."

He took one step toward me, gauging my reaction. I stayed put, unwilling to let him see how he affected me. Another step, and we were only a foot apart. "And if I don't?"

Frustration built in my chest, aching to get out. But I wouldn't give Bailey the satisfaction of taking it out on him. He wanted me to come undone, and I wouldn't give that to him.

He closed the distance and I arched my neck to look up at him. He brought his hand up, his fingertips grazing my cheek before he pushed my hair behind my ear. God, I hated how that sent shivers down my spine.

"Hmm, Lettie? What are you going to do?" His green eyes searched my face for any reaction. He was so close I could see the small ring of hazel around his pupil. Were his eyes always this damn beautiful?

He wasn't wearing his cowboy hat tonight. Instead, his hair was messy, the top just a little shorter than the sides. My hands in his hair when his face was buried between my legs flashed through my mind and I pushed it away. Now was not the time to think of that moment in the hotel. I could think of that later tonight when I was alone. Right now, I needed to imagine him standing in front of an ax throwing target, if only to keep my hands off of him.

"I see that war raging inside your head," he said, his voice husky. "Which side is winning, Lettie? Your head," he brought his finger to my temple, tapping it twice, "or your body?" His other hand settled on the curve of my waist before sliding around to my back. He tugged me closer to him, to the point our chests touched.

My breath hitched, but I stayed silent. It was fucking hard not to give in when his hard chest was pressed against my breasts. I felt my nipples pebble under my bra, my body betraying me.

His tongue ran over his bottom lip. "Get on your knees."

Was he fucking crazy?

No, I was fucking crazy, because next thing I knew, my knees hit the sheep skin rug on my hardwood floor.

"Bad girls who leave the room mid-conversation deserve to get punished, don't you think?"

He traced my jaw until his finger stopped under my chin. He angled my head up toward him, and the second our eyes met, I saw his burn with need. I nodded in response to his question and reveled in the fact that he loved how I looked kneeling before him, completely at his mercy.

After a minute passed, I realized he was waiting for me to make the next move. I bit down on my bottom lip, my body screaming at me to take, but my mind yelling at me to stop. I was quickly losing control when it came to Bailey, and I couldn't bring myself to hit the brakes.

28

BAILEY

I stared down at her before me, those blue eyes wide and fucking jaw-dropping from where she sat on her knees. She drew her bottom lip into her mouth, her teeth working it. Unable to help myself, I pressed my thumb against her lips, pulling the bottom one free.

Her lips parted and I slid my thumb in, her tongue swirling around it as she closed her lips around the digit, pulling it deeper. I cursed as my dick throbbed against the zipper of my jeans. I wanted her to initiate whatever was going to happen, but I didn't know how much longer I could hold myself back.

Lettie made fire course through my bloodstream at just the sight of her. If just having my damn finger in her mouth did this to me, I would be a goner once my dick parted those sweet lips.

As if she read my thoughts, she pulled her head back, releasing my thumb as her hands shot up to work at my belt and zipper. Her urgency in the way she yanked my jeans and boxers down caused another curse to slip past my lips.

She kept her eyes on me as she gripped my shaft, pumping it once, twice, then bringing her tongue to the head to lick the moisture off that built there. I threaded my fingers through her hair, wrapping the silky strands around my fist.

She swirled her tongue around the tip, then down to the base, and up again. Her lips parted, and that was my undoing. She took me into her mouth, burying it so deep I felt her tongue twitch as my tip hit the back of her throat.

She began sucking, her cheeks hollowing out with the action. Her head bobbed and then she took me down the back of her throat, a small choking sound coming out of her. She held it, then pulled her mouth off of me, looking up at me with parted lips.

Once she settled the reflex with a few swallows, she took me in again, but this time I held her head in place as I thrust my hips, testing how far I could go. She opened her mouth, bringing her hands around to my ass to urge me further. I did, tilting my hips until I hit the back of her throat. I pulled out, a string of saliva coming with.

"You like taking my dick in your pretty little mouth, baby? Like feeling it slide down your throat? Because feeling you choke on it makes me want to fucking explode."

She nodded. "I want more," she begged, and that was all it took.

I thrusted back in, my hand fisted tight in her hair as I fucked her mouth. She made small gagging noises, but kept her hands gripped on my ass, giving no indication she wanted me to stop. I quickened my pace, the back of her throat feeling like fucking heaven. I'd never had a blowjob as intense as this, and I knew that none would ever compare.

I pulled out again and she spit on me, the saliva falling down to the floor as it slid off my length. "Do you want me to fuck you, Lettie?"

She shook her head. "Just my mouth."

That was fine for now. But mark my word, I'd claim her one day.

She opened her mouth again, letting me slide my length back in. Seeing the sheen on her chin, her pretty pink lips stretched around me, the small choking noises she made, the hum of her moan against my tip, I lost it. I tried to pull out before my release, but she refused and held me in place as I came down her throat. She swallowed every drop, keeping her eyes on me as pleasure pulsed through me.

Fuck.

This side of Lettie was all new to me, and I fucking loved it.

I let go of her hair and she pulled her mouth off of me. I reached down to grab her under her arms, hauling her up to standing. I cupped her face, saliva still coating her chin.

"I'm sorry that what I said hurt you."

Her forehead creased, my apology coming at a surprise after what just transpired between us.

"It's okay," she said, more like a question.

I shook my head. "It's not, but I promise I won't say shit like that again. It was uncalled for."

She nodded, and I brought my mouth to her swollen lips and kissed her. Compared to the blowjob she just gave me, our mouths were gentle. She pulled back and used the top of her shirt to wipe her chin dry.

"Do you think it'll be obvious when we go out there?"

I chuckled, dropping my hands. "I told them I was going to use the restroom, but I'm sure they didn't buy that for a second."

Her cheeks turned pink again. "Great. Just what I need. My brothers aware that there's something going on between us."

I pulled my pants back up, situating myself. "Guess we'll have to get used to it."

She froze in place. "Uh, no."

"Huckleberry, I didn't just come down your throat for you to try to keep us a secret."

"First off, don't use that nickname in such a sexual sentence. Secondly, there is no *us*." She threw air quotes up around the word.

I heard plates clinking down the hallway, indicating they were getting ready to serve the food. I bent to kiss her forehead. "We'll put a pin in it for now, but don't think you won this battle." I turned and headed for her door, pausing before I walked out. "And Lettie?" She met my gaze. "Might want to fix your hair."

She scowled and grabbed a pillow off her bed, chucking it at the door. I closed it right before it could hit me, laughing as I made my way down the hall.

There was no way in hell I could get a taste of Lettie and then be cut off. She was like the most addicting drug. One hit and I was hooked.

29

LETTIE

Five Years Earlier...

My hair was still wet from my shower when I finally emerged from my room at five o'clock. Brandy and my mom had told me not to come out until five p.m., so I'd taken the longest shower of my life and did every possible thing I could between shaving my legs, using my sugar scrub, doing a hair mask, and then painting my nails after I got out.

I hadn't bothered to do my hair since I wasn't expecting a big celebration for my eighteenth birthday. I'd specifically told everyone I wanted it to be lowkey, and I hoped they'd listened.

I still wasn't sure if I wanted to accept the offer for the school in Boise, so I wanted my head clear tonight. If I did choose that school, I'd have to leave as soon as possible, but that meant leaving my friends and family, the only people close to me.

I didn't know anyone in Boise, and the thought scared me. But did I want to spend the rest of my life in Bell Buckle? I could choose a closer college and commute daily, but if I did that, I was sure I'd never leave. Bell Buckle was the only place I knew, and if I wanted to spread my wings, now was the time.

But if I didn't decide on Boise and did end up staying closer to home, I'd be doing the same routine I'd been doing daily my entire life. As scary as leaving was, I couldn't keep playing it safe.

But safe was comfortable.

"Happy birthday!" a chorus of voices shouted as I rounded the corner of the hallway.

Stopping in my tracks, I took in my family and Brandy, all grinning from ear to ear with those cheesy cardboard party hats on.

"Thanks, guys." I awkwardly smiled. "I didn't want anything big this year," I reminded them.

"Oh, please. This isn't big. Plus, you could be leaving us soon. We wanted to go all out," my mom said with a wave of her hand as she brought me a party hat.

Lennon emerged from the kitchen with a bowl of chips. "We have to celebrate our little sister, no matter what milestone it is."

"I'd hardly call it a milestone," I said.

Brandy rolled her eyes. "Call it whatever you want. You're legal!" She squealed, running over to me to wrap me in a tight hug.

"Legal? Please," Reed scoffed. "She can't even drink yet."

Brandy narrowed her eyes at him after letting me go. "We're still going to the Watering Hole tonight."

"No drinking for the kids," my dad grumbled as he stole a chip from Lennon's bowl.

Lennon frowned at him, setting the bowl on the table. "You've reminded us twenty times now, Dad."

Callan snorted from the kitchen where he was checking on some food in a slow cooker. "It's not like they've never been there before."

"Or drank before," a deep voice added from the front entry way behind me.

I spun on my heel to find Bailey standing there with a cake in his hands. Light purple frosting was messily coating the outside of what appeared to be white cake.

Bailey *baked* a cake?

Bailey *baked* in general?

Did I hit my head in the shower?

"Happy birthday, Huckleberry," Bailey said with a soft smile.

My eyes searched his green ones, confusion clearly written on my face. "Is that for me?"

He chuckled. "Yeah, Huckleberry. It's for you."

"A cake?"

"It is your birthday, isn't it?" he asked, though he knew the answer. He always remembered my birthday, but he'd never baked me a cake before.

"Let me take that from you." My mom squeezed in between us, gently grabbing the cake from Bailey. He let her, keeping his eyes on me the entire time.

"Come out on the porch with me?" he asked, something flashing across his face that reminded me of a cross between fear and longing.

"Uh, the party's in here," I stuttered, hooking a thumb over my shoulder.

He flashed his stupid beautiful smile at me. "I'm well aware, Lettie."

I looked over my shoulder, then back at him. "Don't you want to stay in here then?"

"We both know you hate parties," he pointed out.

Damn him for knowing me so well.

"Right. Let me grab my coat?" Any excuse to put this off. I didn't want to know what he had to say. Not when he kept looking at me like I wasn't just his best friend's sister right now.

"It's not cold out," he reminded me.

"Right," I clipped. "Shall we?" I gestured to the front door behind him.

He nodded once, opening the door for me. I passed him, my shoulder touching his chest and sending electricity shooting to my fingertips.

The door closed behind me as I walked to the edge of the porch, leaning my elbows on the railing. I was usually fearless, so why was I standing here like Bailey was someone to be afraid of?

He came up beside me, copying my position against the railing. "You choose a school yet?"

I shook my head. "Can't decide."

He shrugged. "Go with your gut feeling."

I let out a nervous laugh. "Easier said than done."

He faced me, standing up straight as he leaned one hand on the railing. "You don't trust your gut?"

"It's not that I don't trust it. I just don't want to make the wrong choice. It's a lot of pressure," I stated.

He nodded like he was contemplating that. "Then stay close to home."

I looked up at him. "What?"

"If you're not sure where to go, why risk moving so far and then regretting it?"

I straightened, still having to tilt my head back to meet his eyes. "Wow, you're really helping."

He held his hands up in mock surrender. "Sorry. I never had to make a decision like that."

"You never wanted to go to college?" I asked.

"No," he said matter-of-factly. "I always knew I was right where I belonged."

I looked back out at the property and the setting sun casting an orange-pink glow over the land. "How'd you know?"

"Some things just feel right," he said.

I wasn't sure what felt right to me, but I did know that staying in my parents' house with my siblings all close by would mean they'd still be suffocating me with their concern for my health. How could I truly live my life if I was being kept in a fish bowl under twenty four hour surveillance, constantly being reminded to take my supplements, always being watched in case I got dizzy, or my skin went pale? God forbid I chew on a single ice cube without the entire household being alerted.

The front door opened and my mom poked her head out. "We're cutting the cake so you guys can head out early."

I nodded to her. "Thanks, Mom. We'll come in."

"Are you feeling okay?" she asked, concern knitting her brows.

"Yeah," I said, trying to hide my sigh.

"If you don't feel good, you can skip the bar-"

"I'm fine, Mom. I'll be okay," I interrupted her.

She nodded, disappearing inside.

"She just cares about you, you know. We all do," Bailey pointed out.

I didn't meet his eyes, but I knew he was staring down at me with that damn concerned look on his face. "I know. I just hate that I can't even step out of a room without someone thinking I'm going to pass out. It's not even that common, anyway."

"Passing out?" he asked.

I faced him then, narrowing my eyes up at him. "For someone like me."

"Well, that's your problem right there," he said, like I was supposed to know what that meant.

"What's that?" I asked.

"You treat yourself like you're not normal, either. So naturally, why would anyone else?"

"I am normal," I argued.

He reached up to shove his cowboy hat lower on his brow. "I don't know about that," he joked.

I lightly hit him on the arm, then walked by him to head inside. Before I reached the door, he rushed around me, opening it for me.

We walked inside to join the party and eat the cake Bailey had baked for me, but I couldn't help feeling like our conversation wasn't done.

***

The music was loud and the lights were low. The typical setting for Outlaw's Watering Hole.

Though Brandy and I were still too young to drink, we still had fun drinking virgin margaritas and watching the boys royally fail at playing pool.

"The table has a tilt," Callan huffed.

"Oh, please, Cal. You just suck. Admit it," Lennon said.

"He's not the only one," Reed called from where he sat at the high top table.

Beckham was still on tour, so he wasn't able to come home for my birthday, but he had sent me a video of him singing happy birthday with the biggest smile on his face.

I couldn't wait for him to be home.

Lennon scoffed. "Like you're any better."

Reed took another swig of his beer, then slammed it down, standing from the table. He grabbed Cal's cue from him, stalking over to the end of the table.

"Rack it," he instructed Lennon.

Lennon rolled his eyes. "I am older than you, you know."

"By two years," Reed grumbled. "That doesn't even count. I can still boss you around."

Bailey came back from the bar with shots of tequila, setting one each in front of Brandy and me. "For the birthday girl and her best friend."

"Oooh shots!" Brandy shrieked.

"Bailey," Reed warned.

He waved him off. "Have a little fun, Reed."

I looked up at him from where I was sitting. "Thank you," I said with a smile.

"My pleasure. It's not like you've waited until you were twenty-one, anyway," he pointed out, reminding me of the times he's had to save my ass while I was tipsy before.

"That camping trip was so much fun. We have to go again," Brandy said before holding her shot glass out to me for cheers.

I tapped mine against hers, a soft clink vibrating off them, then we tipped them back.

My face scrunched against the burn, and I quickly used my virgin margarita to wash it down.

"Taste a little more like a real marg?" Bailey asked, watching me gulp it through the straw.

"Little bit," I croaked.

"Another?" Brandy gleamed.

"No," Reed clipped from where he was bent over the pool table, deep in the game.

"Don't listen to the party pooper," Brandy mumbled to Bailey.

I laughed at the look Reed gave Brandy's back. Even over the music, he could hear her. She was oblivious to it, but I swore I saw something other than hatred there.

"One's enough for you ladies. Lettie?" He faced me. "Care for a dance?"

I gulped. "Uh, sure."

"Blue" by Zach Bryan played over the speakers, slowing down the mood for the couples on the makeshift dance floor. Really, it wasn't a dance floor at all. Just a section of the bar with an abundance of boot scuffs on the hardwood floor where there weren't any chairs or tables.

Once we were in the center, Bailey stopped, turning to face me. He set both hands on my waist as I draped mine around the back of his neck. We swayed to the music, a little off beat, but clearly the two of us couldn't be bothered to keep up with it.

His green eyes seemed to get lost in mine as the bar drowned out and all I saw was Bailey.

Bailey, my brother's best friend.

Bailey, my childhood annoyance.

Bailey, the guy who just baked a cake, probably the first one he'd ever made, just because it was my birthday.

My heart rate picked up and I dropped my forehead to his chest, unable to keep my eyes on him.

He was looking at me the way someone looked at their first love, and I was far from that.

He was always playing pranks on me growing up, doing whatever he could to get under my skin. But maybe I was taking his signals all wrong. Maybe he didn't do it because he couldn't stand me, but for solely the opposite reason.

Maybe he did it to get me to see him.

To give him my attention, regardless if it was negative or not.

And that fucking scared me.

Bailey was always there when I needed someone to cry on or rant to, and I was the same for him, but that was all this ever was. All it ever could be.

I couldn't ruin what he and I had by testing how far we could go.

What if we didn't work out as more?

What if I fucked it up and he ran like all the other boys I'd had in my life in the past?

Then I'd have no Bailey.

And I'd rather keep him how he was in my life, at arm's length, than let him in further. It would crush me if something tore us apart.

His hands squeezed my hips lightly and I lifted my head, finding his gaze.

"You doing okay, Huckleberry?" he asked.

The song ended and I dropped my arms, taking a step back from him. "Why does everyone need to ask me that a million times a day?"

His brows furrowed with confusion. "You just seemed tense, is all."

"Of course, I'm tense, Bailey. I have a lot of decisions to make right now."

"Like?"

I sighed, looking around the dance floor at the few couples already moving to the beat of the next song. "You know what."

It wasn't just the school. It was us.

His face dropped, and I wanted nothing but to bring his smile back. "Lettie, don't think about that right now. It's your birthday."

I looked down at my boots, then behind his shoulder at the bar. I couldn't see the look on his face again knowing that I put it there. "I think the party's over."

He was quiet for a moment, watching me to gauge if I was serious, then his shoulders fell, and I fucking hated myself. "Okay."

I turned, heading back to my brothers and Brandy as Bailey followed a few feet behind me.

I'd already upset him, and even with something so small, it fucking crushed me.

I couldn't let us go any further, and staying in Bell Buckle would only make that more difficult.

I guess that made my decision.

I'd start packing for Boise tonight.

30

LETTIE

After dinner, Beckham invited us all to the bar for old times' sake. I agreed to go as long as Brandy could tag along. I didn't want to be stuck around a whole bunch of guys by myself, brothers or not.

I rode with Callan and Bailey. Reed, Lennon, and Beckham took a separate vehicle. Since we'd stopped on the way there to pick up Brandy, the three of them got to Outlaw's Watering Hole before us. Callan pulled into a parking spot and killed the engine, all four of us getting out.

I stared up at the orange neon sign out front of the wood building. Not a thing had changed about the outside in the last five years. Nostalgia hit me in the chest, and I realized just how much I missed this small town. Bell Buckle ran in my blood.

That ranch and the rescue were my entire life. I was a fool to leave.

"Coming?" Bailey asked.

I snapped out of my thoughts to catch him watching me. "Yeah."

Callan held the door open and I followed in after Brandy, Bailey's body so close behind me I could feel the warmth radiating off him. We found Reed, Lennon, and Beck at a high top table near the pool tables with seven beers sitting atop it.

"Went ahead and ordered you guys some Coors Banquets," Reed said.

Brandy grabbed one off the table, taking a long pull. She set the glass on the table with a clang and grabbed a pool cue, arranging the balls into the rack.

"A simple thank you would be nice," Reed muttered.

I grabbed a beer, the glass cold in my hand as I walked over to Brandy.

"You want to do teams?" I asked.

"Sure. I'll take Callan, you take Bailey?"

"Why do I get Bailey?"

She shrugged, busying herself with lining up the rack to hide the smile on her face.

"Just thought you might want to be with him, is all."

I didn't miss the innuendo in her comment. I took the five steps back to the table and set my beer down. "Callan, Bailey, you guys care to play?"

Bailey smiled down at me. "With you? Always."

I was half convinced he didn't just mean the game. I rolled my eyes and turned back around, the two of them following. I didn't miss the hard look in Reed's eyes from where he sat at the table across from Beckham.

They grabbed their cues off the wall. "Ladies first," Brandy said as she bent over to hit the cue ball.

It hit the balls with a crack, sending them scattering. None went in, so I chose my shot. After the cue ball bounced off the side wall, missing every single one on the table, Bailey frowned at me.

"Am I on the wrong team? What happened to your game, Huckleberry?"

"I've still got it."

"You sure about that?" he asked as Callan took his shot. He got stripes, and took aim for another ball. After missing, Bailey was up. "I'll show you how a pro does it."

"Oh, don't flatter yourself," Brandy said from across the table.

He bent at the waist to take the shot, shooting two solids in the corner hole. He turned to me, holding his hands palms up, elbows bent, with a smirk on his face.

Show off.

Maybe I should play worse so he'd have to show me. Bend me over the table, my ass rubbing right where I knew we both wanted it.

No, I should definitely stop.

"Well, looks like you and Cal have it under control." I grabbed Brandy's hand, tugging her with me towards the dance floor where "Me and My Kind" by Cody Johnson played over the speakers.

"I need something stronger than beer," I said to her. I needed something other than Bailey to make my head spin. He was making me fucking crazy.

"I know exactly what you need." She winked before dragging me over to the bar.

Out of the corner of my eye, I saw Bailey leaning on his cue, watching me as Callan bent over the table. Could I have been any more obvious running away from him like that?

Good ol' Lettie. Always resorting to running.

Fuck me.

"Four shots of tequila, please," Brandy shouted over the music to the bartender. He was middle-aged, cute, a little shorter than Bailey. I shook my head, as if that could clear my thoughts. Now I was comparing men to Bailey?

"Four?" I asked her.

"You've got two hands, don't you?"

The bartender lined four shot glasses up in front of us, pouring them to the rim with Patrón. Once he was done, he set the bottle back on the shelf. "There you are, ladies."

Brandy offered him a sweet smile, assumingly forgetting how much of a lightweight she was. I grabbed for the tequila, downing both shots one after the other. The alcohol warmed my chest as I grabbed the lime he'd set on the napkin in front of me.

"Better?" Brandy asked before she tipped her head back to finish her second shot.

I nodded. "Much."

She leaned on the bar, knowing it pressed her breasts together, giving the bartender a clear view of her cleavage peeking out of her burnt orange romper.

The outfit was cute on her, with bell sleeves and a flowy bottom. It landed mid-thigh, showing off her long legs, but the v-cut top left little to the imagination. Brandy was all confidence and sass, and I loved that about her.

I'd opted for a denim blue sundress, pairing it with my "going out" cowgirl boots. I knew Bailey loved my outfit because when I'd changed into it after dinner, he couldn't keep his eyes off of me. Much like the way he couldn't keep his eyes off me right now.

With the buzz of the tequila working its way through my blood, I pulled on Brandy's arm, leading us to the dance floor just as "This One's for the Girls" by Martina McBride started playing. We screamed the lyrics to each other as we danced.

God, I missed this. The familiarity of being in this bar with my best friend, Bailey, and my brothers. As much as I hated them looking out for me, I knew they'd never let anything happen to me. I could let loose and not worry. Not with the six of them standing by.

It felt weird being able to legally drink here now. The bar hadn't changed one bit in five years, but other things did.

Things that couldn't be seen with the naked eye, like my feelings for Bailey and my love for Bell Buckle.

I'd thought starting over was the answer, but I'd quickly come to find that everything I could ever need was right in front of me the entire time.

31

BAILEY

Lettie in that dress would forever be ingrained in my mind. She never used to dress up or wear anything other than her usual jeans, boots, and tank top or tee. Don't get me wrong, she was goddamn beautiful wearing worn-in boots and dirt-stained jeans. But in a dress? With her hair all curled and running down her back in waves? I was surprised I was still breathing right now.

She danced with Brandy in the middle of the makeshift dance floor, the lights dim and the music loud. Her dress bounced as she moved, and while I definitely wanted a peek of what was underneath, no other guy in this bar needed to see that shit.

"You sleeping with my sister, Cooper?" Beckham's voice filled my ears.

I kept my arm casually slung on the table, my hand wrapped around my beer, and faced him. "If I am?"

He smiled, shaking his head. "I fucking knew it." He lifted a finger off his beer, pointing it at me as he took a sip. "You better treat her right. If I'm on the road and find out you hurt her, I won't hesitate to come back and kick your ass."

I chuckled, thankful he wasn't pulling the overprotective brother shit on me. Lettie's brothers had known me my entire life. I was the least of their worries when it came to her.

"You act like your brothers can't handle me."

"Oh, I'm sure they can. I just want to be here to watch your ass get beat," Beck said.

"Ah, you're just butthurt you lost every fight growin' up."

"You know how much muscle it takes to stay on a bucking bronc?"

"Please, enlighten us, Beckham," Callan said as he came over and reached across the table to grab his beer.

"Beck talkin' about rodeo again?" Lennon interrupted, making his way over from where he was playing pool with Callan.

Reed sat along the half-wall with his arms crossed. I wasn't sure if he'd overheard our conversation. If he did, he wasn't giving any reaction as he watched the dance floor.

"Eat shit, Lennon. At least it's not sales numbers," Beck remarked.

Lennon took a seat, taking a long pull from his beer. "Now, that's a conversation I'd happily take part in."

"Always was the boring brother," Callan mumbled.

I scoffed. "You guys talk like you're not damn near thirty. Hell, Len and Reed already are."

"Bailey, you're fucking twenty-seven. Shut your mouth before I shut it for you." Beck grabbed the pool cue from Lennon and got up to rack the balls for another game.

I grabbed Callan's cue, coming to the opposite side of the pool table. "Speaking of being almost thirty, you thinking about retiring soon?" I asked Beck.

"Not sure. I enjoy the rush and being on tour. I'm not sure what else to do once I do decide to retire."

"You could work on the ranch. Could always use an extra set of hands," I offered.

He moved the balls around, arranging them just right. "I could."

Beckham removed the rack and bent to take his shot.

"You and Parker still talk?" I asked as he shoved the cue forward, missing the cue ball entirely.

He pursed his lips and straightened. "Haven't heard from her since she left on a cattle drive a couple weeks ago."

I didn't press further, getting the feeling it was a sensitive topic.

"That's it, I'm cutting them off." Reed pushed off his chair, aiming for Brandy and Lettie.

I set my cue on the felt tabletop and grabbed Reed's arm before he could get any further. "Let them have their fun. They haven't been able to do this in years."

He shrugged me off. "You're fine with them taking their sixth shot right now?" He nodded his head in their direction. I moved my gaze over to where they were propped at the bar. I'd lost track of how much they'd been drinking, but it was clear Reed had been counting. I did *not* feel like carrying them out of here tonight.

"I'll get Lettie," I said. He took off in their direction and I followed suit.

"Oh, if it isn't buzzkill number one," Brandy slurred as we approached.

"Who's buzzkill two?" I asked.

"No one. There's just one. And I'm unfortunately face to face with him right now."

Reed ignored her jab as he gave the bartender a look to cut them off. The guy nodded in response, filling two glasses with water and setting them on the bar.

Reed and Brandy shot daggers at each other as I faced Lettie, her eyes glistening up at me. "Care to dance, Huckleberry?"

I held my hand out to her. I didn't think she'd take it, but she didn't hesitate for even a second, setting her dainty hand in mine. She followed me out to the dance floor, "It's Your Love" by Tim McGraw filling the room. I turned, facing her and placing my hands on her hips. She wrapped her arms around my neck, giving no indication that the alcohol was affecting her.

"When you call me huckleberry, do you just see me as a giant, blue ball?"

I laughed, pressing my forehead to hers. "No, Lettie. But you *are* wearing a blue dress."

She tried to hide her smile as she pinched my shoulder.

"It's denim," she whined.

I feigned hurt, drawing her closer to me. I was so lost in her, I didn't see when Brandy stomped past us, or hear when she told Reed she wouldn't get in his truck.

All I saw was Lettie, with her blue eyes, in her blue dress.

Blue was my new favorite color.

"I may be a little drunk," she said, doing her best to hide her slur but doing a bad job at it.

I rubbed the tip of my nose against hers. "I know. Which is why I want you to know I've liked you since the day I laid eyes on you when we were little."

Her eyes met mine, a small gasp passing her lips. "Even after I landed in a bucket of huckleberries?"

I couldn't help the laugh that escaped my lips. "Even *more* after that. Blue ass or not, you're beautiful, Lettie Bronson." Our hips swayed in time to the music, our bodies touching in places I'd always dreamed of.

"You're not so bad yourself."

She closed her eyes, laying her head on my chest as we danced in our little bubble. I brought my hand up to stroke her hair.

"I'm so grateful you came back," I whispered.

I didn't think she'd heard me over the music, but a few minutes later, she mumbled, "Me too."

32

LETTIE

I handed Lennon the rescue's credit card after he rang up the supplies Brandy and I came into town to grab.

"How's the barn coming along?" Lennon asked as he waited for the receipt to print.

"We're making good progress. If we keep at it, it'll for sure be done by the first snow," I replied.

"Thank goodness, because we've got some old ones that will need the shelter once the temperatures drop," Brandy said.

"Good to hear. I'm glad Bailey's helping you out with it. I don't know what Dad was thinking putting you on it alone."

"I think he knew Bailey would step in," Brandy admitted.

My eyebrows pulled together. "How would he know that?"

She frowned. "Please. That guy is so gone for you, he'd tie your damn shoes if you didn't wear boots all the time."

Lennon held the card and receipt out to me, and I grabbed it with a little too much force. Brandy didn't know what she was talking about.

"Thanks for loading the truck, Len."

"Anytime, Lettie. You two drive safe."

"Will do," I said, turning for the door. Brandy walked around the front of the truck, getting in the passenger side as I got in the driver's seat.

"We have to get diesel and then we can head back," I said to her, noticing the gauge was almost on empty.

"Alright. We can hit the pumps that are right on the edge of town."

I headed in that direction, driving through the main strip where privately owned shops lined the street. Fully bloomed flowers sat in window boxes that framed some of the windows, and most of their doors were propped open to let in the cool air. A few people walked along the sidewalks, window shopping as they strolled.

With the rapidly cooling temperatures, I had a feeling winter would come early this year. I hoped it wasn't too brutal. A drastic change in temperature could cause horses to colic, and while we were still getting meat on their bones, it could be fatal.

I pulled up to the diesel pump, hopping out of the truck to fill the tank. Brandy stayed in the truck with the windows rolled down, scrolling on her phone.

Was it that obvious to everyone that Bailey was into me? I didn't think they suspected we had done anything as more than friends, but Brandy made it seem like the way he looked at me was clear as day.

Images of him helping me into the house the other night after the bar flashed through my mind. The way his hands felt unzipping my dress, helping me into his t-shirt he gave me on our trip.

Callan had taken Brandy home before we left, so Bailey, Reed, Lennon, Beck, and I rode in the other vehicle. Bailey had dropped Lennon off at his house right outside of town, then swung by the motel to unload Beck. Reed hopped out of the truck after we entered the property, walking the rest of the way to his place.

It was well past midnight when we got back to my parents' house. The only light on at the house was the porch light, indicating my parents had gone to bed hours ago and assumed I'd be getting home late.

"Up you go," Bailey said after opening my passenger door and unbuckling my seat belt. My head was spinning, all three Baileys equally attractive. I'd snuck another shot when Bailey had gone to grab my purse from the table. I'd desperately needed it after dancing with him.

I hopped out of the truck a bit too eagerly, staggering forward into him. He caught me by the waist, directing me out of the way so he could close the passenger door. "That alcohol finally gettin' ahead of ya?"

I giggled. Fucking giggled. I was never drinking again. "I'm blaming Brandy."

He chuckled. I leaned against his side as he walked us up the porch steps, his arm wrapped around me to keep me from stumbling.

"Maybe Reed's been right all along about her."

I shot a glare up at him in response.

He unlocked the front door with my house key, leading me inside. My shoulder rammed into the wall in the hallway, causing a picture to swing on its nail. "Shh," I managed to get out through my uncontrollable laughing.

"I'm not the one who needs to shush, Huckleberry," he whispered as he managed to get me through the doorway to my bedroom.

I landed on my bed face first in a fit of giggles, but the moment I stilled, my head spun faster. "Ugh."

"Please don't throw up on me." I tossed up a hand to wave him off. "Let me get you out of that dress, Huckleberry." I turned my head to the side, raising an eyebrow at him. He frowned in response. "I'm not trying to sleep with you, but I don't think sleeping in that dress will be very comfortable."

I pressed my face back into the pillow. A second later, I felt his fingers at my back, easing the zipper down. I hadn't worn a bra, but it wasn't like we hadn't seen pieces of each other before.

The dress was strapless so it wasn't difficult for him to slide it down my body when I lifted my upper half a few inches. My black thong hid nothing, but he didn't falter as he stood up and hung the dress over the back of the chair in the corner. I watched as he opened a drawer, his lips lifting slightly as he pulled the shirt he'd given me on our trip out of my dresser.

His eyes didn't drift to my ass or anywhere on my body. In fact, he simply gestured for me to sit up. I did, not bothering to cover my chest. He slipped the shirt over my head, his fingertips brushing my skin as he tugged it down my torso. He adjusted the shirt, then brought his hands up, pulling my hair out from the neckline where it was trapped.

"We're not having sex?" I asked, trying my best to focus on one of the Baileys filling my vision.

He cupped my cheeks, pressing a gentle kiss to my forehead. "Not while you're drunk, Huckleberry."

I frowned. His touch woke me up inside to the point I wasn't sure if I was more buzzed off the alcohol or him.

"Get some rest. I'll see you in the morning."

"For sex?"

He laughed, his chest moving with the action. "No, Lettie. For the barn."

"Oh. Right."

I laid back on the bed and he pulled the blanket up over me, brushing his lips across mine. I fell asleep to the memory of his lips. How soft they were on my mouth. How rough they were between my legs in the hotel.

"Lettie?" A male voice interrupted my thoughts at the same time the pump clicked, indicating the tank was full.

I snapped out of the memory to find the man standing a few feet away from me.

"Charles?"

The worry that was etched into his forehead eased, his features softening. "Hey. I haven't seen you since…"

"Since the bar," I filled in for him. The bar in Boise. Charles was the guy who'd puked all over me. Ruined a damn good pair of boots, too.

"Yeah, you didn't tell me you were moving. I tried swinging by but your apartment was empty."

I set the pump back in the holder, pressing a few buttons on the screen before turning back to him. "Sorry. Kind of a split-second decision."

"You living around here?" He looked around as if this was the middle of fucking nowhere.

I mean, I guess it was.

"Yep. Grew up here."

His eyes landed back on me. "Ah. Bell Buckle. I was just passing through. I'm on my way to Jackson Hole for a trip with the guys."

I forced a closed-lip smile. "Sounds like fun."

He rubbed at the back of his neck. "You know, uh, if you'd be up for it, I'd like to take you on a proper date. Dinner, movie, all that."

I sucked on my teeth, unsure of how to turn him down. I had no interest in going on a date with Charles, and not only because he vomited on me. It felt like a betrayal to Bailey, and right now, my focus was all on Bailey in that department.

"I'm kind of… seeing someone," I said.

His eyes widened. "Oh. Sorry, I didn't know."

"It's kind of new." I pulled my keys out of my pocket, taking the two steps to reach for the driver's side door. "It was nice seeing you, though."

"You too, Lettie."

I opened the door. "Take care."

He nodded once and turned around, heading back to his SUV. I slid into the seat and started the truck, rolling up the windows.

"Who was that?" Brandy asked.

"That guy I was telling you about." I knew damn well she heard the conversation.

"Oh my gosh, vomit guy?" She erupted in laughter. "That is so awkward."

I pulled out of the gas station, aiming in the direction of the ranch. "Tell me about it."

After a few minutes of silence, Brandy spoke up. "So, when were you going to tell me you were seeing someone?"

I glanced at her, a frown on my face. "When were *you*?"

"I'm not seein' anyone."

I raised an eyebrow. "You've been fighting with my brother quite a bit recently."

She turned to me in her seat, mouth agape. "Lettie Bronson, do not tell me you just insinuated I am with Reed. Don't mistake our fighting for flirting. I'd rather sleep on a bed of horse shit for the rest of my life than touch him."

She could play it off however she wanted, but I wasn't blind.

"Can't say I feel the same."

"About your brother?"

I shot her a glare. "No. About you-know-who."

I didn't miss her eye roll out of the corner of my eye as she rested her head back against the headrest. "You can say his name, you know. Hell, even a blind person could see what's going on between you two. You guys aren't too good at hiding it."

I went to gnaw on the inside of my cheek, but stopped when I remembered what Bailey said all those weeks ago. *"You're gonna chew your cheek clean off if you keep at it."*

God, even if he wasn't around, he consumed my thoughts.

If Brandy was insinuating what I thought she was, that meant everyone at the ranch saw it, too. We obviously couldn't keep our attraction to each other a secret, but I wasn't sure if I was ready to tell my entire family about us. There were still so many things we needed to talk about and figure out.

Was that even what he wanted, or was he just enjoying messing around? He'd never straight up said he wanted a relationship or any type of commitment, but I couldn't imagine Bailey *not* wanting more with me. He never seemed like the guy to mess around behind a girls' back, but what did I know? I avoided that side of him my entire life, being too afraid to know if he was with anyone.

The only way to find out was to ask him, but there was never a right time. Whether we were around people or busy working on the barn, I didn't want to catch him off guard. That could ruin everything, and if things between us went south, I'd have no choice but to leave again. I couldn't stay in Bell Buckle and see him on this ranch everyday if we weren't together, not since we'd clearly become much more than just childhood friends.

33

LETTIE

After parking the truck, Brandy and I got out to unload the supplies we'd picked up in town. As we were bringing the bags of supplements, electrolytes, and grain into the barn, a familiar deep chuckle sounded from the Chevy parked by our storage shed. Swiveling in that direction, I saw one of our volunteers, Valerie, with her hand on Bailey's arm as they both laughed together.

I audibly swallowed in an attempt to push away the pang of jealousy that was creeping in. She was just being friendly and making small talk while he helped her load the truck for the fundraising event tomorrow. There was no harm in that, right?

Brandy noticed me watching them and failed to hide her shit-eating grin. I ignored her and got back to work unloading our truck, grabbing the last few bags of dewormer from the back seat.

With my hands full, I kicked the door shut with a little too much force. I turned around to find Valerie looking over at me. She waved, her white teeth flashing as she smiled.

I raised my hand in a poor attempt to wave, the plastic handles on the bags squeezing the life out of my palm. Brandy had to have grabbed more than just dewormer. It felt like these things were loaded down with horseshoes.

Realization dawned on me and I dared a peek inside, but right as I maneuvered one of the bags open slightly, Brandy swooped in and grabbed them out of my hand.

"Hey!"

"Poking your nose where it doesn't belong, Lettie," she said over her shoulder as she brought them into the barn.

"I know that's not just dewormer!" I shouted after her.

There was only one man on this ranch that needed horseshoes, and if my guess on what was in those bags was correct, she'd be hearing it from me. I was sure Reed wasn't the one to ask her to buy them, though. My dad tried to keep horseshoes on hand so Reed didn't have to dip into his own stash when he worked on our personal horses. Reed never minded, but my dad insisted.

Bailey was loading a folded-up plastic table into the bed of the truck, but I knew Valerie was more than capable of loading the rest, seeing as Bailey already did all of the heavy lifting.

I debated going over there when I saw Beckham perched against the fence, watching the rescue horses graze. The horse he'd had us pick up was a few feet from the fence where he stood, content as he chewed.

I walked in Beck's direction, coming up beside him. "Hey."

"Hey," he replied.

"Going to do anything with him?" I jerked my head in the direction of the bay.

He shook his head. "Nah. The guy deserves to retire, live out the rest of his days in a wide open field. He's already put in more work than some horses do in their entire lives."

He was right. The best thing we could give these horses was freedom and food.

I glanced behind me at Bailey and Valerie chatting.

"Why don't you just go over there?" Beck asked.

"Huh?"

He faced me, keeping a hand on the fence. "I see you looking at him."

"And? He's just helping her." But I knew he caught the slight bit of jealousy in my tone.

He turned away, looking back out at the field. "Won't go anywhere if you don't confront your feelings." I hated that he was right.

He was one to talk, though. He'd hid his feelings from the one person in his life we all knew he felt something for, and now she was off the grid.

Knowing bringing her up wouldn't do any good, I decided to listen to Beck. "Talk to you later?"

He nodded, the movement jostling his black cowboy hat slightly. I turned and headed in Bailey's direction.

I came to a stop at the corner of the tailgate. "Hey. Can I borrow Bailey?"

Bailey was wearing a baseball cap *backwards* instead of his typical cowboy hat. The fact that he was all sweaty, sexy, and around a woman other than me grinded my gears. Bailey wasn't mine to be jealous over, but I felt it all the same.

I didn't miss the smirk that lifted the corner of Bailey's lips. I also didn't miss the way his ass looked with his bandana sticking out his back pocket as he jumped off the edge of the tailgate. "You good with the rest, Val?"

Val?

She totally ignored me, instead reaching down to lift the tailgate and acting like it was too heavy. Bailey lifted it for her, slamming it closed. How do you volunteer at a horse rescue and you can't close a tailgate?

"I can load the rest into the back seat. Thanks for your help, Bailey." She flashed him a sweet smile, all her teeth on display. "Nice seeing you, Lettie." She regarded me for less than two seconds before walking around to the back door of the truck.

Bailey wiped at the sweat on his forehead with his forearm as he faced me, the moisture glistening on his tan arms.

Before I could say anything stupid, I grabbed his hand, tugging him behind me over to the halfway repaired red barn. Once inside, I dropped his hand, spinning around to face him.

"What's the emergency?" he asked.

"I didn't like that."

His brows furrowed in confusion, but a few seconds later, a smile reached his mouth as realization dawned on him. "Are you jealous?"

I crossed my arms. "Jealous? Please."

He took a step closer, towering over me. "You're jealous of Volunteer Valerie."

How many more nicknames did he have for her?

I pursed my lips, then threw my hands down to my sides. "Okay, fine. I'm jealous."

He shook his head, a small chuckle coming out of him.

"What?" I demanded.

"You don't need to be jealous of her, or anyone, in fact."

"Why do you say that?"

He lowered his head slightly. Fuck, I wish he wore backwards baseball caps more often. I didn't think he could get any sexier, but twist that hat around? I'd drop my panties in this damn barn if he asked.

"Because I only have eyes for you, Lettie. It's always been you."

I barely had time to swallow before he pressed his lips to mine, cupping my face in his hands. My fingers wrapped around his wrists as I met his pace, our lips melting together.

I wanted to be able to kiss him whenever and wherever I wanted, but that wouldn't happen unless I admitted how I felt and what I wanted. I needed to start voicing my feelings and stop hiding from them. That was the only way this would work.

I pulled back, his hands lowering slightly to cup my jawline, his thumbs rubbing circles on my cheeks.

"It's always been you, too, Bailey."

His eyes narrowed the slightest bit. "Really?"

I nodded. "I don't want this to ruin us."

"No ruination can come from the two of us being together. I promise."

I searched his face, seeing that he meant it. There was no hint of humor or sarcasm in his voice. "How do you know? How are you so willing to risk it?"

"Because I don't think I could go through this life *without* risking it for you."

Within a breath, his lips were back on mine, devouring me, a sense of urgency and demand in the way his hands tangled in my hair, pulling me closer. Now that I knew what he tasted like, how much he truly wanted me and me alone, I never wanted this to stop. Kissing, touching, whispered sweet-nothings, I wanted it all.

His tongue slipped past my lips as he brought one hand down the side of my body to fist my shirt at my waist.

"Fuck, Bailey, you make it so hard not to ride you in this damn barn right now," I mumbled against his mouth.

He smiled into our kiss before pulling back an inch. "What's stopping you?"

"Only the fact that it'd be so obvious to anyone who saw us come in here."

He shrugged like that wasn't a big deal. To him, it probably wasn't.

He licked his lips, my eyes following his tongue as it trailed along his slightly swollen lower lip. He reached up to the bill of his hat, pulling it off to run his hand through his hair before fixing it back in place, still backwards, *thank God*.

"Come to my place tonight," he said.

I was at a loss for words for a moment, my mouth opening and closing like a fish out of water. "Like..." I cleared my throat. "Like a date?"

He nodded. "Like a date."

"Do I need to dress up?"

"Wear whatever you're comfortable in. I honestly wouldn't mind if you wore nothing at all."

I shoved at his shoulder playfully, hard enough to make him take a step back. He grabbed my chin, tilting my head up to him. "My house at eight."

I couldn't say no to those green eyes, but his mouth was on mine before I could respond. He already knew what my answer would be.

He pulled back again, scanning my eyes for a moment before turning around without another word and heading out of the barn.

I was tired of letting my overthinking get the best of me. From now on, I'd keep saying yes to Bailey Cooper.

34

BAILEY

Exiting the barn, I headed to my '85 Chevy K10. It may be old, but there wasn't a day it wasn't running. I'd keep daily driving it 'till its last leg, then probably swap the motor for one with less miles. The truck was my grandpa's before he passed, so there was no way in hell I'd ever scrap it.

Starting the engine, I drove over to my parents' house to get a few things for tonight. Shifting the truck into park out front of their house, I got out and made my way up my parents' porch steps and through their door. I didn't bother to knock because every time I did, my mom gave me guff about it.

I found my mom in the small office they'd added onto the house a few years ago. She raised an eyebrow, skepticism shining in the look on her face when she saw me. "Home in the middle of the day?"

"Yeah, got everything pretty much done for the day at the Bronsons'. Where's Dad?" I asked.

She heaved a sigh. "Outside stress working."

Taking a seat on the recliner in the corner of the room, I leaned back. "What's to stress about?"

The corners of her mouth tilted down the slightest bit. "What's *not* to stress about?"

I didn't miss the concern shadowing her features. I leaned forward in the seat. "Mom? What's wrong?"

She looked down at the paperwork in front of her, picking one up and handing it to me. "I'm afraid we may lose the ranch."

Complete shock froze me in my place, my hands unable to move to grab the paper she held out. "What do you mean we may lose the ranch?"

She set her hand down, leaving the paper on the edge of the desk. "We're not bringing in enough money to make ends meet. We're running out of savings to pull from, and we can't keep living off dipping into our money set aside for retirement."

"Why didn't you guys tell me sooner?"

A look of sorrow shone in her eyes. "Honey, we don't want to worry you with these things."

"Mom, I can help. You and dad aren't alone in keeping this ranch afloat. I'm sure the Bronsons would help out if they knew."

She shook her head. "As much as the Bronsons have helped us over the past years, I don't want their money. It's one thing to offer labor, but cash? I can't ask that of them."

We couldn't lose this ranch. It'd been in our family for four generations. There was no fucking way I'd let us lose that. Land was only getting more expensive. If we lost the piece we had, there was no telling if we'd get another.

"I'll think of something." I grabbed the paper on the desk as I stood, folding it in fourths and shoving it in my back pocket.

My mom stood from her seat behind the desk as I came around, pulling her in for a hug. "I don't want to put this burden on you," she mumbled, her voice muffled from my shirt.

I let go of her. "It's not a burden, Mom. This is my home, too. We all fight for what we love. We stick together. That's what families do."

She reached up to set her hand on my cheek. "You've always had a big heart, Bailey. One of the best things about you."

I pursed my lips as she dropped her hand. "Speaking of big hearts, can I borrow a few things from your dining set?"

"Of course. Take whatever you need."

"Thanks, Mom. I'll bring it back tomorrow."

"You're welcome, sweetie. But Bailey, please don't put this on your shoulders, too. You already have so much on your plate."

I frowned. What was it with people thinking I did too much? I liked to keep busy. What was the problem with that?

"My plate will never be too full, Mom. Not when it comes to the people I love."

She sat back in her seat as I turned and headed toward the door of her office. I strode through the house, stopping by the cabinet that held all of their finer cutlery and dining sets.

I sifted through all of the holiday sets, finally finding what I was looking for. The set that made me think of clear skies, wildflowers, and Lettie.

I wouldn't accept moving, even if it was only a few miles away. Lettie was in my grasp, and I wasn't letting go.

There had to be a way to keep this place. I'd figure it out, no matter what it took.

35

Lettie

Painting the doors on the barn had taken longer than I'd anticipated and sunset was quickly approaching. Bailey had left shortly after he asked me to come over to his house tonight. I assumed it was a spur of the moment question and he had to run home to prepare, but knowing the gentleman he was, he most likely had it all planned out.

I dipped my hair under the shower head one last time before turning the water off and stepping out to dry off. I had no idea what to wear tonight. Bailey and I had known each other basically our entire lives, and I'd never given a second thought to what I wore around him. Boots, jeans, and a t-shirt were all I typically wore on the ranch, so he was used to seeing me in that. But for a date with someone I'd known my whole life, who'd seen my ass covered in huckleberry juice and my hair coated in mud from the creek more times than I can remember?

Was a dress too much? I'd worn a sundress to the bar the other night, so surely wearing one tonight wouldn't be overkill. Or would that be trying too hard, and I should play it safe with my usual clothes?

Snap out of it. It's just Bailey.

But that was the thing. He wasn't *just* Bailey anymore. He was so much more. We'd jumped fifty feet over a line I'd imagined up due to fear of giving in and messing up, and now we were going on a date.

A lifetime of never letting my mind think of him as anything more than a friend, and now I was wrapped in a towel standing in the middle of my room overthinking something as simple as clothes.

He probably couldn't care less about what I wore tonight.

Rouge was asleep on my bed, exhausted from a day out with the volunteers. He was attached to me - and Bailey, of course - but was always running around with new people, begging for extra attention. That much hadn't changed about him in the last five years, which was also why I didn't want to take him away from the ranch when I left. He loved it here, and it would have been more selfish for me to take him from the place he loved just to sit in a small apartment all day while I was at my classes.

Sifting through my closet, I settled on a paisley print bandana top with light wash jeans and a pair of boots that weren't coated in dirt. I debated grabbing a jacket, but thought better of it. Though it was warm out, I still felt cold. I blamed it on my dripping hair, which I'd decided to let air dry to its natural waves, afraid that if I put any effort into doing it, I'd overthink it and not go altogether.

Leaving Rouge in my room, I made my way out of the house to find my dad and Reed riding in the direction of the white barn. If they saw me wearing this, they'd know I was going out, and I didn't feel like dodging around who I'd be with.

I beelined for my SUV, trying to keep my boots quiet on the ground.

"Going out?" I heard Reed call out.

My fucking luck.

I stopped to turn in their direction, taking a few steps. They closed the distance on their horses, my dad wearing his signature frown as always.

"Meeting up with Brandy. I'll be home late," I said.

My dad nodded, but Reed narrowed his eyes at me from under the brim of his dark brown cowboy hat.

"You always dress up to see Brandy?" Reed asked.

It was my turn to narrow my eyes at him. "Since when does it matter what I wear to go see Brandy?"

He shrugged, the reins in one hand with his other arm casually draped over his opposite wrist. "I get the feeling it ain't Brandy you're goin' to see."

My hand moved to rest on my hip. "Why's that?"

He tipped his head in the direction of the white barn. "'Cause Brandy's still in there working with one of the rescues."

I pursed my lips together. *Twice with my luck tonight.*

"Fine. I'm going on a date, but the *who* is none of your business."

Reed scoffed. "The hell it isn't."

Travis shot Reed a look. "Give her a break, son. You know your sister will be safe."

I wanted to gag. I did *not* need the birds and the bees talk from my dad.

Reed stared at me, sucking on his teeth before clicking his tongue and pulling on the outside rein to spin his horse around. He trotted off toward the barn without another word.

My dad shook his head, bringing his gaze back to me. "I trust that you'll use protection."

My jaw dropped. "Dad! Please!"

He cleared his throat and mumbled, "This is why I leave this kind of thing to your mother."

"Yes, please. For all our sakes, leave that part of parenting to her," I pleaded.

He nodded once, then clicked his tongue at his sorrel, spinning him in the direction Reed took off in. He stopped a few steps later, looking over his shoulder at me. "I'm glad you're giving him a chance, Lettie. He's a good man."

I swallowed the emotion that climbed its way up my throat. Bailey *was* a good man, and while I always knew that, I was glad I wasn't keeping him off limits anymore. He was giving me a second chance, the opportunity to make things work after all those years away, and I was damn sure going to make it count from here on out.

I waved my dad off, turning on my heel to get back to my SUV. He could always read me like that damn newspaper, as if I had headlines of my thoughts sprawled across my forehead.

I started up my car, turned on my headlights since the sun had begun to go down, and headed over to Bailey's parents' property. He lived next door, but with the acreage both our families owned, it wasn't feasible to walk, and I didn't want to ride back in the dark later tonight.

As I drove down our long driveway, the nerves began to settle in. Bailey was my childhood friend. We'd both seen each other at our worst. But something had changed between us in the past couple weeks.

Something I wish I would have been open to all those years ago.

36

BAILEY

Stabbing the thermometer into the slice of meat, I checked that it was close to rare. One thing I could never forget about Lettie was that she liked a red piece of meat. She'd order the dang thing still moo'ing if she could. I liked my steak, but I preferred it cooked to some extent.

Grabbing it with the tongs, I pulled it off the grill to set on the clean plate I had ready. My mother's scalloped potatoes were inside in the oven with ten minutes left on the timer, and the salad was prepped and ready for dressing.

I didn't have to go all out with this dinner for Lettie. Hell, she'd be happy with to-go tacos from the Mexican joint in town. But I needed her to know I was taking this seriously. I didn't want her to think all I wanted was a hookup. What I wanted was far from that.

I wanted her to take my damn last name.

Nothing with Lettie and me was 'too fast.' If anything, we took things way too fucking slow. I'd been falling in love with her throughout our whole lives, and the last thing I wanted to do was lose her again because I didn't make my intentions clear enough this time around.

This was my second chance with Lettie, and I'd be damned if I fucked it up.

But that didn't mean I'd be proposing to her tonight. Sometime in the future, of course. Tonight was to prove to her that we could be more than just childhood friends crushing on each other.

It was no secret she felt the same way. She may think she was hiding it well, but I saw right through the walls she tried to put up, and I was determined to break them down one by one.

I could win her over and figure out a way to keep this ranch in my parents' name. They needed more land in order to grow more, which in turn would bring in more profit. But the acreage around this part of Idaho was going up in price each day.

We weren't the only ones falling on hard times, though. The locals were feeling it just as hard. The Bronsons had the rescue bringing in extra funds on top of the money Reed and Callan brought in for them, so they were better off than the lot of us.

We'd figure it out. We always did. But tonight wasn't about that.

After another minute, I pulled my steak off the grill, dialed the knobs down, and kept the lid propped open before heading inside with the plate of steaks. Using the toe of my boot, I slid the slider door shut, then set the plate on the island to slice the steaks.

There weren't too many five star restaurants around Bell Buckle, but this would come pretty darn close to one. My mom's scalloped potatoes and these steaks? Could never go wrong with that.

I sliced through the meat with a knife. My mouth salivated at the thought of digging in. Hopefully, Lettie got here soon because I was starving.

The timer for the potatoes rang out. I spun around, grabbing an oven mitt and opening the door. I pulled the glass dish out, turned off the oven, and set them on the stove to cool while I dressed the salad.

I drizzled the honey vinaigrette over the summer salad containing strawberries, corn, avocado, and an assortment of other vegetables to bring the dish together. It sounded like an odd combination, but once Mrs. Bronson talked me into trying a bite a few summers ago, I was hooked.

Grabbing the potato dish, salad, and plate of steaks, I walked back out onto my porch. I carefully went down the porch steps and headed for the white gazebo I'd built about a hundred feet from my back porch a couple years ago.

It was nice to come out here after a long day on the ranch and enjoy a beer. I'd purchased more high-end outdoor furniture for the gazebo since the roof protected them. The chairs were far more comfortable than what I had on my back porch, so this was my go-to spot ever since I completed it.

I arranged the dishes on the white tablecloth to fit in between the array of candles I'd set out.

After adjusting a few things, I stood back, checking off my mental to-do list to make sure everything was perfect.

Salad fork, dinner fork, knife, spoon, plates, water, wine...

I forgot the damn napkins.

Making sure I had foil over all of the dishes in case pesky bugs decided to ruin all of my hard work, I headed in the direction of my parents' house on foot.

I'd moved into their in-law unit on the property shortly after I'd turned eighteen. It was convenient with working on the ranches, and rent was decent, so I never thought about leaving here.

Thinking about it now, it may seem odd that I was still technically "living at home" at the age of twenty-seven. It was the same property, just not the same house. That counted for something, right?

It's not like I sat around playing video games in my parents' basement. I worked my ass off every day, rain, snow, or shine. Working was like my therapy. Keeping my hands busy kept my mind from spiraling.

When I found out Lettie left Bell Buckle, I'd mucked stalls, filled water buckets, swept the barn, cleaned the damn cobwebs from the rafters. Anything you could think of doing on a ranch, I did it, and I didn't stop for sixteen hours.

My hands were to the point they were nearly bleeding, but I knew if I stopped, the thoughts would take over. The overthinking. *Was it me? Did she hate me that much, after everything we'd been through?*

Unfortunately for me, there's only so much the human body can handle. I hit my breaking point physically, which in turn made me hit my breaking point mentally.

Lettie may never understand how much her leaving affected me, but now that she was back, I was past that. I wanted this new beginning with her, regardless of the past.

For all I knew, she may have been running from her mental breaking point, too.

Making it to their house, I headed inside and found my mom doing dishes in the kitchen, my dad beside her drying off each one she handed him.

"Hi, sweetie," she said over her shoulder.

"Hey, Mom. Do you happen to know where those light blue napkins are?"

She handed my dad a plate before turning off the sink and facing me. She wiped her hands on a rag, drying them off. "Oh, you're bringing out the fancy napkins, huh?"

I frowned to hide the smile that tried to creep up on me. "Just need some sort of napkin, Mom."

My dad set the dish in the upper cabinet and closed it. He faced me, folding the dish towel he'd been using, as my mom dug through a drawer in the corner of the kitchen.

"Finally putting that gazebo to good use, I see," he said.

"What do you mean? I hang out in there all the time," I defended.

He chuckled. "Drinking beer in the thing ain't breaking it in, Bailey."

My mom closed the drawer a little too hard, an obvious smile pulling at her lips despite the look of shock she wore at my dad's comment. "Eddie Cooper, you did *not* just insinuate that Bailey needs to-"

I held up a hand to stop her. "Please don't put words to it, Mom. We all know what he was getting at."

And if I got lucky, that would most definitely be happening tonight.

Hell, I considered myself lucky that she even said yes to a date with me. She probably thought I was too damn dumb to set up a proper date all on my own. She was sure to be surprised when she showed up tonight.

My mom crossed the kitchen, holding the napkins out to me. "Wash them before you return them, please."

"Yes, ma'am. I'd stay longer, but I have to get back before some coyote decides to dig into a nice steak dinner. Made your recipe for the potatoes."

She pulled me in for a hug, her head barely reaching my chest. "I always knew you liked that girl. 'Bout time you admitted it."

I laughed. "I didn't admit anything."

She pulled back, an eyebrow raised. "You may have gotten away with fooling me when you were a kid, but not anymore, Bailey. I know love in your eyes when I see it."

My mom was good at jumping into people's personal business. She also loved love, so it wasn't a surprise to me that she was happy that I was finally showing interest in a woman. My eyes had always been on Lettie. I'd just been waiting for her to look at me the same way, too.

I looked over her head at my dad, mouthing, "Help me."

He chuckled again, shaking his head as he headed toward the living room.

My mom smacked my arm with the dish towel my dad had set on the counter, a big smile on her face.

"Thanks for the napkins."

"Of course, honey. Let me know how it goes. And bring Lettie by for dinner sometime. I haven't seen her in forever."

I bent to kiss my mom's cheek. "That is if she doesn't run for the hills after tonight."

"Ah, you two will be rollin' around in the hay in no time," my dad said from the brown leather couch.

"Eddie!" my mom shouted at him in disbelief.

Oh, if only he knew.

I walked back out their front door and headed in the direction of my house, the napkins shoved in the back pocket of my jeans. I'd opted for no hat tonight, solely due to what Lettie had said to me at the bar in Montana.

"Stop covering those eyes."

"Why?"

"They're beautiful, is all."

If she hadn't said that, I'd be wearing my dirt-and-sweat-coated cowboy hat. It was like a safety blanket at this point. Without it, I felt naked.

After I'd asked her over to dinner earlier today, I'd got to work on decorating the gazebo as soon as I'd left the Bronsons' ranch. I'd hung fairy lights from the roof to line the arches, set up the table with candles, flowers from the field, and a tablecloth.

I'd gone the whole nine yards, power washing the concrete slab it sat on, getting the cobwebs all swept away, and dusting the dirt off the railings.

Everything I did when it came to Lettie was spur of the moment because I lost my damn mind around her, and if I had to be honest, I didn't want to find it. But tonight would be different. I needed her to know how serious I was about her.

As I approached my house, I noticed Lettie's SUV was parked out front on the gravel driveway, the headlights off. Seeing that she wasn't with her car, I walked around back.

Coming around the side of the house, I stopped in my tracks at the sight of Lettie standing there, her silhouette lit up by the fading sun and the lights decorating the gazebo.

Her caramel-colored hair was loose, hanging down her back and almost reaching the hem of her jeans. Her shoulders were bare, the dark orange top she had on barely held on by a knot, showcasing her back to me.

She looked like an angel standing there with the lights in front of her.

If this was as good as tonight got, seeing her standing there, the clear surprise shown in her posture as she was unaware I was behind her, I'd be completely content.

After all those years apart, Lettie was here. Back in my orbit.

37

Lettie

My boots were frozen to the dirt as I stared at the spectacle in Bailey's backyard. He'd gone all out. The fairy lights and candles created a warm glow that illuminated the field, making the scene look almost unreal.

The table was centered under the pitched roof, an array of blue and white flowers from the fields spread throughout the arrangement. I could smell whatever food was waiting on the table from where I stood. I was lost in the idea that someone put this much effort into a date with me. That *he* put so much effort into this.

An arm snaked around my waist a moment before my back connected with a warm, hard chest.

"You're early," Bailey said in a low voice, his breath against the shell of my ear causing a shiver to spread down my spine.

"I was going to offer to help with dinner but..." I kept my back to his chest as I turned to look up at him.

"I asked *you* on a date. That means I do the work, Huckleberry. Not you."

I studied his face, the lights reflecting in his eyes, making them appear a few shades darker than their typical mossy green. "You didn't have to do all this."

He let go of me, his hand finding mine before leading me toward the gazebo.

"This is our first official date, Lettie. No way in hell was I going to order a pizza and turn on a movie. I want you to remember our first date night for the rest of your life." He pulled the chair at the end of the table out, gesturing for me to sit.

Bailey didn't know that regardless of what he did tonight, I'd remember it. I never forgot one moment with him growing up. All those times he'd conditioned my boots, cleaned up my saddle in the barn, or always made sure to bring an extra towel to the creek because I always forgot mine. He may think I didn't notice the little things, but I did.

I thought about them every day while I was gone.

"Don't knock pizza and a movie. It's actually pretty romantic," I joked.

He scooted my chair a few inches forward, then went around to the opposite side and took his own seat. He lifted the foil from the dishes set out on the table, the scent of food making my mouth water.

My eyes landed on the steak and I smiled. "Typical cowboy, always eating steak."

He frowned at me from across the table. "We've had steak together twice in the past few weeks. That's not every day."

"That was just when you're with me. I bet you've had steak at least five more times since then. I can even bet you've got a freezer full of steaks inside right now."

"You're just trying to find things to pick on me about because you can't believe I did all this." He grabbed the bowl of salad, dishing himself up a portion.

"Why would I need to do that? My list is already miles long."

He pinned me with a glare, doing his best to hide his smile.

"But, in all seriousness, this is amazing, Bailey. Thank you." He held the bowl out to me and I grabbed it from him, piling the summer salad on my plate.

"It was no biggie. I needed to do something with this thing anyway." I dished up the rest of my plate as he did the same.

I hadn't even known this structure was back here. "When'd you build it?"

He finished chewing his bite before speaking. "Couple years ago. Wanted to keep myself busy and figured this was the best way to do it."

"On top of all the other things you do?"

He rolled his lips together as our eyes met, his gaze burning into my skin. "I'd love to add one more thing to that list."

We held each other's gazes for a few silent seconds before I snapped my eyes away, focusing back on my food. He stared a few moments longer before taking another bite of steak.

"I wasn't sure what to wear," I said in a sad attempt to make conversation.

"You look beautiful, Lettie. You always do."

I gave him a small smile before loading my fork with salad.

"Oh, I almost forgot." He pulled something out of his back pocket, setting one on the table beside my plate, the other on his lap. "Napkins."

"Let me guess, blue for huckleberry?" I laughed as I unfolded the napkin and laid it out across my thigh.

"No. Blue because they remind me of your eyes."

My laugh immediately ceased and I froze with my hands on the napkin from where I was flattening out a crease. I was too scared to look up at him.

He was saying all these sweet things and being so fucking romantic, it made my heart want to jump out of my damn chest. This was a new side of Bailey I wasn't used to. He'd do small gestures growing up, always silent with the way he cared about me, but now that he was voicing those feelings, my mind was having a hard time processing the fact that they were coming out of his mouth.

I refused to let my mind take over, though. I was done overthinking this. I wanted Bailey. Why was I so damn scared to give in to those feelings?

Looking up, I found him watching me, gauging my reaction. He was scared I would run again. I knew that. But I needed to reassure him somehow.

As much as my head wanted to talk me out of crossing that line again with Bailey, my heart wouldn't let it. Neither would the heat building between my thighs at the way he stared at me.

Fuck it.

I stood from the table and walked over to him, lifting my leg to straddle his lap.

His hands naturally fell to my hips as he gazed up at me, an intense fire blazing in his eyes.

"I want this, Bailey."

"I never thought I'd hear you say those words," he said, and a second later, he crashed his mouth to mine, slipping his tongue past my lips. His fingers dug into my hips as I slid my hands up his chest to tangle them in his hair.

I moved my hips forward, feeling his dick straining against his jeans.

He lifted me with him as he stood, wrapping my legs around his waist. His mouth never left mine as he walked us up his porch and into his house. He kicked the slider door shut before setting me on the kitchen island.

His eyes scanned me, lowering until they landed on my shirt. "You know what would make this outfit look even better?" His voice was rough with need as he spoke.

"What?" I breathed.

He looked at me. "If it was laying on my floor."

His hands came around my back, pulling at the knot that held the shirt together. He tugged on the fabric, the knot coming undone. The shirt fell down my torso and he tossed it to the kitchen floor.

"Fuck, Lettie. No bra?" His hands came around to palm my breasts before he brought them down to the hem of my jeans, his fingers working at the button and zipper.

I set my hands on the counter, lifting my hips so he could slide my jeans off.

He cursed once they landed on the ground, taking in my already wet, gray lace panties. "Already soaked for me, Huckleberry?"

I pursed my lips together as he set his hands on my knees, pulling my legs apart. My panties pulled to the side, exposing some of my pussy.

He kept his eyes on the sight between my legs as he worked at the buttons of his shirt, undoing them one by one. I watched his fingers, closing my legs slightly, heat creeping up my cheeks from his stare.

He pulled them back apart, his hard eyes landing on mine. "Uh-uh. No getting shy on me now. You can't hide anymore, Lettie."

He pulled his shirt off, the fabric landing in a heap on the floor behind him. He took his time taking his jeans off, kicking off his boots and socks.

He grabbed a condom from his jeans and I raised an eyebrow. "You always keep condoms in your pockets, at the ready?"

"Wasn't sure where we'd be doing this tonight. I don't keep condoms in my kitchen drawers," he said as he ripped open the foil and slid the condom on.

He stepped forward, coming back between my legs. I stared up at him as he tipped my chin up with his finger. "I know who you are out there, Lettie, but I want to know who you are in bed. I want to memorize every inch of your body, know how you like to be fucked, if you like it slow or fast, gentle or hard. I want my name to be the one on your lips when I make you come undone tonight and every night after. You've always been mine, Lettie."

I audibly swallowed, then said, "Hard."

A smirk pulled at his lips. "I had a feeling you'd say that. Now, be a good girl and lay back so I can give it to you how you like it."

He set a hand on my shoulder, easing me back until I was laying flat against the cool countertop. "Hold on to the counter," he commanded.

My hands found the edge and I grabbed it. His fingers hooked in my panties and he pulled them off, letting them fall to the floor.

He slid me forward an inch, my legs spread around him. I watched as he fisted his cock and pumped it twice before dragging it along my center. The warmth of him made my head fall back against the counter.

The head of his cock brushed against my bundle of nerves. My breath picked up pace as he slid it lower, positioning himself at my entrance. "Eyes on me, Lettie. I want to see you."

I tilted my head slightly, our eyes meeting a moment before he thrust inside in one swift motion. I gasped, my lips parting. He gave me a moment to adjust to the size of him inside me before pulling out slightly. He shoved back in with such force, my fingers almost lost the edge of the counter. He thrust in and out of me, fucking me like I'd never been fucked before.

"Like that?"

"Yes," I moaned.

"Such a good girl, taking all of me in that sweet little pussy. I knew you'd feel so fucking perfect wrapped around my cock."

His hands gripped my legs behind my knees, keeping me positioned just right as he thrust against that sweet spot deep inside of me.

"Touch yourself for me, baby. Show me how you like it."

My right hand let go of the counter and I brought it between our bodies to rub circles over my bundle of nerves as he fucked me mercilessly. My head fell back as pleasure coursed through me, pressure building deep inside of me.

He leaned forward, his body covering mine as he slid one hand up my belly to my neck, squeezing with just the right amount of pressure. "You think of me when you touch yourself?"

"Mhmm," I managed to get out on a moan.

"Such a naughty girl," he whispered into my ear. "You want to come on my cock?"

I nodded as his fingers flexed on my neck.

Fuck.

He picked up his pace, my body sliding up the counter. I added pressure with my fingers, and then I exploded.

"Bailey!" I tilted my head back, squeezing my eyes shut as stars danced across my vision.

He kept his pace as the waves crashed into me, coursing through my body in blissful pleasure. As I began to come back down, he exploded, his head tipping back as I watched him unravel with his hand still around my neck. Never in my life did I think I'd get to see this sight, get to feel these things, but now that I had, I never wanted to stop.

His head dropped to my chest after he released my neck, our breaths evening out.

After a few moments, he sat up, looking down at me.

"You're more than I ever could have imagined, Lettie." He grabbed my hand, helping me to sit up. He grabbed his button-up from the ground and slid my arms into it, buttoning the middle button.

I slid my hands up his bare chest, admiring every inch of it. His body was evidence of how hard he worked on the ranch. He was like a perfectly sculpted statue, all hard lines and deep curves.

Before crossing the line I'd so carefully drawn with Bailey, I had tried to move on from having him in my life, thinking I could forget about the way I felt around him.

But after being with Bailey, burning that invisible line to the ground, I was ruined. Ruined in the best way possible. Now that I had him, I didn't want to imagine my future without his hands on my skin, his smile aimed at me, and hearing that ridiculous nickname every day.

Bailey was now ingrained into my daily life, quickly making the last five years apart disappear, like it never even happened.

38

BAILEY

The sweet smell of french toast filled my house as I took the last slice out of the pan, setting it on the plate with the rest of the golden brown bread. I turned to the island, grabbing a knife from the block, getting to work slicing the washed strawberries.

Lettie came around the corner from the hallway, wearing only my button up from last night. "Good morning," she said, rubbing the sleep from her eyes.

I smiled. She was so damn cute, all sleepy, hair strewn about. "Good morning, Huckleberry. Sleep well?"

She must've smelled the breakfast I'd put together because her head snapped up. Her eyes landed on the plate of french toast. "Dinner *and* breakfast? I've been missing out all these years."

"Don't forget dessert." I winked.

After we left the kitchen last night, we'd taken a shower, where I'd made her come two more times using only my tongue and fingers. After our hour and a half shower, she'd insisted on toweling me off, which led to her getting on her knees. We could have gone all night, but sometime around two a.m., I'd talked her into getting some sleep since she had to help with the fundraiser for Bottom of the Buckle today.

She slid into the seat at the island and I grabbed a clean plate for her, setting two slices of french toast, whipped cream, and strawberries on it. I placed it in front of her and piled the same onto my plate. Taking the seat beside her, we dug in.

I was wearing gray sweatpants and nothing else, and it was clear Lettie approved, because her eyes kept drifting to my lap while she chewed.

After the fifth glance, I smirked. "Like what you see?"

She cleared her throat, struggling to swallow the bite in her mouth. After a sip of coffee, she said, "I thought the cowboy outfits did it for me, but I think you've proved it can only get better as the clothes come off."

I chuckled, shaking my head. Once we finished, I grabbed our plates and brought them to the sink.

"So... What does last night make us?" Lettie asked hesitantly.

I faced her, setting my hands on the edge of the counter behind me. "What do you think it makes us?"

She bit her bottom lip. "I was hoping you could tell me."

I let go of the counter and crossed to her in three long strides. Grabbing her chin, I angled her head up toward me. "You know, Lettie."

Those blue eyes stared up at me and I wanted to melt into a puddle. "Say it. Please," she whispered.

My thumb rubbed along her jawline. "You're mine. You've been mine since the moment I laid eyes on you, and it's killed me having to wait for you to realize it. You were always so scared of us, Lettie. But I'm not. The only thing I'm scared of is losing you again."

Her eyes searched mine, and she must have found what she was looking for, because she arched her neck toward me. I met her halfway, dipping down to press my lips to hers. She tasted like coffee and cinnamon as her tongue slipped past my lips.

I slid my hand into her hair, angling her head to give me better access. Lips, teeth, tongues clashed as we tried to get more of each other, but before we could go any further, her phone began ringing from down the hall.

She pulled back. "Shit. What time is it?"

"Eight," I answered.

She cursed, jumping from her seat and hurrying down the hall to grab her phone. While she took the call, I got to work cleaning up the dishes I'd used to make breakfast. I was drying the last plate when Lettie came back from the bedroom, wearing the clothes she'd worn last night.

"I hate that I have to leave," she said.

The sentence sent chills down my spine, but I urged them away.

It was just for the fundraiser. Not another five years.

"Don't feel bad. I have to start on some chores, anyway. This is the latest I've headed out there in a long time. I'm sure I'll get shit for it."

She came around the island as I set the plate in the cabinet and turned toward her. She wrapped her arms around my neck. "Oh, you definitely will. It practically made Brandy's day to tell me she noticed I wasn't at my parents' house this morning."

My hands settled on the curve of her hips like they were made to be there. I leaned forward to nuzzle my nose against the tip of hers. "What are you going to tell her?" I asked, mostly because I wanted to know if she'd be open about us. I wouldn't force her to be, but it'd make me feel better.

She nibbled on her bottom lip and I kissed her, only to bite her lip myself, tugging on it slightly. She pulled back, her eyes full of desire for more.

"I'm going to tell her the truth," she finally said.

I pressed my lips to her forehead. I didn't know how I was going to go all day without touching her once she left.

"I've gotta get going, but I'll text you."

I nodded. "Good luck, Huckleberry. Say hi to Brandy and your mom for me."

She stepped out of my hold, heading for the front door. "I will."

I watched her jean-clad ass disappear, already wishing she was back in my arms.

That whole thing about being addicted to Lettie?

Yeah, I was sure I was going to overdose.

Thank fucking God. It was about damn time.

I didn't want to go out any other way.

39

LETTIE

The sun was out, fighting against the morning chill. After I'd left Bailey's house, I'd quickly changed into my Bottom of the Buckle Horse Rescue t-shirt, and then drove Brandy and I to the fundraising event. We'd opted for my SUV instead of Brandy's '69 Bronco because she didn't trust break-ins with the out-of-towners that came to these kinds of events. Reed promised to keep an eye on Rouge out at the ranch while I was gone, but I knew he'd make his way over to the volunteers and beg for belly rubs all day.

There was an Art & Wine festival on the main strip in town. Nonprofits and small businesses lined the streets with booths, showcasing the products they sold or the cause they supported.

"Lettie," my mom said from behind our canopy tent. I turned from the table where Brandy was talking with an elderly woman. "I want to show you this."

I made my way to her, seeing the paperwork she had in front of her. "Here's a copy of last year's budget and expenses. You can take a look at that while we have some free time today. Animal rescue is always going to be financially difficult, but we save a lot of money having Brandy gentle the horses, growing our own hay, and with Reed as our farrier. Callan donates a portion of the funds his riding lessons bring in, which is way too generous of him, but he refuses to stop. We're very fortunate, but I want you to see how close to rock bottom we've almost hit before."

"Thanks, Mom. I'll take a look at it."

"Of course, sweetie. I'm confident you can get into the groove of things with BOTB, but I don't want to throw it all at you at once. It can be overwhelming," she said as she stuffed a few papers into the folder she brought with her to every rescue-related event.

"I'm really glad I get to be a part of it on a bigger scale. I love working with the horses in any way that I can, but I'm ready to learn this side of things."

Her eyes softened. "I'm happy you're back, sweetheart. That ranch didn't feel like home with you so far away."

I did miss the ranch while I was gone, but I wasn't sure if it was the reason I came back. Home wasn't just this town or that ranch. It was Bailey. He was my home, the person I felt most myself around. Being away made me finally realize that.

My mom pulled me in for a hug, rubbing her hands up and down my back. I swallowed, clearing the emotion that was creeping up my throat. It'd been too long without one of her hugs.

***

Five o'clock was fast approaching, which meant we were that much closer to diving into a home-cooked meal at my parents' house and cracking open an ice cold beer. The morning chill had disappeared all too quickly, leaving only the miserable heat. This time of year was the worst for freezing mornings and blazing afternoons.

We'd had people at our booth all day, asking about the rescue, how we got started, how long we'd been doing it. Everything you could want to know, they asked about it. My voice was tired from talking all day, but it felt good connecting with people. The more people we talked to, the more people would be aware of horse rescue and how much work went into it. There were no days off when it came to rescue.

"You finally going to tell me where you were last night?" Brandy asked once we finally had a moment with no one standing at our table.

I rolled my eyes. "I'm sure you know."

"I'm just wantin' to hear you say it out loud," she confessed.

I leaned against the table, facing her. "I slept at Bailey's house."

A knowing smile crept up her face. "*At* Bailey's house or *with* Bailey?"

"What do you think?"

She shrugged. "I wouldn't know."

"*With* Bailey," I admitted.

"It's about time!" my mom shouted from behind me.

My cheeks heated. *Of course, she heard.*

My mom came over to us and Brandy held her hand up to her for a high-five.

"Uh, excuse me?" a quiet feminine voice interrupted.

I turned away from Brandy and my mom, focusing my attention on the woman who'd approached the booth. Her amber hair was tied back in a high ponytail, and freckles sprinkled her nose and the apples of her cheeks.

"Are you guys hiring?" she asked hesitantly.

"No, sorry. We do need volunteers, though, if you're interested. I can tell you a little bit more about the rescue, if you'd like," I replied.

"I would, but I'm really trying to find a job around here. You don't happen to know of any, do you?"

Brandy nudged my arm. "The feed store," she mumbled.

I smiled. "Oh, yeah! My brother is hiring. He's the manager over at Tumbleweed Feed. I can give you the address. Just walk on in and apply. I'll put in a good word. What's your name?"

I grabbed a pamphlet for the rescue and flipped it over, scribbling the address on the back. "Oakley," she said as she took the pamphlet from me.

"Lettie," I replied. "Nice to meet you."

Her eyes lit up, a smile stretching across her mouth. "You too. Thank you for this." She held up the paper.

"Of course. And if you get the urge to spend some time with the horses, just let us know. All the information is in there for Bottom of the Buckle."

She nodded, stashing it in her small purse. "Will do. Hopefully I'll see you around."

She walked off, getting lost in the sea of people littering the street.

"She seems sweet," Brandy said.

"If that son of mine has half a brain, he'll hire her," my mom added from behind me.

I turned around, raising an eyebrow in question.

"It's about time my kids start settling down," she said, as if that was enough explanation.

"With an employee?" I asked.

She shrugged. "Better that than some city girl."

Brandy's jaw dropped. "Mrs. Bronson," she gasped.

"Nothin' wrong with them. But Lennon deserves a sweet girl, and from what I saw, she fits the bill."

"Mom, you can't go around playing matchmaker for us," I griped as I gathered up the papers on the table to start packing them away.

"Isn't that a mother's job?"

Brandy laughed while she began folding the table cloth. "It better not be. My mom has terrible taste in men."

Brandy's dad had left their family when she was twelve after her mom found out he'd been cheating on her their entire marriage. There was a backstory with her father I didn't know much about other than his tendency to sleep around. He wasn't home much when we'd hang out at her house, and if he was, Brandy would ask if we could hang out at my parents' ranch. Thankfully, Brandy was an only child, so he didn't leave her to raise a bunch of children on her own, but even being a single mom to one child was hard.

Ms. Rose was like a second mom to me and I was now realizing it'd been too long since I'd seen her. I'd have to plan a visit as soon as I had a free moment. Brandy no longer lived with her, having moved out shortly after she turned eighteen, but she visited her every other weekend, regardless of whatever boyfriend she may or may not have around.

My mom got to work loading the truck as Brandy and I took down the canopy tent.

Brandy eyed me. "Was he good? You're not giving me any details, girl! I'm practically chomping at the bit here."

I started working on the metal leg opposite of hers, collapsing the tent. "I don't kiss and tell."

She scoffed as she worked on her pole, trying to maneuver her hand without using the finger that she'd broken. She'd already taken off the splint. "Oh, please. You told me about vomit guy. Plus, I already know you two have kissed. I mean the rest."

Brandy was my best friend. I couldn't *not* tell her about it.

I made sure my mom was out of earshot and told her about last night, leaving certain details out, like how his hand felt wrapped around my neck, or the words he'd muttered with his head between my legs.

Just thinking about what he did to me made my cheeks heat.

I couldn't wait to get back home to Bailey.

40

BAILEY

I decided to get some things done around my parents' ranch before heading over to the Bronsons'. With winter fast approaching, we had a lot of tasks to take care of to prep the property, like emptying the water tank, draining all the sprinklers so they didn't freeze over, and making sure we were stocked on essentials for the animals for winter.

Then, once I was done doing that here, I'd do the same over at the Bronsons'. They had their hands full with the rescue horses in the winter, so I did my share of winterizing to help out in preparation of the unforgiving season to come.

Winter always stressed all of us out because many of the horses in Bottom of the Buckle Horse Rescue were thin and malnourished when they came in. They took in less during the winter solely due to the fact that travel was too risky in the cold for them.

Every now and then, Mrs. Bronson would find a neglect case she couldn't turn down, and we'd do our best to get the animal here, but it was too often that we lost them on the way.

Winters were hard on these animals, and if not given the proper care to begin with, regardless if they were in a trailer on their way to the rescue or in a field with no food, their chances of making it were slim.

After I all but kicked the sprinkler system for being the most frustrating and finicky thing on the damn planet, I checked my watch, seeing that it was almost time for her to arrive.

I'd called Billy's daughter this morning before I started on my chores to see if she'd be willing to meet to discuss her late father's property next to Bottom of the Buckle Ranch. I'd found her number on the listing online, and thankfully, she'd been free, so I decided to delay my trip over to the Bronsons' by another thirty minutes.

I wasn't going to let my parents lose their property because of money. We could always make more. It was just figuring out how to do that was the problem.

It wasn't like you could snap your fingers and bring in more income when it came to ranching and farming. The Bronsons had a chunk of income from their cattle, hay, and rescue, though the rescue ate up a bunch of the money itself, but my parents relied on farming alfalfa.

If there was a way I could find more property and open us up to more income, I'd do it. I didn't want my parents to think it was all on them, even though the ranch was theirs. I didn't own the land itself, but I put my heart and soul into keeping it running alongside them. This ranch was my entire life, and I wouldn't let it be taken away from any of us.

There were too many memories here, and I wanted my children and generations to come to have the same memories. Even if they did have to sell it, I had the option to buy the portion of land my house sat on, but it wouldn't be the same. The Cooper ranch couldn't be split apart.

A blue Ford Edge drove up the drive, kicking up dust in its path. With my hands in my pockets and my hat low on my head, I approached her car as she killed the engine and got out.

She had blonde hair that almost reached her hips and a cream-colored cowgirl hat with the brim flat, not a roll or curve to be seen on the thing.

"Good morning, ma'am," I greeted, holding my hand out to her.

"Please, call me Bea. Ma'am makes me feel old," she said with a shy smile as she shook my hand. She didn't look a day over thirty.

"Alright, Bea. Well, I don't want to take up too much of your time, but I did want to talk to you about Billy's old place."

She leaned into her car, grabbing a piece of paper with a photo of the property entrance on it. She held it out to me and I took it, skimming over the information.

"Honestly, if you're really interested, I can lower the price. My brother doesn't quite care what we sell it for, he just wants it to go to someone who will take care of it. And by the looks of it," her eyes skimmed my dirt-covered jeans and stained work shirt, "you'd be the perfect fit."

I folded the paper, stuffing it in my back pocket. "No offense to Billy, but that property would be in the best shape it's ever been if I took it over. I just need to get some things in order before I can make the jump," I stated. I wanted to surprise my parents, but I'd have to get a loan before I could decide if the price was something I could do. I didn't want them to lose money by lowering the price, either.

"Is it your parents looking to buy it?" Bea asked, blocking the sun with her hand over her eyes. The morning sun was no match for her hat.

I rubbed the back of my neck, glancing at my parents' house to the right of me. "Not necessarily. I'm the one interested, but it'd be to help them out."

She nodded, understanding what I meant. "Well, like I said, I don't mind lowering the price if it's something you want to discuss."

I shook my head. "Price isn't the problem. Just have to talk to my bank and then I can let you know."

She smiled. "Well, you have my number. I'll talk to my brother and wait to hear from you?"

"Sounds good to me. I'll hopefully know within the next few days."

She held her hand out again and I shook it. "Sounds like a plan, Bailey. It was nice meeting you."

I nodded, dropping her hand. "Nice to meet you too, Bea. And I'm sorry about your father. Billy was a great guy and an even better farmer. He was always over here helping out if we needed it. Never met such a giving guy."

She gave a closed-lipped smile. "He was always talking about that rescue next door, telling stories about your dad and Travis. The three of them had a lot of fun, it sounded like."

I let out a small chuckle. "They sure did."

She turned back to her car and said over her shoulder, "Say hey to Lettie for me."

I watched her as she slid into the driver's seat. "You heard?"

She smiled up at me, pressing the button to start her car. "Small town, remember? Plus, it's not like you and Lettie have ever been a secret, even if I don't live in the county line."

News traveled fast, that much was for sure.

"Drive safe, Bea," I said.

"Thanks. Talk to you soon," she replied before closing her door.

I watched as she pulled down the driveway, heading to the main road. Maybe things weren't going to be so bad after all. I'd figure this shit out for my parents, and I'd get the girl.

That's all I ever wanted in life.

My home and Lettie Bronson.

Together.

***

Shifting my Chevy into park, I killed the engine and hopped out.

"Hungover?" Reed called from where he was bent over a horse's back hoof.

I chuckled, smiling down at the ground as I fixed my hat. Not even a foot out of my truck and I was already getting shit for being late.

I wasn't sure if Lettie wanted me to tell Reed or not, so I kept my mouth shut about last night.

"Had a lot to do at my parents' place," I said, closing the distance between us and leaning against the outside wall of the barn as he straightened, setting the horse's leg down.

"You need any help over there?" he asked, grabbing the file from his bag in the dirt next to him.

"Nah, I think we've got it handled. You guys need anything for winter for the rescues?"

He shrugged before bending over and grabbing the horse's ankle, propping his hoof against his leg. "Brandy should know. She's been writing everything down on that damn notepad."

My eyebrows shot up. "What'd the notepad do to you?"

He sighed as he filed at the hoof. "She should be resting her hand, not going around like a mad woman taking inventory."

I crossed my arms, shifting my weight to my other boot. "It needs to get done."

He set the hoof back on the ground, tossing the file on top of his bag as he stood up straight again. "There's five other people always around that can do inventory. Over thirty volunteers who can do it themselves. Yet she insists."

"Brandy's a workaholic," I pointed out. "On the bright side, at least she's not dealing with that gray."

He brushed his hands off on his leather chaps. "I'm not letting her near that thing. I don't know why you let Lettie bring him home."

I frowned. "I'm not going to be the one to tell your sister no."

"You scared of her, Cooper?" Reed snorted.

"Something like that," I mumbled.

I wouldn't say scared. More like infatuated and willing to give her anything she ever wanted.

"The barn's looking good," he said, changing the subject.

"Yeah, it's almost done. Should only take a little more and it'll look good as new."

He grabbed his bag of supplies, then walked around to the passenger seat of his truck, tossing the bag on the seat. "You guys made good progress."

I thought back to the times we got little work done in that barn and fought the smile that pulled at my lips.

Teasing Lettie was my favorite pastime activity.

"Yeah, we sure did." I kicked at the dirt before pushing off the wall.

"Dad's making dinner tonight if you don't already have dinner plans," he offered.

I snorted. "I never have dinner plans."

Well, minus last night. I'd make Lettie a fancy dinner every night if it ended with us in my bed the way we did. Just thinking of her body under me had my dick getting hard.

I cleared my throat, trying to discreetly adjust myself. Reed looked over his shoulder from where he was zipping his bag up on the passenger seat, his black cowboy hat shading his eyes. "You good, Cooper?"

I nodded. "Yep. All good."

"Don't be getting weird on me now. It's not a date, just my dad's cooking."

"Reed, we're past the weird stage, don't you think?"

He smiled. "A lifetime of friendship will do that to you."

41

LETTIE

The sun was setting when we pulled up to the ranch. Callan and Reed helped us unload the truck while my mom headed inside the house to help my dad finish cooking dinner.

As soon as she opened the front door, Rouge darted out of the house, beelining it for me. He knew he wasn't supposed to jump on people, but he did it anyway, the excitement taking over. Aussies were too smart for their own good. It was like they knew when they wouldn't get in trouble for breaking the rules. I rubbed his neck, then instructed him to get down and came around the back of the truck.

I closed the tailgate to the truck after Reed pulled the bag the canopy was stored in out of the bed.

Brandy came around the side of the truck and Rouge took that as an opportunity to nudge at her hand, begging for an ear scratch. She did just that, and he closed his eyes slightly, leaning into her. "I'm going to turn in early tonight, but I'll see you tomorrow."

"You sure you don't want to stay for dinner?" I asked.

She shook her head. "I'm pretty tired after today. Going to try to sleep early."

"Alright. Text me when you get home?"

"Always do." She wrapped her arms around me in a quick hug, then made her way toward her Bronco.

"Have a good night, Brandy. Drive safe," Callan said as she passed him.

"Goodnight, Cal."

Reed popped out of the storage shed and I caught him watching her drive away.

"Wouldn't kill you to say goodbye to her," I said.

He grunted, pulling the door to the shed shut behind him.

Callan, Reed, and I crossed the driveway, Rouge on our heels as we headed up the porch into the house. Bailey came out of the front door right as we approached.

"Where are you heading?" I asked him.

Callan slipped inside the house after giving a quick nod to Bailey in greeting.

"To the hardware store real quick. Have to get paint for tomorrow morning. Wanna come?" The barn was almost complete, save for a few last minute touches and the paint.

"What about dinner?"

"It shouldn't be done for another twenty minutes. Won't take us too long," he said.

I looked at Reed. "Can you let mom know we'll be back in time to eat?"

Reed nodded, heading inside. Rouge followed him, his snout in the air as he sniffed at the smell of food wafting from the house.

We strode over to Bailey's truck and he got behind the wheel as I slid into the middle seat. The nice thing about these old trucks was that they didn't have center consoles. Unfortunately, most of them didn't have cup holders because of it.

Bailey started the engine and spun the truck around, heading down the driveway. His hand found my thigh, his thumb running circles on my jeans as he headed toward the hardware store.

"How was the fundraiser?" he asked.

"It went well," I responded. I was too distracted by his hand to give him any more details about the day.

"Lettie?"

I faced him. "Yeah?" My voice was breathy.

He glanced at me. "You good?"

"I just missed you." My cheeks heated at my admission.

The corner of his lip quirked up. "Missed you too, Huckleberry."

I took him in, from his hair down to his boot on the gas. Bailey made me feel like a teenager with my hormones out of control.

As if he could read my thoughts, he slid his hand higher on my thigh while keeping his eyes on the road.

I sucked in a breath, then reached over to his belt, undoing the clasp.

He glanced at me again. "What are you doing?"

"Making up for the hotel."

I tugged at his button and unzipped his jeans. "You've more than made up for it already," he said.

"Don't care."

He gave in, keeping one hand on the steering wheel as he helped me free his cock. It sprang out, my mouth watering in anticipation.

I used to hate giving blowjobs, but with Bailey, all it did was turn me on.

I bent down, grasping his shaft with one hand and lowering my lips around the head. He let out a breath and I saw his hand shift on the steering wheel from the corner of my eye.

Pulling him deeper, I began sucking, the fullness in my mouth almost too much. He brought his hand to the back of my head and lightly pushed down, shoving himself to the back of my throat.

My pussy throbbed in my jeans from his hand in my hair and his cock in my mouth. I ached to feel friction there as I continued bobbing my head up and down, taking him to the back of my throat.

"Such a naughty girl, taking my cock wherever you want it."

I moaned and his cock twitched in my mouth.

I heard his blinker flick on, and the truck jostled. He shifted it into park and pulled me up off of him, pushing me back so I was laying on the seat.

He worked at my jeans and slid them off with my panties.

"Don't have a condom," he said as he eyed me.

"I don't care."

He didn't hesitate. He shoved into me and my head tilted back, a moan escaping my lips.

"Always so fucking wet for me." He pulled out, sticking two fingers in me, then brought them up to my lips as he thrusted back inside me.

"Suck," he commanded.

I leaned forward slightly, taking his fingers into my mouth and sucking just as hard as I had on his cock. He shoved them deeper so they hit my throat for a moment before pulling them back out.

He grabbed my legs, positioning them on his shoulders as he thrust deeper. His hand came around to my neck, adding just enough pressure but still allowing me to breathe.

"You like choking on my dick, don't you?"

I nodded, unable to form words as pressure built between my legs.

His fingers pressed into the sides of my neck, and I brought my hand up, squeezing his wrist and bringing his hand down harder on my neck. The pressure made me explode, my pussy clenching around him as I released.

"That's my good girl. Come for me."

Pleasure coursed through me as he kept thrusting in and out. On a grunt, he reached the edge, pounding into me relentlessly.

Once his pace slowed, he let go of my neck and sat back, bringing my legs down.

"For the record, I really did just want to get some paint," he said.

I laughed. "You didn't want that?"

"Oh, no. Trust me, I always want you. I just don't want you to think I only invited you along because I expected this."

I sat up, gathering my jeans off the floor of the truck. "I'll take you anywhere I can get you," I said, confirming his earlier comment.

He smirked. "I can find some places to hold you to that."

I didn't care where it was. I was done hiding.

***

We pulled back up at the ranch forty minutes later. If my family didn't guess why it took us so long, they had to be blinder than a bat.

I got out of the truck, and Bailey came around and grabbed my hand. We walked to the house, hand in hand, and headed through the front door.

As soon as we entered the kitchen, all eyes landed on us. Reed's gaze shot to our hands and I inwardly cringed.

"What the fuck?" Reed barked, causing Rouge to perk up from where he laid in the kitchen.

"Uh oh," Beckham muttered from the island.

I swallowed the anxiety that crept up and tamped down the urge to pull my hand out of Bailey's. This would happen sooner or later. I had to take whatever they threw at me.

"Oh, please. As if you guys didn't see this coming." Callan rolled his eyes.

Beckham raised a hand. "I definitely did."

Lennon entered the kitchen from the hallway, noticing the tension and following everyone's gaze to Bailey and me. "What's..." His eyes darted between the two of us. I could see the realization hit him. "Oh."

"Oh?" Reed practically shouted. "That's what you have to say about Bailey holding hands with our fucking sister?"

"Watch your tone, Reed," my dad warned, his frown harder than usual.

Reed shook his head. "When did this start? Is that why you were late this morning? Because of my sister?"

Bailey gripped my hand. "When did it start, or when did it become official?"

That was definitely not the right thing to say. Redness crept up Reed's neck. "You've been messing around with her behind my back?"

Bailey dropped my hand and went to take a step forward, but I shot my hand out, my palm colliding with his chest as I angled my body in front of his. "None of this was behind your back. I'm my own person, I make my own decisions. I don't need your permission."

"Like hell you don't."

Callan's face went hard. "Reed, take it down a notch."

"Personally, I don't think there's a better person for Lettie," Beckham piped in.

Reed crossed his arms. "You think Bailey is best for her? He hasn't been in a relationship longer than three days."

Bailey stiffened behind me and my dad looked like he was about to interject from where he stood by the oven, but he was cut off by Bailey's voice. "None of them were Lettie."

Reed pointed a glare at him. "As if that's supposed to make me feel any better?"

"I'd never mess around with her feelings, Reed. I've felt this way for a long time. It's not some new, summer fling."

I braced myself for his response, but suddenly, his face softened, his eyes drifting to me. "And you like him?"

My eyes landed on each of my brothers, then I looked over my shoulder to find Bailey watching me. Our eyes always found each other, always held a thousand words our mouths couldn't say.

I turned back to my brother. "I always have."

His eyes were glued to me as he pondered my response. Reed was always the most protective of me, even though Lennon was the oldest.

After a few seconds of silence, Reed swallowed, his Adam's apple bobbing with the action. He nodded and crossed to me, wrapping me in his arms. Once he let me go, he pinned his stare on Bailey. "If you even think about hurting her, just know that this ranch has a lot of places to hide a body."

Oddly, that made Bailey smile. "I'd be more worried about Lettie hurting me."

My dad must have been satisfied with the change of mood, as if Reed's comment was somehow comforting, because his signature frown softened a bit before he turned around to pull the foil off the dish set on the counter.

Reed pulled Bailey in for a hug. In my twenty-three years of life, I'd never seen them hug each other. They slapped each other's backs before they pulled away.

Beckham clapped his hands together. "Thank God that's over with."

Lennon chuckled, coming over to grab the plates from the cabinet. "I thought Reed was going to burn the damn house down with the smoke comin' out of his ears."

"I've got to look out for my little sister," Reed said.

"She's an adult, Reed. Let her live a little," Beckham said before stuffing a tortilla chip in his mouth.

Reed shook his head. "I don't care how old she is, I'll always be there to protect her."

My mom came into the room from her bedroom down the hall. "What'd I miss?"

A snort bubbled out of me. "Nothing. Can we eat, please? I'm starving."

"Me, too," Callan said.

Beckham held his hand up again. "Me, three."

Bailey wrapped an arm around my shoulders, pulling me back against him. "I knew they'd be okay with it," he whispered in my ear.

My hands hung on his arm draped across my chest. "I thought Reed was going to behead you."

I felt Bailey shrug behind me. "A little headless horseman roleplay might be fun."

I rolled my eyes and kicked at his shin. He laughed, pressing a kiss to my hair.

We stood there, watching my family set the table and bring dishes of food over on hot pads.

This was what I was missing.

I was home.

42

LETTIE

Red's muscles vibrated under me after I slowed him to a walk. We'd galloped through the field and once we hit the end of the property, I sat in the field to enjoy the sandwich I'd packed for the ride. I missed coming out here alone and listening to the sounds of the birds chirp as the wind rustled the leaves in the trees.

This was the only thing I wanted to do today. Since it was my birthday, Bailey had made a rule of not working on the barn today. There were a couple more minor details I wanted to finish inside, like screwing the name cards for the horses into the stall doors, and tidying up all the sawdust everywhere.

I'd get to it tonight, whether he liked it or not. I had to take advantage of my energy when I had it. There were too many days I forced myself through our work when I'd much rather be in bed. I took on the barn project not realizing how big of a chore it would be, but working on it with Bailey made it bearable.

Shifting to lean down to open the gate to the pasture, I undid the latch and pulled on the fence, the metal groaning as it swung open. Red stepped through, sidestepping to allow me to close it behind us. He was a natural with gates, doing the moves perfectly without me having to instruct him what to do.

"I thought you'd never come back," Brandy yelled as I swiveled my head to find her ambling over to me.

"I debated it," I admitted. Every time I was out there on Red, the thought crossed my mind. Everything was simpler out riding. The chaos of thoughts swimming through my mind ceased, and the world quieted. It was a peace I'd never stop chasing after.

She stopped in front of Red, looking up at me. "I can put him away for you. Head on inside."

I arched a brow, suspicion creeping in. "Why?"

She shrugged, and it was anything but casual. "Figured you'd want to shower after a long ride."

"Brandy..."

She grabbed the reins, a smile stretched across her face. "C'mon. Get off the damn horse."

Swinging my leg over, I dismounted, reveling from the ache in my legs. "Please tell me you didn't-"

She held up her hand with the reins to stop me. "Go inside before I drag you in there myself."

I pursed my lips, accepting my fate. I wasn't oblivious, I knew they had something going on in there, and I had the biggest suspicion it involved my birthday.

She walked off in the direction of the barn as I made my way over to the house, slowly easing up the porch steps and through the door. As soon as I stepped into the entryway, my eyes landed on the house full of people.

"Surprise!" Hands were thrown in the air, confetti went flying; someone was even blowing one of those noisemakers where the paper unfolds and it makes an obnoxious sound.

Despite not wanting a party, I couldn't help but smile. It proved how much they all missed me, and just how much I missed all of them. When I was in college, my friends barely texted a happy birthday and went about their day. But the people I loved in Bell Buckle? They went all out.

I couldn't help the tears that welled in my eyes, but I blinked them away, taking everyone in.

"Happy birthday, sweetheart," my mom said as she wrapped her arms around me. She had one of those cardboard party hats on her head, the string damn near choking her out.

"Thanks, Mom." She let go, and I took in the rest of the room. There was a sign that read "Happy Birthday, Huckleberry" that hung from the ceiling, blue and white streamers strewn about, and a blue tablecloth on the table that was lined with all kinds of blue snacks that I had no doubt were all huckleberry-flavored. In the center sat a cake that looked just like the one Bailey made me on my eighteenth birthday.

Moving my gaze, I found Bailey standing in the corner with the biggest grin on his face. He uncrossed his arms and closed the distance, wrapping me in his hold as he lifted me off the ground. A shriek passed my lips as he swung me around, then angled his head up to me and planted a firm kiss to my mouth.

"Happy birthday, Huckleberry," he mumbled against my lips.

I pulled back, looking down at him. "Did you do all this?"

His green eyes gleamed up at me and I wanted to fucking melt. "Did it all for you. Thank God you went on a long ride."

He set me down as my brothers came up, one by one telling me happy birthday, hugging me, joking with me. All of this - the party, the people, the laughter - it ingrained into my bones that there really was no place like home.

"Personally, I thought a birthday card would have been enough," Beckham joked.

"I know what to get you for your birthday," Lennon grumbled.

Beck placed a hand over his heart. "Aw, you're getting me something? That's so nice. I'm not getting you shit for yours."

Lennon scoffed. "That's fine. I wouldn't want it even if you did get me something."

Callan popped in between them. "Guys, guys. We both know Lennon's just salty that Beck is leaving soon."

My eyes flew to Beck. "When?" I didn't know he was leaving, especially soon.

His expression softened. "Couple days."

Bailey's hand rubbed circles idly on my back, but it did little to soothe the sadness that crept in. I hated when Beck went back on the circuit. I wanted him here to know he was safe and not breaking his spine in half being thrown off a bronc. I can guess that's why no one wanted me to leave Bell Buckle in the first place, minus the bronc stuff. They just wanted to know I was safe and I should have never punished them for caring about me by disappearing.

Callan's gaze landed on me, seeing the shift in my demeanor. "C'mon, Lettie, let's not think about it. Let's enjoy the day and celebrate you."

I nodded as Beck said, "Yeah, no getting all sappy about me leaving. I'll be back before you know it, and I can promise it won't be five years." He winked at me.

Lennon landed a soft punch on Beck's arm as Callan turned to head into the kitchen. Brandy came in the front door behind me, and I made room for her beside me as we got lost in conversation with my brothers and Bailey.

It was a tradition of ours to have cake before the main food on birthdays. Afterall, eating the sweets was part of the celebration, not the savory food. My mom lit candles on the cake, and Reed picked it up, bringing it over to me as everyone sang "Happy Birthday." Once they were done with their off-pitched harmony, I blew the flames out.

I blinked, and suddenly my entire face felt wet. *No, not wet.* Reed threw the goddamn cake in my face.

Everyone burst into laughter as I wiped the cake from my eyes and nose. "Did you really think you got away from our pranks?" Reed said through his fit of laughter.

"No. Just thought maybe I could get a break on my birthday," I griped.

Someone handed me napkins, and I rubbed the frosting from my face as best I could. I caught Bailey smirking as he watched me clean myself off. "I made a second cake just for this."

"Thank God because I really wanted a slice," Callan said from the kitchen where he was getting plates out of the cabinet.

"Bailey Cooper, that is no way to treat a lady," Bailey's mom exclaimed.

He waved her off. "She's used to it, Mom."

The deep rumble of my dad and Bailey's dad's chuckle filled the room. Our mothers pointed glares at them, and they both said, "What?"

"Don't you remember when I'd prank you back in the day, honey?" Eddie asked.

Debby shot glares at him. "All too well."

I hiked my thumb over my shoulder. "I'm going to go shower."

Bailey leaned down, muttering, "Want me to come with?"

I frowned. "You need to clean up this mess."

He straightened. "This is *technically* Reed's mess."

"Then you can help him," I said sweetly before turning and heading down the hall for the bathroom.

I never minded the jokes they played on me, but they did it to get a reaction. Whatever it was, they were always the ones to clean it up. Just because Bailey and I were together now didn't mean I was going to let that part slide - as much as I did want him to join me in the shower.

43

LETTIE

After cake and a few gifts, we'd all moved to the back porch to eat our official dinner. Who didn't eat cake as an appetizer on their birthday?

"The barn is looking really good," my dad said from the end of the table.

Bailey grabbed his fork, stabbing at his potato salad before saying, "I can't take the credit. Lettie's been doing all the hard work."

"Not true. Bailey's been doing twice the amount of work as me." Though I'd been getting a lot done to help, my energy drained so fast working in the heat. Most days, before afternoon even hit, I was finding some task I could do sitting down in the shade.

"Regardless, it looks great, you guys," my dad assured us before cutting into his steak. What was it with cowboys and their steaks?

Brandy set her too-full glass of wine down. "We'll be able to move rescues in there in no time."

Reed was eyeing her drink like it was poison when Callan said, "I'm thinking of getting a few more lesson horses after winter. I'm hoping lessons will pick up after the snow melts."

"You can always use Red," I offered.

"Thanks, Lettie, but I don't want to use him if you're riding him. He's getting old," Callan pointed out.

"That's why Brandy's going to break that gray for me."

"You're what?" Reed demanded.

Brandy didn't bother looking at him, she just picked up her wine and twirled it in the glass. "I'm breaking that horse for her in a few months once my schedule opens up."

Reed dropped his fork. "No. That horse is fucking crazy. Won't even let me near him to shoe him." He pointed at me. "You're not riding him." His finger moved to Brandy. "And you're not breaking him."

She set her glass down with a clink before she even took a sip, her furious eyes shooting fireballs at Reed. "You don't get to tell me what to do."

"Like hell, I don't. That horse is dangerous." Reed wasn't going to budge on this, and with the two of them, this would turn into all-out war.

Bailey, sensing the situation heading south, piped in. "Alright, guys. We can discuss this another time. We'll see how the gelding behaves in the coming months and re-evaluate then."

I looked at him in shock. What in the mature just came out of his mouth?

"I'm going to get a beer," Reed grumbled, pushing back from the table and disappearing inside.

My mom sat at the end next to my dad, her lips pursed as she watched all of us. She knew there was something between Brandy and Reed, but none of us ever bothered to ask what caused them to hate each other so strongly. Whatever it was, they weren't letting it go.

"I know what will cheer him up," I said.

Bailey must've seen the up-to-no-good look in my eye because he narrowed his. "What's that, Huckleberry?"

I smiled. "You'll see."

Through the glass doors, I saw Reed popping the top off his beer and taking a long swig. I stood from my chair, taking note that everyone had a heaping portion of potato salad on their plates. Grabbing the bowl with the remnants of potato salad, I casually headed for the door like I was going to bring it inside, but as I reached the slider, Reed opened it, stepping out.

I lifted the bowl and dumped the contents over his head, the potato salad sliding down the sides of his face. He didn't even bother to squeeze his eyes shut as he glared at me. The corners of his mouth quirked as everyone laughed behind me from the table.

"Gotta be able to play at your own game, Reed," I sniped.

"I'll get the hose," Bailey said from behind me, his chair scraping against the porch.

Reed reached up and grabbed a fist full of potatoes. I took a step back, knowing his intent. He came closer, and I spun, running down the porch steps. As my feet landed in the grass, I was sprayed with freezing water. My screams filled the air as Bailey chased me with the hose, soaking me from head to toe. I caught Reed standing at the top of the stairs, holding the potato salad as a threat if I decided to climb the stairs to the safety of the table.

"Not very good at getting us back, are you?" Bailey said through a laugh as he grabbed hold of the back of my shirt and pulled me to him so my back was to his chest.

I turned, wrapping my arms around his neck and reaching up on my tiptoes like I was about to kiss him, but as he closed his eyes, I snatched the hose from his hand and aimed it at him. His eyes flew open and he reached for me, his laugh filling the air as I struggled to keep the hose out of his reach. With my height, that was impossible.

I stumbled back, and we both fell to the ground, the hose falling out of our reach as it flooded the grass. But I didn't care about the mud, or the bugs, or the running water. Not with Bailey on top of me, his weight making my body light up like the night sky on the fourth of July.

We laid there, our breaths evening out, our smiles never waning, as we got lost in each other. Bailey Cooper made me the happiest girl in the world.

44

BAILEY

The porch lights on the house illuminated all of the bright smiles around me as everyone relaxed at the long table after the best birthday party Lettie's seen in her twenty-four years. At least, it better be. I put it together, after all.

I could hear Lettie in my head now. *"Stop stroking your ego."*

I would if she was stroking something else.

I shook the thoughts from my head as Brandy came back outside without Lettie. They'd headed in over ten minutes ago. Something about having to pee together?

I'd never understand women.

As Brandy passed behind me, I leaned back in my chair. "Where'd Lettie run off to?"

She made a motion like she was zipping her lips and throwing away the key as she resumed her spot between Callan and

Lennon. Reed was opposite the table of her, but pretended like he didn't notice when she sat back down as he spoke to my father about some horseshoeing shit I couldn't begin to comprehend.

Sliding the chair a few inches back, I mumbled to my mom that I'd be right back, yet I didn't think she heard me as her and Charlotte had been lost in a gossip hole ever since we sat down.

Heading inside, I slid the slider closed behind me and took in the mess. I'd cleaned the cake off the ground earlier, per Lettie's request, but there were wrappers and napkins all over the table, bowls and plates stacked near the sink, and party hats littering the ground.

Figuring it would be nice to clean the Bronsons' house since I'd been the one to bring the chaos here, I got to work. I started with the trash, grabbing a plastic bag from under the sink. Once that was taken care of, I loaded the dishwasher, packed any leftovers into containers and set them in the fridge, and folded the table cloth.

I scanned the room, satisfied with the quick clean.

I wasn't sure where Lettie was right now, but I had the strongest feeling that if I checked the barn, she'd be there. I'd told her to leave the work for tomorrow, but I saw that rebellious glint in her eyes. She had things she wanted to get done, and she wouldn't let me get in the way of it. She was stubborn in all aspects of the word, a force to be reckoned with.

If Lettie was a bear, I'd be right there poking her despite all the warning signs. Even a neon flashing light that said "beware, broken hearts possible" wouldn't have kept me away. Hell, I pined after her even after she broke my heart the first time. Nothing would get in my way when it came to Lettie.

I made my way out front, seeing a dim light coming from the barn.

I knew her so well.

She could change her hair, get plastic surgery, botox, you name it, and I'd still know who she was. My heart called for hers like a damn mate. Even a pitch black world couldn't keep me from finding my Huckleberry. She was my light at the end of every bad day. Just thoughts of her were enough to keep me alive.

But I'd always want more. Just one more hit. One more kiss. One more taste. I couldn't get enough of the woman.

Crossing the driveway, I peered inside the door to the barn, finding her crouched by a stall, screwing in a name card with Zach Bryan playing on her phone lying next to her on the ground.

Between the sound of the drill and "I Remember Everything" blasting through the tiny speaker, she didn't hear me when I slowly came up behind her, bending down until my mouth was inches from her ear.

As soon as her finger eased off the drill, I said, "Working on your birthday, Lettie?"

She shrieked, the drill falling from her hand with a thud. She twisted, slapping at my shoulder. "Bailey! I could have hurt you!"

"Hurt me?" I straightened as she stood. "Please. You couldn't hurt a fly."

She crossed her arms. "I'll have you know, I've killed plenty of flies."

"Oh, yeah?" I inched closer until her arms brushed my chest. She dropped them to her sides, angling her head up at me. "I think someone needs to be punished for going against the rules I set."

She scoffed, but I wasn't playing around anymore. My hands gripped her hips, spinning her so her front was pressed up against the wood stall, a gasp slipping from her lips. She turned her head so her cheek was pressed up against the metal bars.

My lips brushed her ear as I spoke. "That little move deserves double the punishment, don't you think?"

My fingers brushed her hair over her shoulder, exposing her rosy cheek. My eyes traced the column of her neck as goosebumps freckled her skin.

"Hmm, Lettie? I didn't hear an answer."

"Yes," she breathed.

I trailed a finger down her spine, tracing the curves of her ass. "Good girl."

Reaching around her front, I unbuttoned her jeans, sliding the zipper down so my fingers could fit between her panties and the denim material. Even through the cotton, I could feel how soaked she was.

"Always so fucking ready for me, aren't you, baby? Your pussy practically begs for me to give you attention like this. But that's going to have to wait." My hand slipped out, instantly going for the hem to yank her pants off, her panties going with. Before giving her a chance to protest, I landed a slap on her ass, the sound combined with her yelp echoing through the barn.

"That's for leaving your own birthday party," I said, the strain in my jeans almost too much.

"What if someone sees?" she asked.

"Baby, nothing could stop me from fucking you in this barn right now."

She audibly gulped as my hands smoothed over the smooth skin on her ass. God, I was so fucking obsessed with her.

My hand came back, another crack splitting the air. "That's for coming to the barn when I explicitly told you no working on your birthday."

This time, her yelp was more of a moan, her teeth clamping down on her bottom lip.

I smoothed over her silky ass again before landing another slap to her opposite cheek. Her hands gripped the bars as she looked over her shoulder at me. "What was that for?"

"For thinking you could get away from me. Now bend over and spread those pretty legs."

She scooted back, ass in the air, as she kept her grip on the bars of the stall. I made quick work of undoing my belt and sliding my jeans down, my cock springing free from my boxers.

I dragged it up her center, her body jumping as the head rubbed over her bundle of nerves. Something about the risk of someone seeing us made this hotter than it already was. Lettie, bent and willing, at my mercy. The amount of times I'd had this fantasy, and now she was before me. I was tempted to give her another slap just for making me wait five fucking years, but I couldn't hold back another second.

Lining up with her entrance, I slid in, earning a moan from her as her fingers gripped the bars tighter. My hands grabbed onto her hips, holding her steady as I drew out, watching the wet sheen appear on my length.

I slammed back in, gripping her hips harder as I got lost in the sea that was Lettie. If love was an ocean, I'd drown right here, right now, if only to see her float. Lettie was my first and only priority, in and out of the bedroom.

"Touch yourself, baby. I want to feel your sweet pussy choke my cock when you come." In response, one hand let go of the bars, reaching between her legs. Immediately, her grip tightened, and I almost came from that alone.

"Fuck, Bailey," she moaned. My name on her lips while I was inside her was the sexiest fucking thing I'd ever heard.

"You like when I fuck you like this?"

"Yes," she breathed, her voice rising in pitch as she got closer to the edge. I could feel it building, feel the pressure from inside of her. I picked up my pace, my cock repeatedly hitting that sweet spot.

"You gonna come, Lettie?"

She shook her head.

"What do you need, baby? Tell me."

She hesitated, her teeth gnawing on her bottom lip before saying, "I need you on top."

Wasting no time, I pulled her down to the ground and came down with her, hovering over her as I slid back in. Her head flew back, her body arching in response. "Fuck, yes. Just like that."

Satisfaction rolled through me as I resumed my pace. In seconds, she got silent, then it was like she exploded, her body unable to hold back the tremors as her orgasm rippled through her. I rode it out, bending down to kiss her neck as she screamed, her hands grabbing at my hair, my back, my ass. It was like she was reaching for a tether to keep her in this world as her orgasm threatened to pull her under.

Her pussy clenched my cock, and I couldn't hold back any longer. My head felt like it was underwater as I spilled into her, my body stiffening with my release. My forehead pressed against her shoulder as I emptied myself, pleasure surging through me like energy through a power circuit.

This was heaven. It had to be.

Lettie had taken my life, and I didn't want to go any other way. My true love's kiss was poison, and I didn't want the antidote.

Lettie's hands found my cheeks and pulled my head up, her eyes staring into mine.

"I love you," she whispered.

A smile crested my mouth. "Say it again."

Her blue eyes shone like the sun reflecting off ocean waves. "I love you."

I brought my lips down to hers, brushing a faint kiss to her mouth. "I love you, too, Huckleberry."

45

BAILEY

I took in the barn before me, all of the wood prepped for a fresh coat of paint.

We'd been working on this barn nonstop for weeks now, getting it done a couple weeks ahead of schedule. Lettie had finished with whatever she wanted to get done inside the barn the day after her birthday.

We deserved a day off.

We'd replaced the roof and most of the siding, redone the stalls and replaced the hardware. The barn had always been red, and I knew Lettie would want to keep that aspect of it. Every ranch needed a good ol' fashioned red barn.

When the Bronsons' personal barn was built, we'd painted it white to easily distinguish to volunteers which barn the rescues were in, and which one the Bronsons' horses were in. Though

Nova was in the white barn, Travis had declared he was mine, and I was fine to keep him here.

Despite knowing Lettie wouldn't want to take another day off, I made my way over to the white barn to start tacking up Red and Nova.

I fed them some grain while I worked on saddling them. Once they were done, I offered them both water from the trough, then worked their bits into their mouths. Thankfully, I'd worked on getting Nova over his hatred for the piece of metal, and he took it willingly.

Leading Red and Nova out of the white barn, I found Lettie making her way over to the paint cans with Rouge on her heels. Her eyes found me, confusion clear on her face. "What are you doing?"

I approached her, holding Red's reins out to her. "We're taking a break today."

She grabbed them from me hesitantly. "But we're almost done."

"And we can finish tomorrow. Come on. I want to take you somewhere."

I set my foot in the stirrup, pulling my other leg over Nova's back. I reached up to pat the dark hair on his neck to reward him for standing still.

Walking off while I got on was just another one of Nova's quirks we were working on.

Lettie hopped on Red, adjusting the length of her reins in her hand. "Where?"

I smiled, adding pressure with my legs. Nova started at a walk, Red following beside me with Rouge jogging ahead of us. "You'll see."

We took the trail on the west side of the property, leading up into the hills.

"Beckham left around four this morning," Lettie said.

He was going back on the Wilderness Circuit, finishing it off before the end of the season. He came home when he could, but most of his time was dedicated to rodeo. I could never do what he did and love it. Being thrown off a horse is the last thing a lot of people want to do. Beckham somehow found joy in it, always searching out the most unruly broncs.

"I made sure to say goodbye to him last night. I'll miss him, but he'll be home again before we know it."

"I know. I just wish he'd stop, find something safer to do. But I wouldn't tell him that. I worry about him," she admitted.

"We all do. Beck's an adrenaline junky. If he retired, I'm sure he'd just go be a skydiver or extreme rock climber or something."

She shot me a look. "Beckham not on a horse? I couldn't see it."

"You never know."

"Maybe he could partner with Lennon at Tumbleweed. I'm sure he'd offer him a job if he asked."

Now I was the one to shoot her the look. "Beck working retail? Do you know your brother?"

The birds chirping in the trees filled the silence that stretched between us before she spoke again. "Speaking of Lennon, I think I may have found him a new employee."

"I know he'd been having a hard time finding one. Who is it?"

"I don't know her, but she came up to our booth at the Art & Wine festival. She was really nice. And cute."

I glanced at Lettie to see her smiling. "I'm sure that will be a plus for Lennon," I remarked.

She let out a small laugh. "My mom seems to think so, too. She's apparently a part-time matchmaker now."

"Is that so?" I grinned. Leave it to Charlotte Bronson to try to play matchmaker with her grown kids.

After about five miles on the trail, we came to a stop at the top of the highest point, a lush green, wide open field before us. You could see for miles, mountains peaking up in the distance. Rouge plopped down in the cool grass, panting from keeping pace with us.

"Bailey... This is beautiful," Lettie whispered.

I glanced over to her, my arms crossed over the horn of my saddle. She was looking out at the land, a slight glimmer in her baby blues, but my eyes were glued on the only view that caught my attention day in and day out.

The breathtaking landscape didn't hold a candle to Lettie Bronson.

"I found this little spot when I took Red out for you. Kept him in shape while I cleared my head. After I found it, we eventually just kept coming back. I'd let him take me in any direction, and he always chose here. It was like if we looked hard enough, we might be able to see you all those miles away."

She looked over at me, a softness to her features I'd never seen before.

I spun Nova around and brought him so his face was by Red's back end. Lettie was right beside me, watching me. Keeping one hand on the reins, I reached over to set my hand on her cheek, pulling her closer to me.

"Even when you were gone, Lettie, we still felt you. You belong in Bell Buckle."

"I know. I wish I'd never left," she admitted, her voice small.

My thumb brushed her skin as I asked the one thing I'd been wanting to know ever since she arrived back in town. "Then why'd you leave? Why waste so many years running from what you knew in your heart you wanted?"

She was quiet for a few moments, her eyes darting back and forth between mine.

"I was scared, Bailey."

"Scared of what?" I asked, dropping my hand from her cheek.

"Of you. Of the possibility of us," she confessed.

My brows furrowed in confusion. "What?"

She took a deep breath. "I was terrified of falling for you and one of us fucking it up. I didn't know if I could handle losing you in my life like that, Bailey. So, I prevented it from happening altogether, and I regret it."

I blinked, shaking my head. "That can't be all of it."

"It is."

"No, Lettie. It has to be something else, too. You can't say it was all me. What is it?"

She pulled on Red's reins, backing him up a few inches and turning him so she was angled slightly away from me.

"What else were you scared of, Lettie?" I asked when she didn't reply.

Her eyes met mine, regret shining in them. "Everything, okay? My brothers, my parents, but especially you. At least with them, their care was stifling, drowning me at times. But you? You were so damn sweet to me all the time, Bailey. I was so used to it. If we had crossed that line back then, who knows if you wouldn't have begun suffocating me, too? Caring for someone can be the worst kind of addiction. You can obsess, worry yourself to death. I didn't want that for you."

My hands tightened on the reins. "I'll always worry about you, Lettie. It's in my blood. But I will never close in on you, control you. I see what it does to you when your brothers do it."

"Those are just words."

"Words are all I have! You never gave me the chance to prove it to you. You just ran away instead of facing your fears." And I couldn't believe I was one of them. My feelings for her scared her, and that fucking hurt.

I shook my head again. "I don't want to hear that you were scared when you should've been here, safe in my arms. Five years of worrying about you tore me apart, but it didn't for one second shake the feelings I have for you, and that has to mean something."

Her eyes glassed over, tears welling in them. "I'm sorry," was all she said before she flipped Red around and took off down the trail with Rouge right behind her.

I wanted to go after her, but instead, I stayed put. Nova pawed at the ground, feeling the same draw to chase after them. But I kept him in place, forcing air into my lungs. I watched as Lettie, Red, and Rouge walked away, the three most important things in my life disappearing before my eyes.

Lettie wasn't going to get away so easily this time, but I'd give her the space she needed for now.

Just not five fucking years' worth. Not again.

46

LETTIE

I made it back home and walked Red to the white barn. Bringing my leg over him, I got off and removed his bridle. He drank from the trough, Rouge following suit, as I loosened the latigo and got to work removing his tack.

I set the saddle on the fence and walked Red to his stall, passing Reed bent over a horse's back leg, filing away at the hoof. Once I locked the gate, I went back to grab the saddle and found Rouge in the trough, splashing around.

Leaving him to do his thing, I made my way to the tack room, hefting the saddle up to set it on the stand.

"Have a good ride?" Reed asked as I passed back by him.

My shoulders were already sunburnt since I'd opted to wear a tanktop today, under the impression we'd be painting right now. The spurs I'd slipped on before our ride clanged with each step down the aisle of the barn. "It was great," I clipped in response.

Reed stood up after gently setting the horse's foot back on the ground. His eyebrows were raised in question.

I ignored him, not in the mood to get into it with him right now. He was already on edge with learning about Bailey and me getting together. The last thing I needed to do was give him the impression we were already arguing.

We weren't arguing, though. I'd confessed to him why I left, confirming his suspicions, but it all came out wrong.

I wasn't scared of Bailey. I didn't want him to think that I was, but saying that I left because of him? That's the only way it could come across.

Bailey was such a constant presence in my life. Always there when I needed a shoulder. He never pressed for information, but he comforted me all the same. I didn't want to ever lose that, and if we had gotten together when I was eighteen and he was twenty-two? I *was* scared he'd come to see me as nothing more than an immature teen and leave me for someone closer to his age.

But I wasn't scared anymore. What I felt for him now was far from it.

Bailey was the life line I hung onto with every ounce of my being. When things got crazy, or my brothers were being overbearing, or my parents were drowning me in their overprotective behavior, he was the one I came to.

I appreciated my family every single day. But sometimes, it felt like my walls were closing in when they constantly asked how I felt, or if I needed anything.

I never once took them for granted. I loved them with everything I had in me.

But Bailey was like my palette cleanser. Yeah, he cared about me. He was protective of me all the same. But he never forced how he felt onto me. Deep down, I always knew we felt more than just friendship for each other, but being in a relationship meant feelings were heightened, and I didn't want Bailey to drown me, too.

The look on his face when he thought I was terrified enough of him to leave killed me.

Those five years mentally destroyed me, and being back here put me back together. Just being in Bailey's presence wasn't enough, but the thought of losing him if things went south petrified me, my heart nearly beating out of my chest at just the thought.

But I could admit that he wasn't the only one who wanted more.

I didn't want to hurt him. He was my best friend, and being more than that didn't change that. I'd give him all the stars in the universe if that would keep a smile on his face, but I didn't know if it was enough. If I was enough.

That was why I didn't want to admit it to him. What if things were better off with me three hundred miles away?

I headed in the direction of the only place I wanted to be right now. The place I always felt closest to him without being in his presence. The spot we last saw each other aside from Outlaw's Watering Hole, all those years ago, before I decided to ruin everything we'd built.

47

BAILEY

After about thirty minutes of sitting in my thoughts, I led Nova back down the trail. Once we reached the barn, I pulled him to a stop to dismount.

I untacked him as he drank water, then brought him into the barn. Red stuck his head through the opening in his stall, eyeing us. I searched for Lettie, but it was clear she wasn't here.

Guiding Nova into his stall, I closed the door and found Reed packing his supplies into his truck outside the barn.

"Did you happen to see Lettie come in here?" I asked him as I bent to unbuckle the spurs on my boots.

"She left a little bit ago," Reed said as he hefted a bucket of used horseshoes into the bed of his truck.

I straightened, my blood going ice cold. "Left?"

"Yeah. Headed off into the trees behind the house all grumpy."

Relief flooded through me knowing she hadn't driven away. If she had, I'd peel after her like a bat out of hell. Lettie was not getting away from me this time.

There was only one place Lettie would be headed if she went off that way.

Reed looked at me then. "You look like you've seen a ghost, Cooper. What's wrong?"

The leather strap attached to my spurs slipped from my fingers, landing with a thud in the dirt.

"I'll tell you later. I gotta go," I said before turning on the heel of my boot and beelining it for the creek hidden in the trees on the east side of the property.

That creek was the last place I saw her aside from her birthday before she drove three hundred miles to get away from me.

It was now going to be the place I made damn sure she knew how I felt, and that running was no longer an option. Not even leaving the room during a damn argument. Lettie and I were endgame, and that meant working through our battles, whether we liked it or not.

I wanted the good and the bad with Lettie, and it was about damn time she realized it.

***

A short walk later, the sound of running water filled my ears. Lettie was sitting in the dirt, facing the creek with her back to me. Her caramel hair cascaded down her back, locks of it draped over her red shoulders.

Once this was cleared up, I'd rub aloe all over her body, touch every inch of her, just to prove to her that she was mine.

I didn't care if addictions could be deadly. I'd let Lettie rip my damn heart out if she wanted. I already had once before, and while it hurt, I was so fucking honored to be touched by Lettie in this lifetime.

We were meant to be, Lettie and I. We were put in this lifetime together, next door neighbors. The universe couldn't have been shouting at us harder if it tried.

I came up beside her, taking a seat in the dirt, leaving a few inches of space between our bodies. We were silent for a few minutes as we watched the water run over the rocks in the creek.

"I'm not scared of you," she finally said.

"I kno-" She held up a hand to cut me off.

"No, Bailey. I'm not scared of you, but I am fucking terrified of losing you. You've always been my rock, and five years ago, I may have been stupid, but I knew that life would never be the same if I lost you. I looked forward to seeing you every day, to sneaking looks when you stacked hay or rode Nova. If all of a sudden that stopped because I messed things up? I wouldn't know what to do with myself. There's no me without you, Bailey."

I looked at her, but she kept her gaze on the water, a sadness in her features, overtaking the exhaustion that had been there the past couple weeks.

"You could never mess things up, Huckleberry." I brushed the hair in her face behind her ear and she brought her eyes to mine.

"You don't know that," she whispered.

"I'd fight for you, for us. I could never give up on you. You're ingrained in my entire being; a constant thought on my mind. There's never a moment that goes by where I'm not daydreaming about you. How do you expect to be happy if you run from the things that bring you joy?"

She swallowed audibly as a tear slid down her cheek. "Leaving you without a goodbye was the hardest thing I've ever done, and I've regretted it every day since I left. I'm so sorry it took me so long to come back to you."

My thumb brushed the tear away and I pulled her to me, wrapping my arms around her. She buried her face in my neck as I rubbed my hand up and down her back in a soothing rhythm. I was so tired of hearing her apologize. "Don't be sorry, Lettie. Be happy. As shitty as it is, life played out the way it was supposed to, and it brought you back to me. That's all I care about."

She nodded, pulling back slightly to look up at me. I kept my arms wrapped tight around her, needing to feel her against me.

"But I don't want you to hide those fears from me. Talk to me about it rather than hiding it inside. It will only eat you alive that way," I said.

She took a steadying breath, and I wiped another tear from under her eye. "From now on, I will. I promise."

"Good."

"Bailey, can I ask you a question?"

I nodded. "Of course, Huckleberry. Anything."

"Why didn't you move on?" she asked softly.

I didn't even hesitate. "You leaving ruined me, Lettie. But I'd rather be ruined by you than be loved by someone else. I always knew you'd come back."

I pressed a kiss to her forehead before laying her back on the dirt. Straddling her body, I looked down at her. "You're mine, Lettie Bronson."

A smile spread across her pink lips. "All yours, Bailey Cooper."

I leaned down, pressing my lips to her softly. Our chests touched, her heart beating faster than I'd felt it before. At first, I thought it was because of me, but as her hands came up to cradle my face, I noticed how cold they were. I pulled back, looking down at her with furrowed brows.

"What's wrong?" she asked, confusion clear in her tone.

"Are you feeling okay?" I knew what cold hands meant, but her heart beating faster than hooves pounding at the races made me nervous.

She nodded, reaching up for my face again. I grabbed her hand in mine, examining her fingers like I could find answers written on them.

"You're cold," I stated.

Her forehead creased. "It's the creek. It's always colder down here."

"Lettie, it's probably eighty degrees out right now." Standing up, I reached down to pull her up. She put a hand out to steady herself, her palm like ice through the fabric of my shirt.

"Let's go," I demanded.

Her glacier eyes stared up at me. "Go where?"

"The hospital."

She ripped her hand back like she was stung. "No fucking way."

"Something could be wrong, Lettie. Don't you feel your fucking heart? It shouldn't be pounding out of your damn chest."

She looked down at the dirt, shaking her head. "I'm *not* going to the hospital."

I stepped forward, grabbing both her hands. "I won't tell your brothers, I promise. Just go for me. Please." I'd get on my knees and beg her if I had to. Her health was my number one priority in this world, whether she liked it or not.

She kept her gaze on the ground so I tipped her chin up with my knuckle. In her eyes, I found her acceptance to go. She was letting down the wall she'd built when it came to people caring about her, and I was the one she was letting in.

That was all I ever wanted.

"Can you walk back?" I asked.

She frowned. "Yes, I can walk. I walked out here, didn't I?"

So damn sassy, regardless of how she felt. "If anyone asks, just tell them I'm taking you to lunch or something."

My hand wrapped around hers, the fit natural, like her hand was made to be in mine.

"Lunch, huh?"

I glanced at her as we walked the dirt path that led back to where my truck was. "Well, obviously you don't have to say lunch. Wait, what's wrong with lunch?"

"You really think they're going to believe you're taking a long enough break to go into town for lunch? Bailey, you barely give yourself a thirty second piss break in the middle of the day."

"That's not true," I retorted. "All guys take at least an hour shi-"

"Okay!" She cut me off. "That's all I need to hear."

I smirked and knew that would be the last time I'd hear her poking fun at me about my inability to take a break during the day. My truck came into view as we cleared the trees. "Do you need anything from inside?"

She shook her head. "We won't be gone long."

I hoped she was right.

Callan was instructing a lesson in the covered arena, a young boy who looked to be about twelve bouncing atop one of their older lesson horses as he trotted. "Where are you guys going?" Cal called over.

Lettie turned, her face red. "Gotta help his dad unclog the toilet!"

I fought to hold back the laughter that wanted to erupt out of me. Opening her passenger door, she got in and saw the look on my face. "What if he asked us to bring him back some food or something?" she asked.

A chuckle escaped as I said, "You're right. He definitely won't be asking for anything from us after we unclog my dad's toilet."

An image of Lettie in a house, doing daily chores like dishes or mopping, crossed my mind as I rounded the truck to get behind the wheel. I could see us in our home, a couple of babies, Lettie's hair in a bun wearing the same clothes from two days ago, and me coming in from working on the ranch. She'd complain about the dirt on the freshly mopped floor, but I'd pull her into my arms, thankful for another day coming home to her. Lettie was my home. The woman I looked forward to seeing every damn day. I was so lucky to have her.

I'd get hurt by Lettie Bronson a million more times in this lifetime if it led me to being right here, where I was right now. With her by my side, just an arm's length away.

48

LETTIE

My forehead pressed to the cool glass of the passenger window as Bailey drove into town. To my surprise, he wasn't driving like a bat out of hell to get to the hospital. In my mind, this wasn't exactly an emergency, but I'd been avoiding the tell-tale signs of low iron for far too long. I'd been pushing my body to its limit working on the barn, going on the road trip, and forgetting to take my iron for a few days.

When I was in Boise, I'd have to get my levels checked every so often, and once, it had ended up in me needing to get an iron transfusion. As scary as they sounded, they weren't all that terrible - as long as you didn't look at the IV full of basically black liquid.

I hadn't told my family about the transfusion because I had the feeling that if they knew, they'd want me to come home.

Not wanting to cause them to worry more than they already probably were, I'd kept quiet.

Going through health problems and not being able to talk to anyone about it was a lonely way to live life. I'd debated going to a therapist, but felt pathetic spilling my issues to a stranger, so I didn't.

Bailey rolled to a stop at the traffic light, waiting for it to turn green. I glanced over at him, one hand on the steering wheel and the other on my thigh. Because of him, I could let my guard down and be open about how I felt and my medical issues. He cared for me, but not in the way that suffocated me like so many others did. He gave me the space I needed while also being by my side.

Bailey was my lifeboat in the sea of waves that crashed against me, making me want to fold in on myself. When the waters were rocky, he threw me a life jacket, keeping me afloat. I was no longer alone.

A few minutes later, he pulled into the emergency room parking lot, finding a space in the front. The lot was mostly empty. That was one of the perks with small towns. Nowhere was ever too busy.

He came around and opened my passenger door, offering his hand to help me out. I took it, folding my fingers around his, and didn't let go once I was on the ground. The uncertainty of what was about to happen made me want to keep him close, his presence grounding me to the earth.

He closed the door, locking the truck, and we began our short walk to the daunting emergency room doors. I wish they had a "slightly urgent" room instead. The word emergency was intimidating in itself. Add a multiple story building full of doctors and medical equipment, and you couldn't help but feel the nerves settle in.

Before we reached the doors, Bailey stopped me, turning to pull me into his arms. My cheek rested against his chest as my arms wrapped around his torso. His lips brushed the top of my head as he gave me a soft kiss.

"We'll be out before you know it, Lettie. Deep breaths," he mumbled against my hair.

I inhaled deeply, feeling my heart practically beating out of my chest. At this point, I couldn't tell if it was from the low iron or the anxiety of walking through those doors.

I didn't miss how he said *we'd* be out. This wasn't just happening to me anymore. This was the two of us, in this together. Bailey put the "in sickness and in health" into our relationship before he even asked me to marry him, and that's why I loved him. He wanted me regardless of all the times I'd tried to push him away, despite all the years spent apart.

I pulled back, placing my hand back in his. As soon as we walked through the sliding glass doors, the smell of disinfectant and rubbing alcohol burned my nose. My body instantly went on alert with all my past experiences in the hospital racing through my mind in a blur.

We walked right up to the counter, the lady at the desk looking up at me from where she sat. She had white-rimmed glasses on, her hair pulled back in a low ponytail, and long, sparkly pink nails. "Medical card and ID, please."

Pulling them out of my purse, I slid them over to her. She typed a few things into the computer, her nails clacking on the keyboard to the beat of my heart in my ears. It was like I was here, but not actually in my body. The emergency room was the last place I pictured myself being today.

"Reason for your visit?" she asked.

"I, uh, I think my iron may be low," I said, the statement coming out more like a question.

Her nails resumed their tapping, and I watched as they flew across the keys. Bailey squeezed my hand, and I looked up at him, a reassuring look on his face. I took another deep breath, leaning into his arm slightly.

She slid my card and ID back to me, and I slid them back into my purse. "You two can have a seat while you wait. A nurse should call you back shortly."

We turned, taking the closest two seats. The waiting room was empty aside from an elderly couple in the corner. I nuzzled closer to Bailey, laying my head on his shoulder as his thumb stroked circles on the back of my hand. I watched his thumb move as I tried to push the what-ifs from my mind.

What if they couldn't do anything to fix me? What if I let it get so bad this time that there was no going back?

Twenty minutes after the elderly couple was called back, the door opened, and a blonde nurse appeared in the doorway. "Lettie Bronson."

I stood, Bailey following suit. He walked me to the door, but the nurse stopped him. "We have to take her back privately first, then we'll come get you. Name?"

"Bailey," he answered.

"Sit tight, Bailey," she said.

He leaned in, his hand coming up to cradle my cheek as his other stayed glued to my palm. He pressed a kiss to my lips, and I wished we could stay in this moment and never part, but all good things had to come to an end. He pulled back, his green eyes blazing with concern as he said, "I'll be back with you soon, okay?"

"Okay," I whispered.

And then I unfolded my hand from his, our tether going from physical to imaginary. But as I walked through that door, I could still feel his love for me like he was right here with me.

He'd been with me the whole time.

49

BAILEY

My leg shook as my foot tapped on the linoleum floor in an uneven beat. Lettie had been back there for what felt like hours, and no one had come to get me like they said they would. I'd asked the woman at the counter twice now for an update, and she said a nurse would speak to me when they could.

That didn't comfort me at all.

I was on edge and worried that something may have happened. Was she still breathing? Did they give her some medication? My service didn't work in here, so I couldn't even send her a text asking if she was okay.

Unable to sit still any longer, I practically tipped the chair over as I stood, then made my way to the woman behind the counter.

"If they come out for me, can you let them know I stepped outside?" I asked, my voice hoarse.

Her face was coated in sympathy but I didn't want sympathy right now. I wanted fucking answers. "Of course."

"Thanks," I mumbled and headed out the doors. The fresh air did nothing to clear my head as every possible scenario flew through my mind. I paced back and forth, from the pillar that held the overhang to the edge of the sidewalk. I was halfway compelled to burst through the back and find her myself, but the last thing Lettie probably needed right now was me causing a scene.

The fact that a door was separating us right now, keeping me from knowing what was going on, fucking killed me. I wanted nothing more than to hold Lettie in my arms and know she was okay.

I'd been pacing for at least half an hour when the doors to the emergency room opened. I turned, my eyes immediately finding Lettie's petite form as she stood just outside the doors, frozen. From where I stood, I could see the tears welling in her eyes, and that fucking broke me.

I ran toward her, pulling her into my arms, pressing her face against my chest. God, it felt so good to hold her.

"Baby, what's wrong? Are you okay?" I asked, my voice laced with worry.

She nodded, pulling back an inch to look up at me. "I thought you left," she said, her voice breaking on the last word.

I cupped her face, shaking my head. "I could never leave you, Huckleberry. No one came to get me. I'm so sorry. I was going crazy in there. I wanted nothing more than to be back there with you. It fucking killed me not knowing what was happening."

She folded into me, pressing her cheek against my chest as my hands stroked down her hair, soothing her. "They gave me an iron transfusion."

"Are you going to be okay?"

She nodded again, holding me a little tighter. "I only have to come back if my symptoms are the same, but they do want to do blood tests more often than I was getting them to prevent it from getting this bad again."

I looked down at the top of her head, and she met my eyes, feeling my gaze on her. "You were getting them before?"

She chewed the inside of her cheek, then stopped. "Yeah. In Boise."

"You tell me when the appointments are, and I'll take you every time."

Her bottom lip trembled as she nodded in agreement. "Thank you."

"Anything for you, Huckleberry." I held her tighter, loving the feel of her in my arms. "Anything."

50

BAILEY

Lettie rolled over in my bed, nuzzling her head into my chest. The sunlight streamed in from the window, casting a spotlight on her bare back as I drew shapes across her skin. If I didn't have raging morning wood right now, I'd think I was still dreaming.

Though it'd been over a week since we'd been at the hospital, the emotions of being unable to get to her still tore through my chest every time I thought of her. It was a stupid thing to be upset over when she was the one going through the medical issues, but I couldn't keep the thoughts at bay. Now that I had Lettie, any thought of losing her again threatened to tear my heart right out of my chest.

I pressed my lips to her hair, inhaling her sweet scent. "Good morning, Huckleberry."

"Mmm," she groaned.

"I have something to show you," I muttered against her hair.

"If it's not a pancake breakfast, I'll be disappointed."

I chuckled as she sat up, her hair disheveled due to last night's activities. "I'll make you pancakes after. Get dressed, beautiful."

I slipped out of bed, pulling on my boxers, jeans, a Carhartt t-shirt, and my boots. Rouge jumped off the bed, beelining for the front door to be let out. Lettie got to work dressing herself in the clothes she'd been keeping at my house as I took care of Rouge's morning routine.

She'd been staying over at my place a majority of the time over the last week and I was loving every minute of it. If all went to plan, we'd have a place to call our own soon.

Dressed and her hair combed, my fingers locked with hers as we headed out of the house and to my truck. I opened her door and helped her in before closing the passenger door and coming around to the driver's side.

I started the truck and headed down the drive. Once on the main road, I passed by her parents' property and continued down the road for another couple minutes before turning down a different driveway. It was a long dirt road that stopped in the middle of a field with no buildings in sight.

Billy had only used the property to farm alfalfa and never built a house on it. He lived closer to town due to his old age, but it was the perfect piece of land to build our future.

With over eighty acres, my plan was to split the property in half and use the spare forty acres to grow hay, giving my parents all of the profits from that portion of the ranch. It would be more than enough to cover the bills they needed to pay, as well as leave some left over.

I killed the engine and got out, coming around to Lettie's side to open her door.

"Is this Billy's land?" she asked as she hopped out of the truck.

"Not anymore," I said.

I closed her door and turned to find her gaping at me. "What do you mean?"

I couldn't help the smile that pulled at my lips. "I bought it. Sale was finalized as of midnight last night."

Her eyes stayed trained on me as she processed what I was saying. Then as if a light clicked on, she threw herself at me, wrapping her legs around my waist. My hands came to her ass as her arms curled around my neck. "Bailey, that's amazing!"

She lowered her head to press her lips to mine before pulling back with the biggest grin on her face. "What are you going to do with the land?"

"I was hoping you could tell me."

"Me?"

I nodded.

"Why me?" she asked hesitantly.

"I want you to help design our house."

"*Our* house?"

"You're mine forever, Huckleberry. Yes, it's our house. I want to build a family with you, get old with you, sit in some damn rocking chairs on our porch and complain about the weather. I want it all, as long as it's with you."

"You gonna ask me to marry you first?" she teased.

Lettie may have been joking, but I was far from it.

Smiling, I set her down on her feet, then dropped to one knee. I pulled the velvet black box from my pocket and held it out to her, revealing the single white diamond set on a gold band.

Before I could get the words out, she angled my head up with her hands on my cheeks and pressed her lips to mine.

I took that as her 'yes.'

With my lips still on hers, I pulled the ring from the box. She pulled away and held her hand out for me to slide it on.

"Lettie Cooper. I like the sound of that," she said.

It was about damn time she took my last name.

I'd planned to propose tonight in the gazebo, but it felt right doing it here, in the place where we'd be building our future.

Besides, everything was spur of the moment when it came to Lettie Cooper.

Epilogue

Bailey

Eight Years Earlier...

My mother walked beside me on the sidewalk as we headed back to the truck with our bags. She'd brought me to the market to pick out a few snacks for my movie night at the Bronsons' tonight. I'd gone a little overboard but I didn't want to show up empty-handed.

They never expected me to bring snacks, but I always did anyway. We'd set up the projector in the backyard and lay on blankets as we watched the movie. Reed, Lennon, Callan, and Beck were my best friends. Lettie was too, but the title wouldn't stick. That girl was too beautiful to let slip out of my hands.

She was so fucking sassy, I couldn't help my smile every time she opened her pretty mouth.

SPUR OF THE MOMENT

We grew up together, and while most people would think that would warrant her to be like my little sister, she was far from it. I didn't miss her little glances. She had a crush on me, and every time her cheeks beat red when she watched me swim in the creek in my boxers or stack hay shirtless, I fell a little harder. A little farther into the chokehold Lettie Bronson had on me.

The day she turned eighteen, I'd show her. Not a second later. I'd wasted too many seconds of my life pausing, hesitating, and not living in the moment.

I couldn't plan how I'd tell her. I'd overthink it, and end up chickening out. It'd have to be spur of the moment with Lettie. Then I knew I'd show her with no second thoughts.

An old man sat on the corner of the intersection under a white pop-up tent. He had a hand-painted sign that read "huckleberries for sale."

I gestured to the stand. "Is it alright if I get some for tonight?"

I was nineteen, but was too scared to drive my grandfather's truck he'd given me in his will. I was terrified of wrecking it, so I opted for my mom to drive me whenever I needed to go into town. If it was on the backroads, I felt more confident. But with the crazy tourists in town, I didn't want to risk even a scratch on the door.

"Of course." My mom followed me to the stand and I pulled out my wallet.

"How much for a bucket load?" I asked the man who's wrinkles were set deep in the freckled skin of his face.

"Ten dollars," he stated.

My mom raised her eyebrows. "A bucket load? Why on earth would you need a bucket of huckleberries?"

"No reason. Just like 'em." But I knew exactly what I'd do with them.

Reed and I loved playing pranks on Lettie, and this was the perfect one.

The man handed me a tin bucket filled to the rim with huckleberries. I was honestly surprised he actually had a bucket, but maybe people asked for them like this on the regular.

Maybe everyone had a girl back home they loved to annoy.

Or people just liked making pie by the dozens.

Whichever.

The bucket swung from my fingers as we continued on our way to the truck. Once there, I set the bags of snacks in the back and set the bucket at my feet in the passenger seat to ensure it didn't tip over on the way home.

About twenty minutes later, my mom pulled up in front of the Bronsons'.

"Have fun, sweetie," my mom said, giving me a smile.

I leaned over to press a kiss to her cheek. "See you tomorrow."

Grabbing my belongings, I hopped out, making my way up the porch steps as my mom drove off, heading to our ranch next door.

"Thank God, you're here," Reed said as he opened the door before I could knock. "They're driving me up the damn wall."

"Lettie one of them?" I asked, raising an eyebrow.

"When isn't she?"

I held the bucket of huckleberries up, a smirk on my face. "I've got just the thing."

Reed eyed the contents, a devious look in his eyes. "This'll be perfect."

Or royally piss her off. Either way, she'd be fuming, and a red, angry little Lettie was just the way to start off the night.

We headed in, Reed taking the bags of snacks from my hand and laying them out on the table on the back porch. I hid the bucket behind the barbeque grill, making sure I had easy access to it.

As if on cue, Lettie ambled out through the sliding back door wearing jean shorts and a white tank top. She could sense I was here, she always could. Her piercing blue eyes darted to me, then instantly, a frown formed when she saw my smile.

"What are you up to?"

I shrugged. "Just excited for the movie."

Her frown deepened. "We watch Fast and Furious every Saturday. It's nothing new."

She came around the table as Reed was pouring M&M's into a small bowl, pulling a chair out as she reached for a bag of chips. As soon as she had her back turned to me, I pulled the chair away, replacing it with the bucket. Right as it was in place, she plopped down, but instead of the hard wood cushioning her, it was the huckleberries, rupturing red juice all over her.

"Bailey!" she screamed, instantly grabbing the table to pull herself up.

Her ass was covered, the liquid oozing down her legs. I couldn't contain my laugh, Reed breaking into a fit snorts and wheezes.

She turned to me, her face the same shade of red as her backside. "I'm going to kill you!"

"Might want to wash yourself off first, Huckleberry. Might slip and fall trying to catch me."

Something like a growl came out of her throat as she hefted up the bucket, and before I could react, she was tossing the contents at me.

The berries splattered all over my stomach, staining my shirt, but I didn't care. It was an excuse to take it off, right in front of Lettie.

As I lifted it over my head, her cheeks turned an impossibly darker shade of red, putting the huckleberry juice to shame.

Oh, yeah. This was definitely worth it.

"I'm going to take a shower," she said, her voice still full of anger, but something else, too.

She turned around, stomping off with her little red ass.

It was cruel of us, really. But I'd do anything to get her attention.

The pranks were never enough to make her hate me. I couldn't fathom the thought of her cutting me out of her life, so while we pranked her every so often, I always made up for it.

Because if I didn't, I risked losing her. And a life without Lettie was not something I ever wanted to experience.

She made me feel alive with just her presence in the room. I was always searching for her, even if I wasn't meaning to. Even in my sleep, she was always on my mind, invalidating the concept that she was my first thought in the morning, and my last before bed. She was in my dreams. Hell, she *was* my dreams.

And I'd do anything to make those dreams a reality.

I just had to wait.

She'd be mine one day.

I was sure of it.

The End

Acknowledgements

A huge thank you to my readers who fell in love with my debut novel and stuck around for more. I hope Bailey and Lettie pulled at your heart as much as they did mine. They're truly one of the most special couples I've thought up, and I know we say this about a lot of books, but I really do wish they were real. I guess I can settle for their happy ever after laid within these pages, and the glimpses you get at them in the next books in the Bell Buckle series.

To my fiance, Alex, you really are my number one. My hype man, my true love, my real life book boyfriend. I wouldn't have the ability to pursue this career if it wasn't for you. I love you.

To Kassandra, of course. How could I ever leave you out? You're one of the biggest, if not *the* biggest, reasons I do what I do. You tell me to go after what I love, and it doesn't matter what anyone else says. Thanks to you, I'm unashamedly myself, and I hope you always are too.

To Kate Crew. Over the past few months, you've dealt with my stressing over deadlines and plot holes and anything else under the sun that comes with being an author, which is a lot. We haven't gone a day without texting in all that time, and I hope you're loving my release day essay to you of how nervous and overwhelmed I am. Thank you for being the best author friend in the entire universe. I couldn't have done this without you by my side.

To Bobbi MacLaren, I absolutely love all your comments on my drafts and promise to give you all the cowboy hat scenes in due time. Thank you for being my little editor mixed with beta reading. I don't think you can ever get rid of me now.

To my cover designer, Ali, at Dirty Girl Designs, I absolutely loved working with you and I can't wait to see what you come up with for the other covers in the series! Thank you for bearing with me through the whole process, you're a dream to work with.

To my parents, thank you for rooting me on from the sidelines. I love you!

Thank you to my Beta readers for reading my raw manuscript. You guys are the best for all your funny comments.

My Arc readers – thank you for reading and reviewing my book baby. It's a very vulnerable thing to put a story out there that was thought up in my mind, but the fact that all of you loved it just makes me so beyond happy. Thank you for sharing, for spreading the word, and being my biggest cheerleaders. I love all of you.

To all my amazing friends on Bookstagram, I love each and every one of you. All of your DM's and comments make me laugh and smile every day, and I truly wouldn't have the confidence to put myself out there without you guys.

And again, thank you, the reader. This wouldn't be possible without you.

About the Author

Karley Brenna lives in a tiny mountain town in the middle of nowhere out West with her fiancé, son, and herd of pets. Her hobbies include writing, reading countless books heavy on romance, and listening to country music for hours. If she's not at home, she's either at a bookstore or getting lost in the hills on horseback. To stay up to date with Karley's future projects, follow her on social media @authorkarleybrenna.

Printed in Great Britain
by Amazon